LEGACY OF DEATH

LEGACY OF DEATH

Judith Cutler

This first world edition published 2020
in Great Britain and 2021 in the USA by
SEVERN HOUSE PUBLISHERS LTD of
Eardley House, 4 Uxbridge Street, London W8 7SY.
Trade paperback edition first published
in Great Britain and the USA 2021 by
SEVERN HOUSE PUBLISHERS LTD.

British Library Cataloguing in Publication Data
A CIP catalogue record for this title is available from the British Library.

ISBN-13: 978-0-7278-8939-3 (cased)
ISBN-13: 978-1-78029-749-1 (trade paper)
ISBN-13: 978-1-4483-0487-5 (e-book)

This is a work of fiction. Names, characters, places and incidents
are either the product of the author's imagination or are used fictitiously.
Except where actual historical events and characters are being described
for the storyline of this novel, all situations in this publication are
fictitious and any resemblance to actual persons, living or dead,
business establishments, events or locales is purely coincidental.

All Severn House titles are printed on acid-free paper.

Severn House Publishers support the Forest Stewardship Council™ [FSC™],
the leading international forest certification organisation.
All our titles that are printed on FSC certified paper carry the FSC logo.

Typeset by Palimpsest Book Production Ltd.,
Falkirk, Stirlingshire, Scotland.
Printed and bound in Great Britain by
TJ Books Limited, Padstow, Cornwall.

For Rachael, Olivia and Thomas, with all my love

ACKNOWLEDGEMENTS

For the first book in this series, I relied heavily on the hard work of other women, who researched and wrote most readable books. I did for this one too. Thank you to Pamela Horn for *The Rise and Fall of the Victorian Servant*; to Pamela Sambrook, *Keeping their Place*; to Jennifer Davies, *The Victorian Kitchen* and to Norah Lofts, *Domestic Life in England*.

ONE

My daily walk takes me to the site of the new model village; it always pleases me to see how fast the work is progressing, despite the shortness of the winter days. But today something is wrong. The labourers are resting on the handles of their picks and shovels. Thomas, the foreman, is wiping sweat from his brow.

He scrambles out of the trench as I appear, and comes towards me, waving his hands as if I am a sheep that has gone the wrong way. I almost expect him to say, 'Shoo!'

But I realize his eyes are full of fear. 'No, Mrs Faulkner. Mrs Rowsley, I mean. No, don't look, ma'am. 'Tis not fit for a lady's eyes. 'Tis a body, ma'am! A dead body!'

Mr Wilson cast his eyes around Thorncroft House's red dining room, where we had gathered round the long mahogany table, watched from the walls by his lordship's ancestors. None of them was welcoming, with two portrayed by Lely particularly disdainful. 'Welcome to this, the first meeting of the trustees of Lord Croft's estate, convened to oversee both its day-to-day and its long-term needs. I believe we are all here now, gentlemen – and ladies, of course,' he added with a patronising smile that could not fail to raise the hackles of at least two of those present, though they both responded with dignified nods.

Irritated though I was – had I not clearly explained to him that all, regardless of rank and sex, must be accorded the same respect? – rather than interrupt, I resolved to speak to him as he left.

'Perhaps,' Wilson continued, as unctuous as it was possible for a solicitor to be, 'in view of the solemnity of our business, before we are seated we might open with a prayer. Mr Pounceman?'

That was an invitation the Reverend Theophilus Pounceman would never decline. A severe attack of mumps in the summer had left him somewhat thinner, but had by no means dented his elegant carapace. In another milieu he might have been a dandy; in the environs of the Church he dressed and lived like a prince, though he was simply the rector of St Anselm's, the village church. The generous living had been bestowed on him by the previous Lord Croft. In his late thirties, his good looks and excellent prospects might have made him seem very attractive as a potential husband, but I had not yet met a woman who even liked him. As for his view, he disdained what he always referred to as 'the weaker sex'.

The long exhortation to the Almighty to restore Lord Croft to health was countered by a plea that we might enjoy a long and profitable association. Perhaps I was not the only one who registered a word that was decidedly suspect; as land agent I wished to be visibly meticulous in a role I had always performed with the clearest of consciences, never taking more than my contractual salary. Hence my discussions with the Family's solicitor, Montgomery Wilson, respected for his probity and probably even his pomposity throughout Shropshire, who had agreed my suggestions for people who were eligible by dint of their closeness to the Family or as noteworthy members of the village of Thorncroft. In addition to Pounceman were our village doctor, Ellis Page; Tertius Newcombe, a prosperous farmer; Samuel Bowman, the butler who had dedicated his life to the Family; Mrs Beatrice Arden, the cook; and my dear wife Harriet, once Mrs Faulkner, the housekeeper.

'I have received an apology for absence from Mr Martin Baines and my clerk has taken note of those attending,' Wilson said. 'So we can proceed to the first item on the agenda: conversion of the Family wing to a lunatic asylum for his lordship and his mother.'

Samuel Bowman writhed. After some fifty years in service, he was, however, so used to waiting until he was spoken to that he could do no more than stare at me.

'I think most of us would prefer a term that carried less opprobrium,' I said. 'Her ladyship is not far from death, I believe?' Dr Page nodded his agreement. 'And his lordship's disorder might well be a result of not his own but his father's indiscretions—'

'Let us call them by their correct name,' Pounceman declared. 'Transgressions! Sins of the flesh!'

'His late lordship, Mr Chairman, is not here to defend himself,' Harriet said with such quiet assurance she might have been speaking at formal meetings like this all her life. 'But I agree, as I think we all do, that we should perhaps refer to the Family wing by another term than lunatic asylum. Mr Bowman was speaking of this earlier.' She nodded across the table to her colleague, her beautiful hair confined under a much less unflattering cap these days, gleaming in the candlelight.

Wilson nodded towards Samuel. 'Mr Bowman?'

'All of us servants have always called it the Family wing. We don't need to change its name, Mr W— Mr Chairman. There are new locks on the doors; there are bars at the windows. It is safe. It does not need to lose . . . to lose its dignity.'

Wilson nodded. His clerk, a sad-faced youth in a suit a size too large, scratched at his paper.

'Family wing it is,' Wilson declared. 'And the changes to the fabric, Mr Rowsley? I believe Mr Bowman has already alluded to some of them.'

'Indeed. The estate carpenter has also installed some extra doors for security. He has gone to great pains to ensure they are in keeping with the House. However, he assures me that as and when it is safe to remove them, it can be done with no major damage to the fabric.'

'So all is well on that front. Does anyone have anything else to add? Very well, let us proceed to the next item: guards – or do you prefer another name, Mr Bowman?'

How would he react to the sarcasm?

'The staff all refer to them as attendants or nurses,' Samuel responded with a slow dignity that matched his unusually sober waistcoat. 'After all, many of them used to be in regular service here, as footmen or maids. Dr Page has had them trained.'

Page was not going to wait to be patronized. 'As a country doctor, Mr Chairman, I did not consider myself sufficiently au fait with current developments in the treatment of such illnesses, so I invited experts from the county asylum and Royal Salop Infirmary to instruct those who volunteered for new roles.'

Wilson, outgunned, nodded. 'And the rest of the staff?' He looked at me.

'I can tell you that all the outdoor staff have remained in place, with the exception of the Family's personal grooms, both of whom have sought and found employment elsewhere. They are very loyal and I am sure they will be discreet,' I added. 'As to the others, Mrs Rowsley is responsible for the maids, Mrs Arden for the kitchen staff and Mr Bowman for the footmen.'

Harriet and Samuel, despite his initial anxieties, reported confidently on changes, only Beatrice Arden showing any sign of nervousness. She too sported a less ugly cap.

'So many staff still employed!' Pounceman jumped in. 'Really, Rowsley, how can you possibly justify that?'

This from a man who employed at least eight servants to nurture him! For answer I looked at Wilson, who peered over his spectacles. 'Mr Pounceman, I would be more than grateful if you would address all your comments through the chair. There would appear to be a large number of people still drawing wages, Mr Rowsley.'

For answer I passed him a copy of the wages bill for the last three years. 'With your permission, Mr Chairman?' I distributed further copies to the others. 'As you will see, the servants, whatever work they are doing, are not highly-paid. A building such as this is not for the present occupier alone; it must be kept in trust for his heir. The fabric and fittings must be preserved in the best possible state, and to do this we must rely on my colleagues' expertise. As and when staff find new employment elsewhere, the posts they leave vacant may or may not be filled – that will be at the discretion of those directly supervising them, or this committee if the members prefer.'

'My opinion, for what it is worth,' Wilson said, 'is that such decisions might well be left to those with the requisite knowledge and experience. Are we all agreed? Ah, Mr Pounceman.'

'We are trustees for a reason, sir. We are to oversee what is done so no one takes advantage of a delicate situation. How are we to know that there is no nepotism, no other sort of favouritism?'

Dr Page raised his pen. 'Mr Chairman, I should imagine that these loyal employees around the table with us have never had much in the way of supervision from anything except their consciences, with which to the best of my knowledge they have imbued their underlings. Perhaps, if any exceptional remuneration is to be made and they are in any doubt, they should report to Mr Rowsley as land agent?'

'Although that has always been the case, Mr Chairman, I am more than happy to cede my powers of approval to those of us gathered here.'

'I still believe we should approve all the accounts, not just wages but other expenditure. We do not want the estates to become Rowsley's milch cow, do we? I see that he has appointed a clerk to assist him.'

I had. Freddie, a bright lad, once the stable hand at the village pub. Harriet had taught him to read, and though I paid him in shillings, not pounds, at the moment – he was no more than eleven or twelve! – I was sure he would one day become a professional man in his own right.

'Mr Pounceman, I would remind you that it was at Mr Rowsley's personal suggestion that this board was formed. I think you might keep such insinuations to yourself in future.' Wilson rocketed in my estimation. 'You will note that he is required by our articles to submit his accounts to us, once they have been scrutinized by one of my more expert colleagues. Now, I fear we have wandered from the agenda.'

Pounceman raised a hand. 'I would like to table a motion.'

Wilson shook his head. 'Then you must raise the topic in Any Other Business, sir. There is something else to be raised then too, so let us turn our attention to the next item: rebuilding Stammerton.' He contrived to ignore Pounceman's still raised hand. 'Mr Rowsley, thank you for submitting these drawings and estimates to us all in advance. Our discussion can now be informed, not a matter of speculation. I am sure you would all like to comment, but I must remind you to comment through me, as chairman. My clerk will take note of everything you say. Dr Page?'

Page acknowledged the invitation with a nod. 'There are those who may consider such a wholesale change an extravagance. However, as a doctor who regularly sees the effects of living in such hovels as pass for cottages, the effects of not eating because there is no food available, I support Mr Rowsley's proposals wholeheartedly. If the foundations could be dug tomorrow it would not be too soon for me.'

'Thank you. Mr Newcombe?'

'I'm glad it's not my money being spent, that's all I can say. But I agree, many of those cottages are a disgrace. Mr Rowsley and I have had conversations in the past, and it can be admitted there are things over which we have not seen eye to eye. However, persuaded by his arguments, I have started to improve my own labourers' places, little by little, and I've also given them plots for allotments. I have to admit, ladies and gentlemen, they are more cheerful as a result. They work harder, too. So maybe there's an element of self-interest in Rowsley's plans. As for the school, they say that Parliament will soon be insisting on free education for all our children, and being a step ahead is never a bad thing. But I warn you, universal education will change things. And not always for the better.' He paused. 'It's a nice little church proposed there – you must be pleased as Punch, Pounceman. Sorry, Mr Chairman. I would imagine Mr Pounceman must be pleased as Punch.'

Whatever the vicar wanted to say, he would have to wait. Wilson invited Samuel, who had bravely raised a hand, to speak.

'Mrs Fau— Mrs Rowsley! – knows more about teaching and so on than I do, but I can tell you this. When we get the youngest servants into the House, they are poor, weedy specimens, weak and pretty well useless. But then they get three good meals a day, and they are transformed. So I say the allotments are a good idea, which means the cottages need a means of cooking this food. A real kitchen. And it's not decent the way families are crammed together, boys and girls, children and grown-ups, so they need proper bedrooms.'

Pounceman was shaking his head. Eventually Wilson noticed, and invited him to speak.

'Our Lord said we would have the poor always with us. It is right to give them alms, to admit them to the workhouse if they are deserving. But these cottages will be given to the deserving and non-deserving alike! How can you . . . how can Mr Rowsley house a man drinks away his earnings next to a sober God-fearing man who comes to church? A school? I agree with Mr Newcombe that it will give people ideas above their station, and cause unrest. A cricket pitch on the village green? That will encourage idle loitering!'

Harriet raised a finger, catching Wilson's eye. To Pounceman's clear chagrin, he was invited to make way for another speaker.

'With due respect, Mr Chairman, I believe a village green complete with cricket team will actually help prevent revolution. His late lordship, for all his faults – some of which have sadly recently come to light – was popular with his workers and his tenants because he had, as they would put it, no side, no self-importance, one might say. He played alongside people earning a pittance and came to care for them. He insisted food parcels were despatched when illness struck a family. He knew everyone by name. I won't say he was a model landlord, and that was partly because his agent was quietly feathering his own nest, I suspect. But because he knew his men and they knew him, if violence had ever arisen, he would never have permitted the militia to lay a hand on them, and I believe his men would have guarded him with their lives.'

Wilson nodded gravely. 'Mrs Arden?'

Although I thought I knew her well, she surprised me. 'Privies, sir. Why not have proper sanitation? Someone I know lost his wife and family to the cholera in Manchester. He says that with clean water from pipes and – forgive the term – water closets, such a dreadful disease could never flourish. And I know this is out of order, sir, but I'd like to see piped water and bathrooms and water closets here in the House, too. Those nurses Dr Page brought in, they say you have to be extra particular where you've got sick people. Beg pardon, sir.' She subsided, her blushes painful to behold.

Wilson produced a rare smile. 'Thank you, Mrs Arden. An excellent idea. We must discuss it further in Any Other Business. Mr Pounceman, I suspect you have not completed your contribution? What are your thoughts about the church, which I gather does not conform to your own ideas?'

They did not.

Finally we reached Any Other Business. By now I was sure I could see another little smile playing across Wilson's austere features. But he maintained his calm and judicious bearing throughout, even as Pounceman embarked on a diatribe against me.

'I cannot disapprove of the measures taken to secure the House during the term of his lordship's illness. But nothing will reconcile me to the wholesale changes proposed during our earlier discussions. His lordship may recover, after all.' He glanced at Page, who responded with a sad shake of the head. 'And *when* he does, he will no doubt expect to find a reasonable amount left in the Family coffers. If the Almighty chooses to call him home, then his heir should find his inheritance intact. Oh, we have heard that it is a second cousin, probably living in the Antipodes. We have heard all about Mr Rowsley's fruitless attempts to find him. But until he does appear, I say we should veto all these pie in the sky notions!'

'How fortunate,' Wilson said quietly, 'that given the urgency of the projects, we will not have to wait long. Ladies and gentlemen, his lordship's heir is already in the country!'

TWO

Mr Wilson's dramatic announcement silenced us all, before unleashing a gabble of questions, even from Matthew, who was clearly as surprised as the rest of us. Sadly the hard facts Mr Wilson had at his disposal were sparse. Apart from a telegraph from London, announcing that the heir had returned to English soil, there had been no communication, and currently Mr Wilson had no idea of his whereabouts or even his plans.

'I suppose you do at least know his name?' Mr Pounceman asked tartly – an appropriate enough question.

'Indeed. I apologize. Mr Julius Trescothick.'

Samuel looked puzzled, and then nodded slowly, a slow smile suggesting a long-forgotten memory.

'He takes his name from one of his lordship's Cornish estates. It has long been rented out, and soon perhaps as trustees we will have to review the situation. As to Trescothick himself, since I know nothing more, I suggest that we adjourn the meeting until I am fully apprised of the situation.'

'We do know that he is who he says he is?' Matthew asked.

'My Australian colleague is convinced that he is genuine – but naturally I will want to see his papers for myself. Now, I will write to you individually as soon as I have further information and convene another meeting if necessary. Thank you, ladies and gentlemen. Heavens,' he continued, as he rose to his feet as if to demonstrate that the meeting was indeed over and that he for one desired a change of subject, 'is that rain I hear?'

As soon as Mr Pounceman realized that Wilson would be staying overnight in the guest wing, he took umbrage, though not until he had eaten one of Beatrice's best dinners, served in the green dining room, the smallest of the three that graced the House. We were waited on not by Samuel, of course, who took his place uneasily next to Mr Wilson, but by his deputy, Thatcher, and young Tim, a kitchen lad currently trying hard to grow tall enough to become a footman.

Once I had been permitted to watch the play put on by the young people at a house where I was working, not unlike the drama enacted in *Northanger Abbey*, though fortunately without the same consequences to the would-be actors. Thatcher would have been in his element in such a group, if his exact mimicry of Samuel Bowman was anything to judge by. It was never unkind, falling into caricature, just accurate. Perhaps, and the notion was very appealing, Samuel and I should encourage our colleagues to mount some sort of entertainment as an acknowledgement of the joylessness of many of their days. There might be music and dancing – something that would turn on its head the usual glitter of the festive season when we were all spectators as the Family and their friends ate and danced. It was something to put before Matthew and my friends. Meanwhile Mr Newcombe was speaking to me about my suggestion for a village cricket team in Stammerton. More accurately he wished to speak about his son's talents. Fortunately Matthew had already told me about the lad's ability, so I was able to sound enthusiastically knowledgeable until it was time for Beatrice and me, as was the custom, to withdraw to leave the men on their own.

'It feels wrong, us sitting here. As if we're getting above ourselves,' Beatrice said, half whispering as if we were in church, though it was only the second-best drawing room. She looked round apprehensively, as if her ladyship might come and throw us out. 'It feels as if we're trespassing.'

'It does. Imagine how I feel when we use the grey bedroom!' It was the least grand of the guest rooms, and Matthew and I only used it on the rare occasions, such as tonight, when we had to stay at the House in our role as acting hosts.

'But you couldn't have him staying there on his own while you sleep in your old bed, and if you had him to stay – it'd be like inviting a man into a convent, bless you!' But her face straightened. 'I just don't feel comfortable here.' She did not look it; in fact, she looked deeply unhappy.

Another time I might have asked what was really wrong. Tonight I simply had to cheer her up. 'We can scarcely invite

Mr Wilson and the other trustees to join us in the room, can we?'

She shifted in her seat. 'Would not the gentlemen prefer to be here on their own?'

'They might. But we are their equals in this endeavour, Beatrice, and it would have been the worst of bad manners if they had not treated us as such, would it not? We could not expect them to give up their port and cigars, but I do not think they will linger long.'

'I don't know . . . Oh! Here they come!'

They did indeed, Mr Wilson and Dr Page still carrying their port glasses – a departure from convention indeed. One might have expected Samuel to try to sit near us, for solidarity if nothing else, but he made for the hardest and most distant chair, where he might have remained had not a glance from Matthew suggested that his gesture smacked of ill-grace. I cannot say that the general conversation was anything other than stilted, but Mr Wilson in particular made an effort to speak to us women. Soon, however, he excused himself, wishing, no doubt, that the sanitation Beatrice hoped for was already in situ.

'I cannot understand how the chairman can be impartial if he accepts the hospitality of some of the other trustees,' Pounceman declared waspishly the moment he was safely out of the room. He had clearly not forgiven him for ruling as inadmissible his motion to exclude former servants from voting on certain subjects.

'My dear Pounceman,' Matthew responded, 'would you have him travel back to Shrewsbury at this time of night? And in this weather? Why, I'm sure a bedchamber could be prepared for you too within five minutes, and night-gear provided. Am I right, Harriet?'

'I shall see to it forthwith,' I declared, ready to leave the room, but remembering I might ring instead. 'Would you prefer me send a lad for your own things?'

'I think not!' He rose, turning towards the door.

'Leaving us already, Mr Pounceman?' Wilson asked, returning to the room. 'Surely not! It's raining cats and dogs!'

His apparent belief in the mortification of the flesh was clearly wavering. Perhaps it had been softened already by a generous intake of the wine Samuel had chosen, enjoying the sight, as I did, of a parson who preached total abstinence to his flock relishing a particularly fine claret.

At last he shook his head. 'Perhaps, however, I might crave the indulgence of a ride in your coach, Rowsley. I beg your pardon, the Family's coach.'

'Alas, sir,' Dr Page said swiftly, 'poor John Coachman is sadly afflicted by his rheumatism in this weather and I would not have him risk a soaking. But I can offer you a place in my dog cart, if you can borrow an umbrella. This is excellent port, Mr Bowman.' He settled back in the clear expectation of more, which he got, though Samuel's face was as rigid as his bow. 'I just hope that the Hunters' baby waits till tomorrow to put in an appearance . . . Now, Newcombe, I hear you are planning to buy Robertson's mare – it will not do, you know . . .'

'I wish we had not made such an enemy of Mr Pounceman,' I said, as later that evening we lay in each other's arms, listening to the rain.

'He made an enemy of you a long time ago,' Matthew murmured. 'And yet you were magnanimous enough to offer him accommodation here overnight.'

'Christian charity, just as Dr Page's was to take him home at last,' I responded. 'Why couldn't the dratted man have driven himself up here? Rumour has it he's just bought himself a brougham.'

'A brougham! A country clergyman driving a brougham! One who wants the smallest, plainest box of a place for a new church!'

'But only for the peasants,' I reminded him sourly.

'And will he tend his flock there himself?'

'No, he'll get a curate in to tend to their needs, won't he?'

'Did I imagine seeing Beatrice mouthing the words "whited sepulchre" at one juncture?'

'Probably. She loathes him more than most. But she and Samuel . . . I fear things are not well between them, Matthew.'

'Really? I thought he was planning to propose to her?'

'And do you really think she would accept? Should accept? They are my dearest friends, and I want nothing more than to see them happy, but the more I understand of true happiness, the less I can see them achieving it together. The world would like to see them growing old contentedly together, but I see a still vital and energetic woman irritating a much older man, made even more staid by his years of subservience.'

'He would certainly prefer her not to speak so assertively in public. But so would a lot of men of his generation. It's clear, though, that he loves her.'

'I'm sure he does – his vision of her. But is it a true vision? Matthew, if you . . . if things had been different, she would have loved you.' Despite everything, I did not dare ask if he would have loved her. 'And you are not at all like Samuel. I cannot imagine her settling for second best.'

'Many people do. And consider – women especially need the security of a man to provide for them. And men like the idea of a free sick nurse as they grow old, of course.'

I could feel the snort of his laughter. 'We will nurse each other!' I linked my fingers with his. 'That book of Browning's poetry you gave me – the latest. Do you recall that very long poem, about the Rabbi?' We had read it aloud, alternating verses. 'What were the lines we both liked?'

"Grow old along with me" . . .'

"'The best is yet to be". Life will have to be very good indeed to be better than this, my love. But growing old! There must be other things to talk of.'

I murmured, 'Or even not talk of . . .'

Living a communal life in a house such as this taught one very early on that any arguments must be quiet ones unless you want the whole body of servants to know your business. Even so, the youngest and meanest boot boy would soon read the silent signs of a falling out, such as the one between Samuel and Beatrice. Now it was clear to all that the mutual tendresse we had all hoped and even assumed would end in a wedding was no more. The meals in the Room became so excruciating that Matthew wanted to abandon them altogether: indeed, what newly-weds would not prefer to dine in the privacy of their own home? For a while we soldiered on, and then hit on the idea of inviting the warring parties to eat with us on what might be seen as neutral territory. Matthew thought that by inviting the chief nurse and Marty Baines, landlord of the Royal Oak, to join us might reduce the tension, but I recalled that Beatrice had alluded to him during her plea for sanitation in the House and wondered if something had happened between her and the widower to make Samuel jealous. Furthermore, if I knew Samuel he would not be prepared to leave what he saw as his army without a general: someone must superintend the servants' meal and in my absence it must be he. Which brought us back to the original problem: if I was still housekeeper, I should maintain the tradition of being present for meals. All of them.

That afternoon, I fell into step with Beatrice as she set out for her afternoon walk, now on Dr Page's list of instructions for the household. 'Fresh air. Exercise!' he had decreed for each and every one of us, requiring the senior staff to set an example.

'I thought the trustees' meeting went very well,' I began.

She snorted. 'So it did. Till His Nibs told me off for speaking in public. Not to mention speaking about sanitation. Not to mention flirting with the gentlemen. I can't be doing with him anymore, Harriet, and that's the truth. One of us must find a different position. And since it'd take a crowbar to get the old bugger away from here, it'll have to be me that goes.'

Despite what Matthew and I had said, hearing the situation in her own unvarnished words was still shocking.

I took her hand. 'Is it truly as bad as that? Do you truly have no feelings for him? Nor him for you?'

'Harriet, you've eyes in your head. To be honest, even if I ever loved him, which I couldn't swear to, I'm now coming to dislike him. Imagine being shut up with him, in some respectable boarding house, all day every day. And he'd be master, don't doubt it!'

I didn't. 'But you'd leave the House altogether?'

'It isn't as if I'm needed here anymore, not now it's half a hospital, half no man's land. I've been trained to cook the finest dishes for the finest people; my skills are wasted. They have been ever since his late lordship passed away and we've had no guests. Now I've seen you two lovebirds settled, I can go and spread my own wings. The only question is where. There are fashions in food just as there are in clothes, and I'm not fit to work in the best establishments, not now. There, don't look so upset!'

'Of course I'm upset. All the more because I know in my heart that you're right. If not London, where will you try?'

'Some gentleman's residence would suit me best. Not too small – I do like the thrill of entertaining – but not so grand that I'd be expected to decamp for the Season. I've had my fill of the country, though – I'd like to be in reach of a town. Remember Hortense? She's really seeing a bit of life in her new position. And I know I'm older than her, but I still have wings, and would love to fly.'

I nodded. I could well understand. Our honeymoon, in Italy, had necessarily been all too brief, given all the circumstances, but it had made me, too, long for wider experience other than through the pages of books. 'Would you like me to ask my new mama-in-law to consider your problem? She has a very wide range of acquaintances, both in the church and outside.'

'I don't like asking for favours.'

'Mrs Rowsley would not see it as a favour. She might be elderly, but she still abounds with energy and has a passion for organizing people. Not interfering. At least I don't think so. Just matching people's needs.'

'Not unlike your Matthew!' Beatrice set us in motion. 'I think perhaps I would like her help. The sooner the better. Before I murder the pig-headed old fool.'

THREE

Within a fortnight, work had started on what was immediately known as the new model village, the foundations being dug at the edges of the existing hamlet. The foreman in charge, Thomas, had worked for years on the estate buildings, and was the first to admit that while he knew all there was to know about housing pigs and cattle, he might need assistance when it came to human habitation. Meanwhile, he could ensure that the foundations were put in right and tight. He and his team had pegged out the outlines of the new cottages and resolved to start immediately, losing no time before the true winter weather arrived. A latrine had been dug. At the other side of the site, Harriet and Beatrice had organized a small field kitchen in a marquee, so the men would get hot soup or stew at midday. All was going well, and I was able to resume my usual estate work, with an eye on the metaphorical clock, so that everything was ready for when Trescothick eventually graced us with his presence.

One morning I heard footsteps hurtling along the corridor leading to my office. Raised voices – the footman clearly did not approve of such haste – came from outside my door, which opened to permit a boy to fall flat on his face in front of my desk.

'Please, gaffer, the missus says to read this note 'cause 'tis urgent, gaffer!'

'Thank you. Now, sit on that chair and catch your breath.' I read the pencilled note in increasing disbelief.

I have ordered all work on the new village to stop forthwith. Please come immediately! HR

'Mrs Rowsley gave you this?'

'Ah, and I run like the wind like she said.'

'So I see. Now go down to the kitchen – walk, don't
– and ask one of the maids for a glass of milk and a b
tell them I sent you.'

* * *

At ten o'clock on the finest morning we were likely to see for months, the men were lolling around drinking cocoa. Thomas looked embarrassed, as well he might. Harriet looked uneasy, but her chin was set in a way I'd never seen before. She gestured. I was to speak to Thomas. She withdrew a few yards.

'A body, you see, gaffer. Well, a skellington, like. But missus said not to move it, nor to dig out any more of they stones, the ones I thought we could use for the church foundations, being so big but fine dressed. So we said we'd start digging there' – he pointed to a spot a few yards away – 'but missus said no, not to touch nothing without your express permission.'

'I'd better go and talk to her, hadn't I?' I might have smiled, but we both knew I was closer to snarling. Nodding, I walked off to where she was standing, apparently quite calm in the face of all the chaos she was causing. 'Well?'

Her chin went up further. '*Well?*'

'*Well*, what on earth do you think you're doing, interfering with this urgent work?'

'*Well*, perhaps you should take a closer look. I believe the men have uncovered a skeleton. Is it not your immediate responsibility to notify the coroner? And not touch the remains until he grants you permission?'

'How dare you tell me how to do my job?'

'How dare you presume to ignore further evidence. Stones? For the new church? Upon my soul, Mr Rowsley, from my note I assumed you might suspect they are more important than that!'

'I beg your pardon! You are truly overreaching yourself.'

She looked me up and down, as if I were a cheeky kitchen boy. 'We will speak of this later,' she declared, 'when you have had a chance to reflect. Meanwhile, I have a telegraph to send.'

An employee, speaking to her master like this! 'How dare—'

'Keep your voice down. I will not be shouted at in public and it does not become you to try. Good day to you.' She turned on her heel and strode off.

It was only the presence of the men that prevented me shouting at her to come back. And then to stop me running after her.

Damn the woman, for treating me so cavalierly in public. At all. Anywhere. My wife. My own wife.

But a tiny thread of a voice whispered in my ear that I must attend to what she had said, with the very best of grace, in public, at least. Attaching a smile to my face, I turned not to Thomas, but to the kitchen maid engaged in gathering up the men's empty mugs. 'I suppose there isn't a spare mug, is there?' I asked.

The fear in her eyes as she bobbed a curtsy and scuttled back to the marquee came as a slap in the face. Had the very sight of me in my rage reduced her to this? And would I be surprised if it had? Maybe she thought I wanted to smash the mug in my temper. Following her, I called in what I hoped was a much kinder voice, 'And Mary-Ann, might I have two spoonsful of sugar? And a bun, too?' I had had to learn that if I had things in my hands, I couldn't ball them into fists.

So as I joined Thomas, I presented the appearance of a man halfway through a late breakfast, speaking with my mouth full. 'Tell me about all this,' I said, sitting on the edge of the trench and motioning him to join me.

''Tain't much to make such a song and dance about, is it, gaffer? Just the skellington and a few bits of metal there – see? All rusted? Just by that – well, looks a bit like a wall, doesn't it? And – though I didn't tell the missus – there's a few more stones over there we dug out yesterday. Big 'uns.' He pointed.

Finishing my cocoa – it was far too sweet, of course – I got to my feet and strolled over. They were actually ideal for the new church's foundations. Thomas had chosen well. Nine-tenths of me wanted to tell him to clean them up and put them to one side. The last tenth made me run my fingers over them. 'Thomas, have you got a broom or something?'

'Oh, you've found the one with the writing cut into it, have you? There's another over there, gaffer, all cleaned up. Shame it's broken. It was hard to move so I took a pickaxe to it.'

I felt suddenly sick. Nonetheless I shrugged. 'You did your best. Now, what was this about not digging any more trenches?'

'Missus said we must disturb no more big stones, gaffer. But to tell you the truth, soon as she'd turned her back and started on her way, I got young Job to have a little dig. Not so as she'd notice, you understand.' He winked.

Suddenly I was joining a conspiracy to mock her. As a woman who didn't know anything? But I should not allow him to treat any senior member of the household as a figure of fun. Damn her for putting me in this position! What on earth could I say without losing face? 'I think in situations like this you should obey orders, Thomas, however illogical they . . . they may seem.' I had almost said, however illogical they are. 'But since you have, tell me what you found.'

'I can do better than that, gaffer. I can show you. Her's a bit stuck – shall I get Job to take a pickaxe to her, and all?'

Her? 'Best not. Let me look.' As I peered into the new trench, the one my wife had expressly forbidden them to start, blood flooded my face. A beautiful woman's arm protruded from the cold earth. 'Give me that broom, man, now.' I swept gently at the ground around her. Elegant drapery gradually appeared. And tresses. All in stone. 'No one is to touch this. Or anything else!' I pointed to the spoil heap. 'Understand?'

'So missus was right then?' he asked with a sly grin.

'Have you not noticed, our missuses often are?'

Did knowing that she was in the right and that I had put myself absolutely in the wrong make me any less angry? Not a jot, though my temper was now directed at myself and at whoever had taken a pickaxe to part of what I now strongly suspected was part of a Roman ruin. She must have realized straightaway what it was. More curtly than necessary I directed Thomas to cover the skeleton decently with a clean tarpaulin and reminded him that henceforth nothing must be touched. Nothing at all. He might dig – very carefully – some trial trenches a hundred yards or so away from the finds, but as soon as spade struck stone, work must stop. No violence was to be visited on anything they found, nor was it to be removed. What had I said? Thomas's broad honest face suddenly wore a shifty expression.

'The lads – one or two – might have picked up a few little things they took a fancy to,' he said.

'In that case, you must collect them all up again. I'll send over a supply of envelopes for you to put them in, carefully labelled. Tell them I'll recompense them twofold if they are honest with me.'

Still aware of the fury seething in me, I made my way not back home but to my office in the House. It was all her fault.

How dared she send me such a dismissive note? How dared she . . . but what was that about a telegraph to send? Whichever way I tried to direct my thoughts, nothing made sense. I strode as fast as I could, almost willing myself to fall over and hurt myself, as I had as a boy, when physical pain was the only thing that might assuage mental torment. Once when I was younger I had punched a tree so hard I broke three fingers: there were trees aplenty here, all calling me to let them draw my blood at least. My forehead? My hand?

I must set an example. I must not resort to violence. But if I did not hit myself, I fear I would hit her.

Safe in my office, I denied myself to all visitors. I managed to despatch envelopes to Thomas at the site, plus pencils and some sealing wax. So far I was thinking straight. But then all I could manage was to sit with my head in my hands. Then I paced, backwards and forwards, like one of the wild beasts they kept in circuses for our amusement. There was a scrap of paper on the carpet. Were standards already so badly falling, that the housemaid had not tidied up? I was about to ring in fury, when it dawned on me that I had seen her curtsying her way out when I had arrived. I had complimented her on the excellence of her work. And the scrap of paper was the same size of that produced by Thomas's messenger.

'*My love, I believe the workmen have found Roman remains like those at Uriconium. So . . .*'

Covering my face, I groaned. What had I done? And what could be done to put it right? I must face the consequences of my folly, or more might ensue. Abandoning my work and my dignity I quit my office and ran home through the busy kitchen, shocking the servants on my way, so fast that I thought my chest would burst.

Dan, our stable lad, was just urging our new pony to take his place between the shafts of the equally new trap when I arrived dishevelled and now bloodstained from an accidental fall. The knees of my trousers were in shreds.

Harriet, immaculate in her best coat and hat, looked me up and down. Then she looked at her watch. 'Can you be clean and ready in three minutes? I'll get bandages,' she added. She nodded to Dan, who was deeply occupied with the pony, and led the way into the house.

By the time I had stripped and mopped at my hands and knees, a fresh suit and shirt had been laid out on the bed. There were two rolls of bandage. Of Harriet there was no sign.

I managed my knees easily enough, but wandered around the upstairs helplessly trying to deal with my hands. Ah, there she was in the hall, pacing in irritation much as I would have done.

Taking the stairs painfully, embarrassingly slowly, I held out my hands. In silence, she took scissors from her chatelaine, tying the ends of the bandage on my left hand in neat knots. The same for the right. She passed me my hat and led the way out.

Dan was still apparently absorbed in looking at the pony, but shot a glance at my hands under his brows and after a second of visible hesitation passed the reins to Harriet. We set off. I did not look back to see what his face said.

'I do not deserve forgiveness. I do not expect it. I publicly humiliated you and undercut your authority. I am ashamed – more, I am appalled at what I did.'

Keeping her eyes on the road ahead, she asked, 'How did you come to hurt yourself?'

'I was running – I had to speak to you. I had to tell you how sorry I am. And I fell.'

'I assume you had just found the other half of the note I sent.'

'I was contrite before then. I only went back to the office because I couldn't trust myself . . . I wanted to hit every tree I found, shout at every undeserving servant. Because I was no longer angry with you, but furious at my folly, my . . . my wrongness in wounding you. I love you, Harriet, with all my heart and all my soul and I do not deserve you. But I still beg you: please forgive me.'

She gave a little snort – or was it a sniff? Was she weeping?

'Thanks to you and your prescience, I believe . . . No, that is wrong. You and you alone saved whatever lies there. Thank you.'

There was still no loving response, just the sort of information a servant might give an employer. 'In a telegraph, I have told Sir Francis Palmer—'

'The Oxford scholar? The historian?'

'Yes. I said that you have taken every step to preserve the site. He is coming by the next train, which is due at one-fifty. Hence our haste – though I do wish you had bought a more willing beast.'

Was that a hint of a truce? I thought not; she was clicking her tongue in irritation at the lugubrious animal. But I doubted if she would use the whip. She never did. I did not dare recommend it now. After all, I was the one who deserved to be horsewhipped.

No more words were exchanged by the time we arrived at the station, half a minute before the train announced its presence in a way that had more effect on the horse than any of Harriet's cajoling. I was just able to hop down and get to the wretched creature's head before it bolted. I held it still long enough for Harriet to dismount and then set it in gentle motion around the station yard. But the guard's whistle alone was enough to set it aquiver, and it was all I could do to control it when the train set off, with the accompaniment of much huffing and puffing, and then a confounded whistle of its own. At last two boys strolled over and seemed to know how to handle the animal.

Hat in hand, I headed as briskly as I dared to the station entrance, to find a strange and very handsome man in his middle years, his dark hair silvering at the temples, who was tucking Harriet's hand under his arm.

'Sir Francis, this is Matthew Rowsley, my husband. Matthew, Sir Francis Palmer. You will recall the piece he wrote on the Uriconium excavations in the *Illustrated London News*.' Gently she released herself so that we could shake hands, though very gingerly, in my case at least. 'As you can see, Sir Francis, my husband has injured his hands and has entrusted the reins to me. Would you care to take refreshment at our home – a late luncheon – or are you happy to proceed straight to the place where they have been digging?'

I had forgotten that we had not eaten – but after all this morning's troubles, I had no appetite.

'Since the days are getting shorter, I think we should go straight to the site, if that fits in with your arrangements, Harriet – forgive me, Mrs Rowsley, I should say.'

'I am happy for you to call me either, Sir Francis. So to Stammerton it is. Despite appearances, the horse is in general very placid, are you not, Robin?'

I think it was her use of the horse's name that humbled me most.

Harriet was much too polite to allow the newcomer any hint that all was not well between us, and I took comfort from her reference to our home. Did I infer that our distinguished visitor would be staying with us, not at the House? Given the situation there, I thought she had, as usual, made the right decision; certainly all necessary preparations would be well in train by now, or she would not have left the premises.

I wondered when and where they had met before. Not as equals, I suspected, or he would not be so free with her name. But I would not speculate; she would tell me what she wanted me to know when she was ready. Meanwhile, we passed the journey explaining the unusual situation where we had to refer all major decisions to the trustees.

'So they will have to approve any suggestions I might make about the site? Very well. I hope they may be more amenable than some of the landowners we have to deal with. Now, tell me – how and why did the digging start? And how soon can it be halted?'

She glanced at me. I was to explain. 'Harriet realized immediately that the stones the foreman wished to use as the foundations of a new church were valuable in themselves. A skeleton confirmed that. She stopped all work immediately and sent for you. Meanwhile, I have ordered the men to return all the little souvenirs they have acquired. I have not yet notified the coroner, but I have covered the skeleton. And I found another body that Harriet has not seen – a stone body, I am glad to say.'

'So this is all your doing, Mrs Rowsley! Why am I not surprised?'

'I think Matthew has overstated my role,' she said, with an amused smile. But she laid her hand on mine for a moment.

The idyllic moment was cut short, however. Thomas was running towards us.

'Gaffer! Come quick! We've got another body! But only just dead!'

Jumping down from the trap, I ran towards him. 'What on earth do you mean?'

But he was too distressed to be coherent. 'Still warm,' he shouted.

'Show me!'

'There! There! Where you stopped me digging! Along with that woman!'

I sprinted. And there, his body in a hideous embrace with the statue, was Samuel.

FOUR

B efore I knew it, Harriet was on her knees, wrestling with her billowing skirts. She leant into the trench, reaching for Samuel's wrist. 'He lives! Just! Is there a lad here who could ride bareback? Ah, Bertie! Get Robin out of the shafts and ride like the wind to find Dr Page. Now!' The smallest of the labourers tugged his forelock and sped off.

Unencumbered by yards of fabric, Palmer and I had jumped into the trench. We stripped off our jackets and were preparing to lift the old man out. But Harriet shook her head. 'Dr Page might prefer to treat him here first.'

'Is there somewhere we could get a stretcher?' Palmer looked helplessly around.

'Thomas, get the men to lift a gate off its hinges. And send another to the House for sheets and blankets!' I shouted, glad to be useful at last. 'And bid them prepare for a patient!' I laid my jacket over the battered body. I turned to Harriet, who was lifting her skirt to reveal a petticoat she immediately tore into wide strips. 'Here!' she said, bunching the cloth into a pad. 'Use this to staunch the blood.'

Thomas peered down at me. 'All done, gaffer. Now, I been thinking: he didn't fall into that woman's arms by himself, did he? Shall I summon young Elias Pritchard? Not that he can do much, of course, but a constable's a constable, whichever way you slice it.'

'Excellent idea! Yes, please. And Thomas, we need to know how this came about here. Why was no one around?'

'I sent the lads off to bring in the bits and pieces you wanted, gaffer. And – this sounds bad, I know, and I beg pardon, ma'am – I had . . . to use . . . the latrine over there. And then I had a smoke of my pipe. So that's when this must have happened. Soon as I saw the poor old gentleman, I well-nigh lost my faculties. But I pulled myself together, got the first lad I saw to round up the others, treasure or no treasure, and the rest you know.'

'Well done, Thomas. Thank you.' I caught sight of Palmer's green face. I fancied he was more used to death and injury in more sanitized settings. 'Now, this gentleman is Sir Francis Palmer. He knows all about stones like this. So I think he might like to take a walk round the other ditches to see all you've found while we remain with poor Mr Bowman. Perhaps you could escort him.'

Both men seemed pleased with the notion. Palmer, first producing a handkerchief to wipe Samuel's blood from his hand, put his arm in the air so that Thomas could heave him up. The unlikely pair set off. Following Harriet's instructions, I continued to work on the poor broken body. But when we felt we could do no more, she held out her hand to me, palm up. I put mine in hers.

Under Page's close supervision, Samuel, still unconscious, was lifted with the utmost care on to the gate, which had been made as comfortable as possible. Then a team of men carried their burden to the House, with others taking their places when their arms gave under the strain. Everything was seamlessly gentle. I was ready to run ahead of them to warn Beatrice but Harriet restrained me. 'She is at our house, preparing afternoon tea and dinner for Sir Francis. I will go to her there. Matthew, they have argued and argued so bitterly she speaks of leaving here altogether. How will she feel now?'

I shook my head sadly. 'I did so hope—'

'I know. We all did. But she said – and I hardly like to say it, even to you – that she wanted to leave before she murdered him. Ah! Enough of this! Is that Bertie and Robin? No, it's Elias!'

The constable, whose whiskers were so magnificent it was rumoured he could use them to catch cricket balls, had commandeered a horse from someone, so seriously had he taken the news. He tethered it firmly before approaching us with a polite salute. But the expression on his face told us how shocked he was. 'All that blood, ma'am! Not just on you, but on that statue. Looks as if the poor lady's just died, doesn't it? But they say it's Mr Bowman that's been hurt. So what's going on, Matthew? Sir,' he corrected himself, for we were not simply part of a flourishing cricket team now.

I shook my head. 'Matthew in private, Elias, though your sergeant might disapprove of it in public, might he not, *Constable Pritchard*?' We exchanged a smile. 'They are carrying poor Samuel Bowman to the House. We thought it best to wait for you here,' I said not entirely truthfully. 'But Mrs Arden is working in our kitchen today and must be told.'

He frowned. 'Didn't I hear they were at daggers drawn? I'll need to speak to her myself, you know – and maybe it's best if I'm there when you break the news. Just to observe, like, Matthew.'

I nodded. How could I argue? 'There's something else – we may need to notify the coroner that the men have unearthed a skeleton, though I would say that was of someone long dead. It's covered with that tarpaulin over there. You see where Thomas is talking to a gentleman? He's Sir Francis Palmer, a noted scholar. Harriet sent for him immediately she saw the old stones.'

'Really, ma'am?'

She smiled. 'I think they're Roman, Elias. You've heard of all the work going on near Wroxeter. We may have something similar here.'

'But ma'am, what about the new village?'

'They may have to build it in a slightly different place. Don't worry. We have to look after the past, but we need to look after people living here too. You will tell people, won't you? And tell them not to be tempted to come here and take bits and pieces away, no matter how small and insignificant they may be. That's very important, isn't it, Matthew?'

'I think people will deserve a reward if they return items they *happened* to find. I'm sure you agree. But to the point, Elias. This attack on a poor old man who may not even reach his home alive. What's to be done?'

He shook his head. 'I'm going to have to call in Sergeant Burrows, aren't I?'

'But in the meantime?' Harriet urged.

'Can you recommend some reliable men to guard the place, Matthew? Enough to patrol day and night? I'm thinking if this is full of treasure, someone might have been trying to steal some when Mr Bowman came across him. That's probably why the poor old man was hit so hard – so he wouldn't ever be able to identify his attacker.'

Since we had a trap but no horse, Bertie not apparently having thought to return here, though he had got the rest of his errand right, we had no option but to walk back to our house. Elias joined us on foot, leading his mount which, he said, had been inclined to object to a strange rider. Fortunately it did not mind having our guest's valise strapped to it. Sir Francis and Harriet fell as naturally into step as Elias and I did. They chatted with the ease of old friends, at one time bursting into laughter, though they quickly stifled it.

'I've been thinking. Before you break the news to Mrs Arden,' Elias said slowly, 'I ought to send off a telegraph to Sergeant Burrows. He can decide about telling the coroner.'

'Of course. You can use my study to write the messages, and Dan will run off to the post office for you. And return that horse.'

'If anyone can ride the damned thing, he can. How long do you think he'll be working for you, Matthew?'

'I don't know. He's wasted in a small household, isn't he? But I shall be sad when he finds a new position . . .'

Sir Francis declared himself in need of no refreshment but the sherry and biscuits which were ready in the library; he was soon looking with satisfaction at the shelves. Harriet and I had perforce to change our garments before we ventured down to the kitchen: we did not want poor Beatrice to assume the very worst, though the truth was bad enough. Polly, the tweeny bringing our hot water, nearly fainted at the sight of us, and had to be despatched to her room to collect herself.

Suddenly Harriet and I were clinging to each other, not with desire but for comfort. At last we kissed. Were we one again?

'We can't keep Elias waiting much longer,' she said.

'Nor Sir Francis.'

'Oh, he and I are old friends,' she said casually. 'We met when I was working for an aunt of his. I was a senior house-maid. We just liked each other; he never tried to take advantage of me, like a lot of young men, or even disturb me at my work.

But should we chance to meet, he would talk about his studies and lend me books.'

'You didn't tell me about this when we read that article.'

'Talk about another man on our honeymoon? Matthew, that would have been bad taste indeed! Now, let us go down. Oh dear, I am really not looking forward to this.'

If Beatrice, cap askew and sleeves rolled up, noticed Elias slipping into the kitchen behind us, she gave no sign of it. In fact, she simply looked surprised when we told her that Samuel had been attacked, and where. 'But what on earth was he doing out there? And why should anyone want to assault an old man like that?'

Before anyone could reply, a shame-faced Bertie appeared, stuttering with embarrassment. He'd forgotten about bringing that pesky horse back. Anyway, it was now safe in the stable, feeding its face.

'Let Robin have the rest of his feed when he returns with the trap,' Harriet said crisply. He looked flummoxed. 'Is Dan there? Well, why don't the two of you persuade Robin to return to Stammerton, get him back between the shafts and bring the trap back here? Don't give him any notion of having a rest – he's got more journeys to make tonight. Good lad.'

'Not the sharpest knife in the drawer, is he?' Beatrice said with a sigh. 'Now, what's all this about Samuel? It doesn't seem to have sunk in properly.' She sat heavily on a chair, mopping her forehead with her apron.

Harriet sank beside her, taking her hands. 'Beatrice, listen to me. Samuel's injuries are very serious. Very serious. That's why we need the trap – to take you up to the House so that you can be with him.'

'If I wanted to go that badly I could walk, couldn't I?' she said fretfully. 'Not that he'd want me, not unless it was to start bickering with me again.'

I knelt the other side. 'Beatrice, he's not going to be bickering with anyone, not for a long time. If ever, to be entirely truthful. He's unconscious. Dr Page is with him, and I know there are trained nurses up at the House. But he's so ill . . . yes, you might want to be at his bedside.'

'But I don't, you see.' She turned to Harriet. 'I told you, we're not sweethearts any more, not that we ever were really. I think having you arrive on the scene, Matthew, sweeping Harriet off her feet, gave him the idea. Or maybe I got the idea first. Who knows? But it's all gone sour, and I want to wish him well and leave.'

'You sure you want to wish him well, Mrs Arden?' Elias asked, emerging from the shadows.

'Of course I do! We worked together in harmony for years, didn't we, Harriet? More or less in harmony. And remember this, young Elias, if I leave, I might need him to write me a reference, so I'd not go hurting him, would I?'

Elias at least seemed convinced. Perhaps he didn't notice the tiny traces of blood round her fingernails. After all, her hands were shaking badly.

'A cup of tea, that's what we all need,' she declared, squaring her shoulders and getting to her feet.

Harriet tried to press her back on to the chair. 'I can make it, Bea.'

'No, it's my job and I'll do it. And if you give me ten minutes I'll have an afternoon tea fit for a king ready in the drawing room. We don't want that professor of yours thinking you can't run your own establishment. I brought young Marjorie down with me, and she's got an even better hand for pastry than I have. As for you, young Elias, your mama herself gave me the recipe for the fruit cake I made, so you'd better sit yourself down and try it before you go and find out who hurt poor old Samuel.'

I was puzzled; she'd obviously registered somewhere what we had said, but seemed not to have grasped the seriousness. Harriet, catching my eye, gave a minute shrug, and mimed a tiny question mark. But it seemed we could do nothing immediately, and I valued Elias' perceptiveness more than his sergeant did, so we did as we were bidden, and adjourned to offer our guest refreshment.

FIVE

'I can't imagine, Mrs Rowsley, how you concluded that I would be staying at the Lion in Shrewsbury,' Sir Francis said, laughing.

'Would you stay anywhere else? Not with the Lion's connection with Mr Darwin,' I said, passing him tea as we sat in the comfort of our parlour. Bea had been correct: she had indeed done us proud. 'Mr Darwin and Matthew's father are regular correspondents, you know. Anyway, if the telegraph hadn't reached you there, I would have tried all the other hotels, in descending order. We met, Matthew, at the coldest house it's ever been my doubtful privilege to work in; we used to say that even the mice needed fur slippers. Oh, my apologies, Sir Francis.'

He shrugged slightly. I had forgotten that like many he was a man happy to criticize his family himself, but was uneasy when others did. 'My aunt was . . . eccentric. She used to go out hunting in the vilest weather, Rowsley, and not even take a hot bath before the vile meal she alleged was dinner. The wine! Rarely decanted properly, so you had to chew as much as you drank. But nothing competed with the cold! Heavens, I used to get dressed to go to bed! The tiniest fires and the smokiest chimneys. I can't imagine what it was like for . . . for the staff,' he added, suddenly embarrassed and apologetic, glancing under his eyelashes at me.

I preferred not to tell him. 'As far as Thorncroft House is concerned, I am glad to say that his late lordship liked warmth. And you can judge for yourself whether we like comfort here.'

Sir Francis smiled. 'I am glad of it. You have a fine library, Rowsley. And your sherry is excellent.'

Matthew waved away the second compliment. 'Poor Samuel Bowman is responsible for the selection of sherry and wine. I would not dare buy anything without his permission. As for the books, you must praise my father's choice – he is a true scholar.'

'The father who corresponds with Darwin . . .' Sir Francis mused. 'Not Archdeacon Rowsley! Heavens, what a fine mind he has.'

'And a kind heart,' I said truthfully, 'which his son has inherited.' I managed to smile. We must not be at war in front of a visitor. And in my heart I knew I had to forgive him. 'My love, I feel I must go up to the House to see how Samuel is, and speak to him if I can. May I ask you to entertain Sir Francis until I return?'

'Mrs Rowsley,' Sir Francis said, 'we have known each other many years. I would be honoured if you would drop my title, and even more so if I might address you both by your Christian names. Yes? In that case, Matthew, perhaps we might accompany Harriet. I would love to see the interior of Thorncroft House, and the treasures it's no doubt home to.'

We agreed that we would take it in turns to show our guest round. I still felt uneasy addressing him as an equal, but Matthew and he fell into conversation about the Family portraits with the greatest ease. Accordingly I chose to visit Samuel first.

He was not in his own room, but one prepared in what he had pleaded to be called the Family wing. Beside him stood Hargreaves, who had once served his lordship as his valet, and had now become his chief attendant. Presumably he had left someone else on duty. Hargreaves had known Samuel since boyhood, and was bathing his forehead with the tenderness of a son. Adjusting Samuel's bandages was the chief nurse, a woman like me in her early forties. In general Nurse Pegg favoured a grim expression, no doubt to improve discipline. Her voice tended to the shrill, but contrived to be harsh too, as if she was somehow forcing it. With her heavy features and raw-boned hands, she would never have been a beauty, but she exuded kindness.

The news was clearly not good. Hargreaves gently ushered me into the corridor. 'Dr Page has just gone to check on her ladyship and his lordship, Mrs Rowsley, before he returns here. Mr Bowman's not regained consciousness and is already in a fever, so I have taken the liberty of having the adjoining bedchamber prepared for Dr Page. I'm to summon him if there's the slightest sign of change. Yes, I'm watching Mr Bowman overnight. He knows me, see – knows my voice. Nurse Pegg, now: she's a wonderful nurse, I dare say, but he doesn't really know her, does he?' He was almost in tears; pompous and irritating Samuel might be, but he treated each and every servant as a son or daughter – stern, yes, but always kind.

I took his hand. 'Thank you. I can't think of anyone he'd prefer beside him.'

He looked at me shrewdly. 'Nor me. Not now I can't. Not now he and Mrs Arden – it's not like a lover's tiff, is it, Mrs Rowsley, if you'll pardon me for speaking so freely. It's more as if they simply don't like each other anymore. You know, like you long with all your heart and soul to take a young lady to the harvest dance . . . but then you manage to meet her the day before to ask her, and you wonder what all the fuss was about. And you're glad you didn't ask her because then you get to dance with a lot of other maidens,' he added with disconcerting candour.

Absolutely adamant that she would not join us at the dinner table, Beatrice produced the most memorable meal, demonstrating quite clearly that her talents were indeed wasted at the House. I told her as much when I left Matthew and Francis to their port.

'It's good to know I can still do it,' she said. 'And without a huge team to help, too. I'd almost forgotten how to bone a leg of lamb. Almost, but not quite.'

'Francis sent particular compliments about that,' I said truthfully, while trying not to think of the blood round her nails.

'Francis is it, now? Hark at you, Lady Muck! Getting above ourselves, aren't we!'

Despite myself, I felt a flush of anger rising. We had worked alongside each other for years as equal voices in the House, and had our positions now been reversed, I would never have sneered like that. And yet, let me be honest, had she won Matthew's heart, not me, I would have felt like it, and might well have succumbed.

'I'm sorry if I give that impression,' I said truthfully. 'And I would much rather you had joined us. Come, Bea, take off your pinny and sit with us for our tea and coffee. That's what I came down to say. Times have changed here, and we must change too.'

'And if you won't come up,' Matthew declared, making us both jump, 'we will come and sit with you.'

She reacted to the teasing note in his voice. 'Invade my territory, would you? I can't have that.'

Stay the night she would not, however, so, rather than rely on the recalcitrant Robin, we all turned out once again to escort her back to the House. Francis and I continued the tour, this time of the by now freezing State Rooms, while Matthew, more or less frog-marching Beatrice up to the Family wing with him, sought the latest news of Samuel.

'I'm not saying this just because we're shivering too much to hold the lamps steady,' Francis said, 'but in the interests of the paintings a more constant temperature is desirable. Small fires, not likely to set the whole edifice alight, might be possible?'

'More easily said than done these days,' I replied. 'The indoor staff have had their roles changed now we have two invalids – three now, alas! – to care for, so there are fewer nightly patrols. It would be a risk. And, to be frank, the Family has never been known for their personal beauty. Would a few cracks in their portraits be a serious matter?'

'It's true that the loss of Sir Palfrey Croft's face would matter little. But the loss of a Lely is always sad. And look round – the furnishings are also works of art, are they not?'

'Not for those who dust them,' I ventured. 'As for the rest of the House, Matthew must show you the attics; he believes they are unopened treasure chests. Ah!' I turned as the door creaked. 'How is Samuel?'

Matthew shook his head sadly. 'He looks dreadfully ill and is still unconscious. Page insists, however, that the body may well work at its best like that – not aware of pain, it can begin to heal itself. But Hargreaves is under strict instructions to wake Page if he is truly alarmed. How well he's turning out, that young man! If only he was young enough to be apprenticed to an apothecary, even a medical man like Page.'

'At least the village schools you plan should help other,

younger versions of Hargreaves to take on tasks we cannot imagine them doing now,' Francis observed. 'Though in truth I can't imagine that being a popular notion.'

'Not even with some of our trustees,' I said. 'But more of that in a warmer place, perhaps. Brrr! I do believe it's colder here than outside . . .'

Never have I felt more frustrated by the need to do my daily work. First having stopped at the House to see how Samuel had passed the night – he lived, that was all Dr Page would say – Matthew and Francis had driven over to Stammerton, to gauge what must be done with the ruins. I had to redraw rotas to enable the House to be heated overnight and consider the amount of coal we would now need. The only light relief – and the words are ironic – was the arrival of Sergeant Burrows, with Elias in tow.

What I wanted quite desperately to do was find out if Elias had noticed the blood around Beatrice's nails, but to do that risked incriminating her. And it was certainly not a question to be raised in front of anyone else. Burrows might be irritating, but he was no fool.

We greeted each other with the affability of old adversaries. I suggested that while I summoned all the staff for questioning, he and Elias might adjourn to the Room, as my former sitting room was still called, for tea or coffee – alas, we could no longer justify buying her ladyship's special blend – and some of Beatrice's biscuits.

Elias looked me in the eye. 'Does she still make them herself?'

'She likes to keep her hand in,' I said carefully, sensing the question wasn't entirely straightforward. 'Not just in cakes and pastry-making, but in all aspects of the kitchen. Why, last night, she even boned the lamb herself, and very good it was too. As she implied to you, she's wasted here, where there's no longer any call for anything except good plain cooking.'

'Boning meat's not women's work, is it?' Burrows asked.

'It is when you've not got a kitchen lad to hand,' Beatrice said, bustling in with a tray. 'There you are. And no, it's not a cook's job to wait at table, but a couple of the maids are down with heavy colds. Two of the others are talking to the head nurse about becoming nurses themselves. Miss Nightingale might be their inspiration but their real enthusiasm comes from that miserable-looking Nurse Pegg. Where on earth did Dr Page find her, gawky great creature? And those guards, too. I know I don't know all the estate workers, but some of them look so hard you could knock nails in with them. Now, Harriet,' she continued with a very slight emphasis, 'Thatcher tells me all the male staff will be gathered in the servants' hall in five minutes. Do you want me to set about bringing all the maids together?'

I had a suspicion that there might not be a right answer. 'If you could organize the kitchen staff, and maybe the dairy and laundry maids, I will round up the housemaids, wherever they may be.'

Before I could move, however, there was a distant peal on a bell – not a staff one, hung on my wall.

I put my head into the servants' hall. 'Thatcher, could that be the front door bell?'

He was on his feet in an instant, pushing Dixon, the most presentable of the remaining footmen, ahead of him. It was the youngster who would open the front door still panting from the exertion; Thatcher would proceed at the more stately pace he had adopted from Samuel.

It was Dixon who returned first, coat-tails aflying. 'Mrs Rowsley, ma'am. He's here. His lordship's heir is here!'

SIX

Watching Palmer at work, giving the workers precise and clear instructions, I tried to forget the trouble I had caused only twenty-four hours ago, and the several disasters that might have ensued, had it not been for my wife. I blessed her foresight and, even more, her generosity of spirit in forgiving me. I could not forgive myself yet for my behaviour, or for the niggling jealousy that insisted in reappearing each time I saw her and Palmer in the sort of conversation that could only take place between old friends. I had known her but a year – less! How could I compete with this handsome, debonair aristocrat who might have been an early love? Compete? I was well on the way to calling him a friend myself, succumbing to the easy charm he combined with scholarship and natural authority. How could Harriet not have loved him, even if she loved me now? And how long would she continue to love me, with him a constant presence? Yes, he had announced that he must stay until he could bring in other academics, other experts in antiquities such as this.

I made myself stroll in his direction with every show – and many feelings – of affability. Apparently he was pointing out what he thought were the outlines of some structure, Thomas nodding in appreciation and jotting down notes every so often.

'The area seems remarkably extensive,' I said, joining them.

'Oh, this is probably just a part of it,' he said airily. 'Look over there, where the land rises and falls irregularly: I am sure we will find more under there. And in that field – I can't wait to investigate those ridges! Now, Thomas, who can you get to paint me some stakes to mark out the boundary? And how many men can you spare?'

In some alarm, Thomas looked at me.

'I fear that that is not a matter for Thomas or even me. The men are employed to build a new village, not excavate an old

one. Yesterday I mentioned the trustees. A task as big as this
will need their approval.'

'Come, Matthew – you're the agent. Surely your word is
enough to get things started.'

I shook my head. 'I can authorize work to stop here on our
model village; I can authorize it to start elsewhere, off your
site. But I cannot take on another team of men without the
trustees' express permission. What I suggest is this: lay out
Thomas's pegs to show what you think is the full extent of the
land you want preserved. Draw a map to scale. Write a memo-
randum detailing the workmen you will need and for how long.
Will they need accommodation? There is plenty of room for
your academic colleagues in the House, but it will be a different
matter if you want to bring in manual workers. Prepare everything as if for a court of law. I will convene an urgent meeting.
I am sure that almost everyone will agree most readily to what
you propose, but . . . yes, there will be those who do not. Make
the case watertight!'

He shook his head in petulant asperity. 'If this is only half
the size of Uriconium it could be of national importance!'

'In that case, it should be easy enough to persuade the trustees.
How long will you need to put your proposals together? A
week? I can offer you the support of my young clerk, Freddie
– he's little more than a child but don't let that deceive you –
and the use of the library at home or in the House. So I will
suggest a week tomorrow as a possible date.'

If he had been about to object, he had to stop, because my
attention was on the young man running towards us as if his
life depended on it. A footman. Somewhere along the way he
had shed his livery jacket, and poor Samuel, had he seen him,
would have rebuked him for his lack of gravitas. Dear God,
let him not be bringing news that my old friend . . . no!

'Mr Rowsley, sir!' the man gasped. He could say no more
until his chest stopped heaving.

'Quietly now, Hubbard – quietly. Just imagine you have hit
the winning run. Yes? You'd be puffed then but not panicking.
Quietly. There. Now, what do you need to tell me? Samuel –
Mr Bowman?'

'No, he's just the same, sir. But I wish he was here. Or rather back at the House! Where he is, but—'

'Yes, yes!' I tried not to sound impatient, but I was ready to shake the news out of him.

'It's someone who's just arrived, sir. The new lord, he says.'

'Mr Trescothick?'

Another gasp for air. 'That's him, sir. Said he's come to take over!'

Did he indeed? I was fairly sure Mr Wilson might have something to say about that. I had a telegraph to despatch before I even spoke to the newcomer.

Thatcher had installed Mr Trescothick in the library, where the usual small fire had been coaxed into a blaze. Beatrice had provided a tray of refreshments, which Thatcher was now serving, with just the right amount of deference. Of Harriet there was no sign, which was, now I came to think of it, just as it ought to be: she would be organizing his accommodation. Would she think he merited the best chamber? On the whole, for his sake I hoped not: anyone coming from a normal life to this might have been daunted, like a bank clerk who had suddenly been transported to Buckingham Palace.

Unlike many of the Crofts, he was tall, his hair a mousy mid-brown to their russet. He had made an attempt to grow side-whiskers, but they did not flourish. His complexion was still ruddy from the Antipodean sun. Were his shoulders broad enough to bear the responsibility he would inherit? It was hard to predict how long he might have to wait. How quickly would he absorb all the information it was my duty to impart?

'Ah, so you're Rowley, are you?' he greeted me, without standing up.

'Matthew Rowsley, his lordship's land agent,' I corrected him unemphatically as I bowed and offered him my hand. 'Welcome to Thorncroft House, Mr Trescothick.'

He looked at me coolly. 'Well, Rowley, thank you for your greeting. You can report to me after luncheon.' He nodded my dismissal.

I hardly had time to fume with rage and, in fact, did not need to. The newcomer was not worth my anger. He was not my employer, and had no power over me. He would soon learn that, but not, with luck, from me. The preservation of the site and getting the trustees to agree to Francis's proposals were more urgent matters. As was Samuel's health. If ever we needed his years of experience dealing with awkward aristocrats it was now. His mixture of the pompous, the obsequious and unflappability was precisely what was required. In any case, I was letting myself down: why should I worry about a man catapulted into a difficult situation who was probably using bad manners to cover his unease?

Wilson honoured me with a reply within the hour. He would arrive on the next train from Shrewsbury: could I send a trap to the estate station?

I could not only send it: I could drive her ladyship's trap myself, with a far more willing beast than Robin between the shafts. As I gave Harriet a hurried explanation, I derived an unworthy pleasure from the news that she had arranged for Trescothick to be accommodated – in the guest wing, of course – in not the least but by no means the best of the rooms. 'A man who does not warn us in advance of his arrival does not deserve the best,' she said tartly, returning my kiss.

'As high in the instep as an old-fashioned earl, is he? Well, if he's been in the colonies perhaps he's picked up the ways there, though I thought their society was supposed to be egalitarian.' Wilson shook his head. 'At least he has good fine weather to see his inheritance. Assuming he is who he says he is,' he said drily, as he passed me a small valise; he knew he was always a welcome overnight guest at the House.

I shot him an amazed glance, but he was engaged in looking about him. On impulse, I asked, 'Would you care to see the latest development on the Stammerton site? I was going to write to you this afternoon asking you to convene an urgent trustees' meeting, but while you have the chance, I would like you to see with your own eyes what we have found.'

'And we will have further opportunity to speak freely,' he agreed. 'The land seems to be in very good heart,' he said. 'And you have got rid of those diseased oaks, I see. Ah, is that the site down there? The village will be very extensive if those white posts are anything to judge by. If you are to be remembered for nothing else in your life, Rowsley, you should be remembered for this.'

'It's not quite that straightforward,' I said. 'Let me explain how the situation has changed . . .'

He listened intently. 'So the future of the model village is at risk?'

'No. Absolutely not. Nothing is dearer to my heart, Wilson – and indeed, my head. But we cannot sacrifice the past to our present needs. Ah! Francis!' I drew the trap to a halt, and Francis strolled over, obligingly taking Rufus' head while I helped Wilson down. A labourer sprinted over to take Francis's place, so I was free to introduce them. 'Sir Francis Palmer, the eminent historian. Mr Montgomery Wilson, the Family lawyer and the chairman of the trustees.'

Shaking hands, the two men sized each other up, for all the world like a pair of bare-knuckle fighters before a bout. Wilson was not a man to be intimidated by Francis's patrician background, but he might be just as susceptible to his passion and enthusiasm as I was. He was, however, careful to endorse my suggestions about written evidence to the trustees. 'If expenditure is to be made, every guinea must be justified,' he said firmly. 'And I should imagine,' he continued, scanning the lines of newly whitewashed palings, 'that quite a number of guineas will be involved. The new village must and shall be built. The trustees made that clear. I for one would be very sorry to see any delay.'

Francis bowed. 'Of course. Do you care to see what we have found so far?'

'Any more statues?' I asked.

'Not yet. But that is not how I want to work, Matthew. I don't want to turn this into piecemeal scavenging. Before I extract artefacts, I want everything recorded in situ – possibly with a camera.'

It was as if he had pressed a spring in Wilson's face. Suddenly it was one huge enthusiastic smile. 'What sort of photographic apparatus do you use?'

Anticipating a long and incomprehensible technical discussion,

I said, 'Sir Francis is our guest in our home, Wilson. I am sure the staff at the House will be killing the modern equivalent of the fatted calf for Mr Trescothick. I do not think we would overstretch Mrs Arden's ability if I arranged for us all to dine with him tonight. And Harriet is more than capable of ensuring that your usual room is aired.'

His exploration of the site having left Wilson less than his usual dapper self, he was clearly reluctant to meet Trescothick until a brush, at the very least, had been procured. Thatcher rose to the occasion admirably, spiriting him away from my office to restore him and his clothes to the state he preferred. A gentle tap at the door announced Harriet, always a meticulous observer of our official ranking within the House. I closed the door carefully behind her and held her for a few precious seconds – it was all we ever allowed ourselves in working hours.

'Samuel is slightly better, according to Dr Page. But I am anxious, my love: surely we should invite his sister to come to be with him. I have only known him visit her once in the last three years, but I wouldn't want us to be lacking in any attention. Had Francis not been here, I would have suggested she stay with us – she might find the size, the grandeur, of this place . . . difficult. And, to be honest, I would find it hard to know which room to give her.'

'I suspect if Francis brings in a team of experts, they would all want to stay here – which means he might decamp to the House himself. But that must be some days, even weeks, off, and I am sure you are right: she should be invited here immediately.'

'And offered – of course she must be offered Samuel's room! Where else? I will ensure it is prepared.'

I paused. 'I assume – has someone written to her? Of course you have.'

'But she may not be able to read. Someone should go. I'll talk to Bea, shall I? Though even if we could spare her, now Mr Trescothick is here, I doubt if she'd be willing to do something that suggests an intimacy between her and Samuel she is absolute in denying. Do you think I should go? Oh, Matthew – do you think we could? Just us, together? Escape for a day?'

Just as her face lit up as if she were a child, so it fell again, almost comically. 'It's just because we can that we can't, isn't it?' She clicked her fingers. 'What about asking Mr Pounceman? Who better than a man of the cloth?'

'Who better than a *good* man of the cloth?'

A tap on the door: it was Thatcher announcing the return of Wilson, and withdrawing gracefully.

Wilson was now considerably sprucer. Registering Harriet's presence, he bowed and kissed her hand. 'May I hope you'll be joining us in our meeting with Mr Trescothick, Mrs Rowsley?'

'That is a pleasure I fear I must forego, Mr Wilson. I offered to take him on a tour of the House while his luncheon was prepared but he declined. He had been here so often in the past, he said, and would be staying for the rest of his life, so he objected to being treated like a visitor in what would become his own home. And Matthew, according to Thatcher, he has registered that he is not accommodated in a state bedchamber, and demands to be moved. Given that the very best chambers are in the Family wing, I said that it was impossible, but before I could explain, he dismissed me, saying that he preferred to speak to the organ grinder, not the monkey.'

'I hope you put him in his place, dear lady.'

She gave one of her devastating smiles. 'I may have to leave that to you, Mr Wilson. You and Matthew are most welcome to join me in the Room for afternoon tea after your audience with his putative lordship.'

'Putative?' Wilson repeated, as if relishing the word.

She curtsied enigmatically and was gone.

SEVEN

Mr Trescothick was pacing up and down the library when I asked Thatcher to announce us. His face just failed to fall into the furious lines he was hoping for, leaving his expression petulant rather than angry.

'I said I would see you after luncheon, Rowley. What sort of time do you call this? And who is that?'

'My apologies, sir,' I said quietly. 'I had to deal immediately with other urgent estate matters. May I introduce Mr Montgomery Wilson, the Family's lawyer, who invited you, as his lordship's heir, to contact him.'

'And why are you here today?' Trescothick asked truculently, shaking hands nonetheless. 'Unless you have a crystal ball and knew exactly when I'd turn up.'

Wilson and I did not so much as exchange a glance: had he not heard of the telegraph system, not to mention the railways? His reply was silky smooth. 'I came here to see how a new aspect of the estate work is proceeding. As the chairman of the trustees appointed to take care of the estate while his lordship is indisposed, I am required by law to be au fait with any radical changes.' He gestured politely as if he were host: we were to sit around the fire. 'How was your journey here, sir? A pleasant voyage, I trust?'

'I have no complaints. I still do not understand why you should be here for a meeting I told only Rowley to attend. I was intending to summon you when I was settled.'

'We are, as I am sure you will agree, in a somewhat unusual situation.'

'Not really. I am the heir and should be treated as such.' He looked hard at me. Clearly what he saw as relegation to an inferior bedchamber still rankled.

'Of course. Provided the paperwork I asked for is satisfactory, as I am sure it will be. And I am sure that Mr Rowsley would be the first to agree. Which is why I have his undertaking to educate you in every part of running an estate – several estates, as it happens – such as Thorncroft. Your time abroad may have prevented you from learning that there is a tendency amongst the aristocracy to employ professional men to do the work – you will find that at Chatsworth, for instance, the Duke of Devonshire was one of the first to do so, and naturally many others have followed his lead. His lordship obviously did, and his father before him.'

'Well, I won't, you may be sure.'

'Very well. If that is your wish, then I am sure that Mr Rowsley, a most conscientious man, will gladly take you on as his most noble apprentice, and give you all the instruction you need.'

I bowed my acquiescence.

Mr Trescothick looked as if I had offered him a particularly sour lemon. 'We'll see. What do you know about art, Mr Rowley?'

'More each time I come into the House,' I said. 'But if you frequented the House when you were young, you probably know a great deal more about the paintings and sculptures here than I do. I hope you'll be kind enough to share your knowledge.'

I actually earned a smile. 'I daresay I learned far more about climbing trees and chasing foxes. Is there a pack of hounds here . . . still?'

While I puzzled over the slight hesitation before his last word, Wilson answered, 'His late lordship conceived a dislike of the sport, sir, and his son had other priorities – dredging the boating lake, for instance. And it has to be said, the whole estate needed a great deal of money to restore it to its rightful condition. Mr Rowsley's predecessor was at best slack and at worst less than honest.'

He responded with an idiom that sounded strangely plebeian. 'And how do you know that Mr Rowley isn't on the make too?'

Mr Wilson's smile was gratifyingly thin. 'My dear sir, I may have been a lawyer all my life, but I employ excellent staff who have been minutely through both agents' accounts. Indeed, it was Mr Rowsley's idea that we should establish a board of trustees for the duration of his lordship's illness to ensure that no misdemeanours could be committed.'

'"The duration of his illness" . . . How long is he expected to live, then? I got the impression he was on his deathbed.' Perhaps such bluntness was usual in the Antipodes: it sounded crass here.

'Dr Page has not ruled out a complete recovery,' I replied, lying with aplomb. 'So we hope this is but a temporary state of affairs. Sadly his mother is less likely to recover, which is why the Family wing is being used as a hospital.'

'You brought me here under false pretences, Wilson.'

He shook his head gently but continued as if there had been no interruption. 'Which is why, sir, you were not allocated what I presume is your customary room in that wing. If your current accommodation is in any way unsatisfactory, please tell me and I will ensure that the very competent housekeeper is informed.'

'I believe,' I added, fantasising again, 'that she would have suggested the Blue Room, but despite all our efforts the chimney still smokes when the wind is coming from the south-west. Now, I understand that you did not bring your own valet. I will arrange for one of our senior footmen to devote himself to you.' Heaven help me, I was out-Thatchering Thatcher in my efforts to mimic Samuel. Dimly I was aware that Trescothick had not yet enquired about him or indeed any of the staff who must have been here when he was a visitor, or about other acquaintances he might have encountered. For some reason I did not want to mention my good friend's name in front of this abrasive man.

'Very well. Now, the weather still seems fine. Have a horse saddled for me, and I'll have a tool round the estate while there's enough light.'

I rang for Thatcher, who appeared with his usual disconcerting swiftness. On this occasion, perhaps I might excuse him if he was indeed eavesdropping. Straight-faced, I repeated Trescothick's orders.

'I will ascertain if there is a horse free,' he said. 'And will sir be needing riding clothes and boots?'

'Put me in the Blue Room? My dear Mrs Rowsley, I have it on the best of authority that no one can stop the chimney smoking.'

Harriet looked from one of us to the other, as we giggled like naughty schoolboys. 'Please do not tell me that you have been telling Mr Trescothick untruths. Ah! Well, it is the work of moments to move you further along that corridor, if you prefer.'

'I will take my chance with the chimney,' Wilson declared. 'Tell me, where is the excellent Mrs Arden? It would grieve me if she did not feel able to sit down and enjoy some of her own cakes.'

I gestured minutely. I would go and fetch her, using every scrap of winsome cajolery I could summon. Instead I found myself sitting at the beautifully scrubbed servants' table talking about problems that six months ago she would have dealt with decisively, but now had her fretting her apron in anxiety. 'I've got Mr Trescothick here and Sir Francis there and now Mr Wilson here too. I can only be in one place at a time, Matthew.'

'Let me make it simpler, Bea. We will dine at the House tonight, bringing Sir Francis with us. You have enough help to cater for that? Because I have been known before now to peel a potato, and Harriet shares your zeal for beating eggs.'

'Lord bless you, I could cook for twenty single-handed, and you know it. It's just that . . .'

'To use a cricketing image, something has put you off your stroke. Is it the attack on Samuel?'

'I don't think so. It's just that when you make up your mind to go somewhere else and then you find you're still needed in the first place – it unsettles you, Matthew, and that's the truth of it.'

'Let's worry about it tomorrow. Come and have a cup of tea. Mr Wilson asked particularly if you would join us.'

'And if I don't I suppose you'll all come traipsing down into my nice clean kitchen. Very well.' She tugged off her working apron, reaching for a clean one which she tied in place as she followed me.

Dinner was likely to be an enjoyable affair if you were an impartial observer. Wilson had categorically insisted that Bea, as a fellow trustee, must join Harriet and myself at the dinner table. I suspect all three of us would have preferred to eat in the Room, or better still at home with Sir Francis and indeed Wilson himself if he cared to stroll down, but that would have meant leaving Trescothick to dine alone, an insult none of us would have offered. Equally Wilson dismissed the notion of a last-minute invitation to Mr Pounceman or even to Dr Page. I would have liked to see Marty Baines present, but perhaps that was a fantasy too far. In any case, he would have been behind the bar of the Royal Oak. However, as our house guest, Francis was invited.

'I cannot imagine, of course, that it will be the marriage of true minds,' said Mr Wilson. 'I must of necessity be there, but believe me it will be far more enjoyable if my fellow trustees are there to share my appreciation of the difficulties involved in the conversation. And I cannot wait to see what our putative heir' – he bowed charmingly to Harriet – 'will make of the discovery that he has become part of a far more democratic society than the one he claims to have been used to. The house-keeper the best friend of a baronet? The cook not merely producing the repast but enjoying it with her colleague the mispronounced agent?' Wilson smote his forehead. 'No! He shall not know. Let us all appear by name only, and we will see what he makes of us. Has he brought evening dress?'

Harriet reached for Thatcher's bell. 'The butler is the one to enquire, I believe.' She despatched him the moment he appeared.

'I took the liberty of recommending a smoking jacket for a relatively informal supper,' Thatcher informed her on his prompt return, as confidentially obsequious as Samuel, 'on the grounds that Mr Wilson and Sir Francis might not have brought tails.'

'Thank you,' she smiled. 'How is young Davies managing his first assignment as a valet?'

'Silently, I would hope, ma'am. Now, I understand that only six of you will be dining so perhaps the green dining room again? With the table reduced in size? Very good, ma'am.' He withdrew.

Wilson smiled at us all. 'I myself will take responsibility for the seating plan if you will permit me.'

Did that mean he had checked the newcomer's bona fides? I truly hoped so.

EIGHT

M r Wilson's offer was timely. Hardly had he made it than Thatcher returned, asking Matthew for a word in private. A moment after he had left the room, he returned, a movement of his eyebrow inviting me to join him in the corridor.

'Sergeant Burrows is here. Thatcher has shown him into my office. Could you spare a few moments?'

I fancied that the sergeant had simply demanded to see Matthew, but was more than happy to accept Matthew's invitation to accompany him. As we entered, young Freddie scuttled out, pausing only to offer a most accomplished bow and a delightful smile. One day he might break hearts.

We presented our formal selves to the sergeant, of course, Matthew retreating behind the vast acreage of his desk and me taking a chair in no man's land between him and the police officers – yes, Elias was there too.

'First up, Mr Rowsley, how is the victim? Is he ready to talk to us yet?'

'I understand he has not yet recovered consciousness: my wife and I are hoping to bring his sister down to be with him.'

'Good luck with that,' Elias said. 'Chalk and cheese, those two, according to my cousin. Well, you know what families are like,' he said, subsiding under Burrows' glare.

'Do you have any news for us?' Matthew asked.

Burrows said, 'We may have found one or two items of interest. Tell me, Mr Rowsley, do you use a walking stick – a very handsome one, if I may say so – and have you mislaid it recently?'

'Never,' he said. 'To be honest, sergeant, I don't have time for such affectations, not here in the country at least. The only one I know who does is Mr Bowman, who suffers from time to time with his knees. But his is as plain and utilitarian as could be.'

'What about your professor friend?' This time he directed his question at me.

I shook my head. 'Not to my knowledge. He wasn't sporting one when we met him at the station. Not that I recall, anyway.' I did not choose to explain that my mind had been on other things. 'Matthew?'

'No, surely not. The simplest thing to do is ask him, gentlemen.'

'We may well do that.'

I coughed gently. 'Sergeant Burrows, Sir Francis was on a train in the company of others. He was with us all the time until we reached the site of the new village. Poor Samuel was already unconscious in that ditch when we arrived.'

'Ah, I told you that cock wouldn't fight, didn't I, gaffer?'

Burrows' lips narrowed. 'So how do you account for the presence of a gentleman's walking stick so close to the murder scene — attempted murder scene? Are you suggesting that Mr Bowman might have borrowed one of his lordship's canes to go awalking with? To impress a lady-friend, perhaps? An assignation by the disrobed statue, perhaps?'

'Mr Burrows,' I said, in the sort of voice I use to more recalcitrant housemaids, 'do you really think that we can answer your questions? Of course we want to identify our friend's assailant. But we came after the event, not before or during it. And no, to the best of my knowledge none of us saw anyone making a quick getaway as we approached. Surely the best people to ask were the men who were by the site or returning to it.'

'I hope you are not implying that we haven't already, ma'am.'

'I am implying nothing. But have you any other questions that we can more easily answer?' I glanced at my watch.

Elias looked me in the eye. 'We've spoken to everyone, ma'am — all the men at the site, all the men in the House, all the maids. And where are we? Nowhere. The girls all just burst into tears, the men — well, some of them are a bit snuffly-like too. But we need to look a bit further afield. Mount a search, like. The outdoor men are all tied up moving their stuff so this professor man can dig up his stones or whatever, so we . . . well, I don't suppose you could spare a few indoor lads? I can't ask Mr Bowman for permission, so I have to ask you, ma'am, or Mr Rowsley, sir.'

'As you probably know, Mr Thatcher is our butler while . . . for the time being. Ask him, but if he hesitates, you can hint that we approve,' Matthew said. Patting a stack of paperwork on his desk, he added, 'I can't assist you myself, as you can imagine, but I'm sure there'll be as much help as Thatcher can spare.'

'I still think that the answer lies in that walking stick,' Burrows said, his lower lip jutting like a child's.

I smiled at him, not just out of politeness either. 'I'm sure you're right, sergeant. We just need to know whose hand last held it. It's a shame it's been so dry recently; if there'd been some mud you might have found a boot print to help you.'

He stared at me, tugging his whiskers. 'Funny you should say that, ma'am,' he said at last. 'No, we've not found anything useful like that. But we did find – well, it could have been anything or nothing. There was a patch of flattened ground, as if someone had put something heavy there – Mr Bowman's body, perhaps. But the patch was a bit small and there wasn't any blood, so we ruled that out. We even brought Elias's old mutt in to help, thinking it might be just an animal lair – but the dog didn't get excited, so it couldn't have been a fox or a badger. Too big for hedgehogs. So all we have is this posh stick and a flattened bit of grass. We need more, ma'am.'

Matthew said, 'I'll ask all his lordship's tenant farmers to let me have a couple of men – work's slack now, so there shouldn't be a problem, especially if this estate pays their wages on their behalf. And I'm sure Farmer Newcombe will offer help. Look. I'll just scribble a quick note that you can give him when you call on him.'

A scribble was not in Matthew's nature. While he wrote, I said, 'Sergeant Burrows, you know we set up a tent where the building labourers could get some food? I'll make sure your team can use it, even when the labourers have moved on.'

'I'd be much obliged, ma'am. We may even unearth some more stuff for this professor of yours.'

Matthew might have been writing, but he had also been

listening. 'If anyone does, make sure he leaves it exactly where it is, and puts one of Sir Francis's white posts beside it. I'll ask him to come and explain why to you all tomorrow morning. By the tent – shall we say nine o'clock? Excellent.'

The meeting was clearly over. The officers got to their feet, and Burrows left with Matthew. To my surprise, Elias dawdled.

'Ma'am,' he said at last. 'I was just wondering – might I have a peek at Mr Bowman? Just to pay my respects.'

'Of course,' I said, 'if his nurse permits it.' I led the way towards the main staircase, but then turned abruptly, heading for the backstairs.

'You know, ma'am, I just have the oddest notion – and I know it's all too late – that it's best that people don't know our friend is still here in the House.'

I stared but slowly nodded. 'You know he's too ill to be moved?'

'You know that; I know that. But there's nothing to stop me setting a rumour going round that he's being taken off to the infirmary tonight.'

I smiled. 'If you start it, I will help you spread it upstairs and downstairs.'

We climbed the servants' stairs. At Matthew's insistence they had been carpeted and the dreary green paint on the walls had been replaced with a pleasing whitish-cream. Better lighting was in place, though not enough to stop me wishing for the day when gas light might be installed throughout the House.

At last we stood in silence at the door of the room where Samuel lay. Keeping his gaze on our friend, Elias bowed his head, as if making a silent promise. I did not need to ask him what it was, because I was making it too.

The nurse followed us out. 'Dr Page said he'd call by later, Mrs Rowsley. Do you wish him to speak to you?'

I exchanged a glance with Elias. 'Let me write him a note, please. It is essential that he reads it before Thatcher brings him down to the main part of the House. Essential.' Elias followed me back to the Room, where I shut the door. 'So we are conspirators in what I hope is a totally unnecessary plot to protect our dear friend.'

'I can't say as I understand this . . . this feeling, ma'am, not really, but something deep inside tells me it's best, if I might make so bold.'

'Let us shake hands on it then.'

NINE

If Wilson had decided to stage-manage the evening, the costumes were meticulously chosen too. Matthew put himself in my hands – metaphorically and literally, since I suspect his own still hurt more than he liked to admit – and looked more handsome than ever in a maroon smoking jacket. I myself stuck to the sober colours I had adopted aeons ago when I embarked on what I suspected would be a long spinsterish existence. Even now, with my life abloom with joy, I couldn't embrace the vivid clothes that many women sported these days, and I could never, ever imagine wearing a garish tartan, whatever Her Majesty and Prince Albert might adore. But the midnight blue of tonight's dress was subtly shot through with another lighter blue which highlighted my eyes; we had chosen the silk together in Naples, where we had found the sapphire earrings that Matthew had given me as yet another belated wedding present. The matching necklace drew rather more attention than I might like to the fashionable décolletage.

Beatrice, the last arrival in the drawing room, might be fanning herself after a hasty journey from the kitchen but was quietly elegant in a dress in so deep a red it might almost be black. She wore the cameo brooch we had brought back for her from Sorrento. Both of us imbued our curtsies with just the right amount of respect: they would be much deeper when Mr Trescothick came into his inheritance. Francis greeted us as old friends, as did Mr Wilson. Mr Trescothick was inclined to play the grand seigneur, especially with Matthew, but Francis engaged him in recollections of his schooldays, encouraging him to join in. Wilson, who had stationed himself between Bea and me, engaged us in a gentle conversation – Bea in particular, I thought.

While he did so, I speculated about his table arrangements. When she still had her health, her ladyship was meticulous in such matters, though she always had a balanced guest list to work from – equal numbers of men and women. Her problem

– one she often shared with me – was getting the social ranks right: who should get precedence over whom.

In the event I was intrigued by Wilson's decision to place me at the head and Bea at the foot of the much reduced dining table, both of us flanked by gentlemen. I would have been very surprised had Mr Wilson not placed himself at Bea's right hand; he clearly enjoyed her company very much. Was he seeking an agreeable companion or a new cook? I hoped poor Bea's affections were not about to be disturbed again, as I was sure they had been by Matthew's arrival. Matthew sat to her left, leaving me between Francis and Mr Trescothick, who was to my right hand.

The former embarked on many tales of our early acquaintance, embellishing them as he went. Never once did he allude to the difference in our status, implying we were both visitors to the appalling Teigngrace Hall in Devon. Perhaps Mr Trescothick might have deduced that we were once lovers; I hoped that Matthew would not be upset by anything he might overhear. It was clear that Mr Trescothick had not yet registered that the agent he persisted in addressing as Rowley and the Mrs Rowsley he was introduced to might be man and wife, though he was keenly aware of Francis's title: inexplicably he was glutinously deferential, which my old friend did not enjoy. I found a girlish fluttering excitement about Roman statues worked well to distract our heir, though I nearly spoiled it by alluding to a statue I had seen in Florence with Matthew. Fortunately Mr Trescothick did not appear to have done the Grand Tour. He did not appear to have done much else, either; perhaps he was naturally taciturn, for he showed no inclination to join in with Francis's renewed attempts at reminiscing about his schooldays. Perhaps he had been educated by a private tutor, who had brought neither joy nor companionship to his life. In various houses I had encoun-tered young gentlemen who had never got over the loneliness of such an existence – and equally, some who had been so bullied at Eton or Harrow that years later mention of the very name would reduce them to consumption-like pallor.

While a silence more awkward than most ballooned, I strove to think of something that might interest him. At last I said, 'I collect, sir, that you might have returned to these isles on the SS *Great Britain*. Such a wonderful vessel, by all accounts.'

I had struck gold! Much of what he said was wasted on me, but it was clear that etiquette was suspended as all the men started to ask what sounded like intelligent questions. Even Bea joined in, to discuss the catering arrangements. Mine were more prosaic, deliberately: how big were the cabins? How were they appointed?

Matthew smiled down the table. 'This is a matter of moment, is it not? One hears the England cricket team will be travelling aboard her for their tour of Australia?'

'They will indeed.' I returned the smile.

But it seemed that our guest had no interest in that topic, so Matthew asked about stability and seasickness. Again, our guest was very informative. But then he made a gaffe.

Thatcher had overseen the meal as if he had been doing it all his life; the footmen were as silent as even Samuel would want. But then Mr Trescothick summoned him with a crooked finger, as one might call a waiter in a tea room, when in fact a discreet nod was all that was called for.

'Pray tell Alphonse that his cooking has lost none of its sparkle!' he said.

'I fear, sir, that Alphonse left the Family some time ago.' Thatcher's bow was immaculate. He did not even permit his eyes to twinkle as he continued, 'But we have a most excellent cook, sir. Would you wish me to pass your compliments to her?'

'Very well. You may serve dessert now.'

The notion of a butler being required to do such a menial task had long since died out in all but the most formal houses. Samuel had maintained the tradition here because it had pleased her ladyship's whimsical tastes, and possibly his as well. Thatcher, whatever he might have been thinking, merely bowed.

Despite the other men's protests, Mr Trescothick insisted on remaining in the dining room to smoke the cigars Thatcher produced, while Bea and I had to leave them. While we waited in the drawing room, taking the best seats, I have to admit, just the right distance from the fire, I told her of our plans to fetch Samuel's sister to his bedside. Had Bea ever met her?

She shook her head emphatically. 'And I'm not sure you're doing right, Harriet. I can count on the fingers of one hand the times he's seen her since I've known him – and you must know that!'

'Yes, indeed. He very rarely spoke of her to me – or to you?'

She pursed her lips. 'You know what a snob he was – is!' she corrected herself hurriedly. 'I'm not sure he thought she was good enough to be his sister. Not good enough to be acknowledged. I think there was what he considered an unfortunate marriage. Funny that she's now a Mrs Fairbrother, isn't it? But blood's thicker than water – My God, what am I saying, with him lying there all black and blue?' She flushed deeply, before going so pale I reached for my smelling salts. But she pulled herself together. 'Perhaps now he is so ill they can be reconciled. Anyway, you'll see what she says and what she wants to do. She'll have Samuel's room if she wants to stay, I take it? Before then we must make sure all those guineas he's squirrelled away are out of the reach of prying fingers, that's all I'll say.' She gave a sudden snort of laughter. 'I remember one family I worked for where it was their custom to summon the cook to the drawing room after their dinner to congratulate her. It's a good job this Trescothick man didn't have that notion, isn't it?' Then her face fell. 'God knows what he'll say when he finds out. I can't see us having jobs much longer.'

I reached over and took her hand. 'Until his lordship passes away, Mr Trescothick has no power at all. We, the trustees, have the power. And I should imagine the first thing Mr Wilson will insist on doing, both as our chairman and as the Family's lawyer, is to check his credentials. In fact he surely must have done so already, or we would not have dined together. But I agree – we should bring this charade to an end as soon as we reasonably can. It is fair to none of us, Mr Trescothick especially.'

'That's up to Mr Wilson, isn't it? It was his idea.'

'I think he would respect our opinions, if we care to express them. The more I see of him, the more I like him, Bea.' I would have teased her about her sudden flush if I had not known how close to the surface her feelings were these days.

'He's very polite – gentleman-like,' she conceded after a few moments. Then, in a much lower voice, she added, 'The trouble with people like him and Sir Francis is that you don't know whether they're being really nice and friendly or if they're making fun of you on the quiet. While they're puffing away at those vile cigars, are they all having a good laugh at us?'

'Do you really think Matthew would permit that? Or Francis, for that matter? I am no more acquainted with Mr Wilson than you are, but it's clear that he treats your opinions with great respect, which is nine-tenths of the way to respecting you. As a person, Bea, not just as a fine cook in the mould of Alphonse!' I cupped my hand to my mouth in mock conspiracy. 'Was there ever a chef of that name here?'

She shook her head. 'I've no idea. Samuel might know. He might know a lot about His Nibs,' she added in a confiding undervoice, the sort all servants used when speaking of people who must not overhear. It was fortunate, because at that moment the doors were flung open to admit Mr Trescothick, talking over his shoulder to Mr Wilson. His manner was decidedly chilly – perhaps Mr Wilson had properly identified us at last, and he did not find the notion amusing. Without looking at either of us, he pushed past us to his chosen chair: assuredly had he been a woman, he would have swished his skirts to show his disdain. I could hardly blame him: he seemed so uneasy, so moody, it felt all the more unkind to unsettle him further. I rang for tea and coffee. Francis and Matthew were soon in animated conversation, trying hard but in vain to engage him too. Mr Wilson made a point of coming to sit beside Bea.

At this point Thatcher padded in, heading towards me, contriving to be both swift and unobtrusive. 'The gentleman in question is in the library, Mrs Rowsley.'

'Excuse me: a slight household hitch,' I murmured to the company at large. Undoubtedly Matthew and Francis registered my exit, but I got the impression that Mr Trescothick could not have been less interested. I no longer saw anger in his face, but something else – something that looked strangely like unhappiness. Perhaps he had had to leave a loved one behind when he made the voyage here.

Dr Page, seated by the fire, was supping port and reading a periodical. He looked at me quizzically as I arrived, rising to bow and kiss my hand.

'When Mrs Rowsley, that most practical of women, writes a note worthy of a work of fiction, I am intrigued.'

I sat opposite his chair. 'Mrs Rowsley is anxious and uneasy, possibly without reason. But she is not the only one to fear for . . .'

'The health of our good friend Samuel?'

'Yes. For some reason I do not . . . I wonder if it might be better . . . safer . . .'

He leaned over and took my hand. 'Dear lady, a doctor's ear is like a priest's in the confessional. Spell it out.'

'Samuel was nearly killed. If his assailant knew his whereabouts, would that make him less safe?'

'The House is like a fortress. Unless you are afraid that there might be someone inside it who . . .? Surely not! He is revered. He may be feared, but he is certainly revered.'

'I believed so. Until we saw him in the ditch. Someone meant him to die, did they not? Do you think there is the chance of him surviving?'

He stood and took a turn round the room. 'There is a chance. But I would not have him moved from here – the jolting . . . I shudder to think of it. That does not mean, however, that I think all the world should know where to find him.'

'If the police allow a rumour to circulate that he has been moved to the infirmary, would you be breaking your oath if you did not deny it?'

He laughed. 'I don't think I ever promised not to lie. You are serious about this, aren't you? Mrs Rowsley, I have never doubted your judgement. So long as I do not have to perjure myself, if anyone should happen to ask, I will allow them to believe that Samuel is in the infirmary. Would you care for me to add an outbreak of some infectious disease that might discourage people from penetrating the Family wing? It would explain my continuing presence here.'

'Would you really?' My voice shook with relief.

'If you think it's necessary. If you even suspect it's necessary.' He looked at my dress. 'Tell me, am I interrupting some grand dinner party?'

'You are interrupting a very fraught one. Please do join us in the drawing room for coffee. Yes? Excellent. You may find it amusing. Let me explain . . .'

His laughter rang round the room.

TEN

Having bade Mr Wilson farewell – he was catching an early train in the morning, which would stop at the estate station especially for him, of course – the three of us walked back to our house.

'I don't recall your telling me that Mr Bowman was now in hospital,' Francis observed. 'But since Matthew seemed to know about it, I thought it best to take my cue from him.'

'I knew nothing,' I said, more grimly than I intended, 'possibly because there is nothing to know. What's going on, Harriet?'

'Elias and I had a conversation,' she said. 'He was fearful that whoever attacked Samuel might try again. Even though the Family wing is locked, people who want to do something can usually find the means. So between us, and with Dr Page's consent—'

'More than consent, surely!' Francis put in. 'He was extremely convincing. I was absolutely taken in, as was Trescothick. What a happy chance you have measles in the House.'

'Diseases always spread when you have a lot of young staff,' she said limpidly.

We were lighting our candles to go to our bedchambers when Francis said, 'Now you have another visitor in the House, would it make life simpler for you if I were to decamp there? There appears to be a most remarkable collection of books to explore. I believe I could live in that library. But I see some of the cases are locked.'

I was about to offer him the key when Harriet said, with an apologetic cough, 'His late lordship insisted that, however much he trusted his friends, he must be present when the rarest specimens were examined. I was the only person allowed to dust them, and if he was not there to supervise me, Samuel had to be.'

'They must be treasures indeed. So if I asked to see them

you or Matthew would have to "watch my every move",' he said, as if acting in a melodrama. But I thought his jocular tone concealed real anger.

'I promised him on his deathbed that the custom would be maintained.' Her voice betrayed both her embarrassment and her deep sense of loyalty.

'Very well. I understand.' It was clear that he did not.

'I'm sure one of us can arrange to be there whenever you want,' I said heartily, though I was suddenly angry with myself for sounding supine in contrast with Harriet's moral probity.

'Thank you. I will be happy to accept your kind offer. But, books apart, as to my moving to the House, I am more than happy to do so if it would make your lives simpler. I wish, after all, to engage Trescothick as much as I can in the future of the investigation – no, no! Rest assured I will not be pressing him to divert resources from the village. Incidentally, in Page, you have a most passionate supporter, Matthew.'

'I have indeed. And in our innkeeper, who has endured at first hand the ravages of bad water and inadequate sanitation. There is one trustee, however . . .' I tailed off, shaking my head.

'That would be your rector? Will he be taking Sunday's services?'

'Assuredly,' I said. 'We always try to go to one of them, and make sure the staff do likewise. Your removal, Francis: you are a most welcome guest in our home, and although you may find your existence here a little . . . peripatetic, you must stay as long as you wish. Or leave when you prefer. The choice is entirely yours.'

'You were right to stick to your promise,' I said, 'but you know that, don't you?'

'It hurt me to do so,' she said, resting her head on my shoulder. 'His late lordship became, despite the difference in rank, my friend. I trusted him. Even knowing about his lordship's terrible disease has not made me forget the good parts of his character. How could it? He didn't betray me when he contracted it, nor even his wife. I suspect he was a single youth, and sowing wild oats . . .' She stopped. 'Did no one tell him of the risks? Or even . . . Oh, women are meant to be pure, are we not, and yet it is almost as if men are supposed not to be.'

'There is a lot of pressure,' I said. 'But some things are truly worth waiting for, are they not?'

We both realized it would be difficult to invite Samuel's sister to stay at the House if Samuel was supposed to have been taken to the infirmary in Shrewsbury. Harriet was penitent; she should not have put about a lie, she declared, however good the reason.

'I trust your judgement implicitly,' I declared. And even if I did not, I was not going to tell her. 'But it would do no harm at all to go and make sure she knows the situation – whatever part of the situation you think it safe to reveal, that is.'

'*We* think,' she corrected me firmly. 'My love, the weather still holds calm and quiet. Our guest is eager to show Mr Trescothick his historic stones. Our intention to see Mrs Fairbrother is generally known and accepted as the right thing to do. Let us make the journey and draw up our plans as we go.' She added, wistful as a child, 'It would be such a treat not to have always to be . . . on duty.'

'It would,' I said, kissing her. 'As soon as my meeting with the policemen is over. So long as we take her ladyship's horse and not that dratted Robin.'

'You have questioned everyone and discovered . . . precisely nothing?' I said, my exasperation no doubt showing. The meeting at the tent was over, Francis was already peering at stones and making notes, and the two police officers and I had fallen into step as we walked away. Now I stopped, arms akimbo. 'While my good friend lies close to death his assailants are still free?'

'Don't think we haven't tried,' Elias said appeasingly. He looked at his sergeant, who was clearly as irritated with me as I was with him.

'I apologize. My feelings got the better of me. Is there anything more the estate can do? Shall we offer a reward for information leading to an arrest?'

Burrows nodded in a manner intended to be sage, no doubt. 'There is always a risk in offering monetary gain, of course. A lot of time-wasters, Mr Rowsley.'

'Of course. But you are discerning enough to sift through the dross. Surely it's worth a try?'

Burrows nodded again, this time magisterially.

Suddenly I sympathized with him; after all, there was nothing else he could do. 'How much would you advise me to offer?' I asked. 'Twenty-five pounds?'

Elias' eyes widened. 'That'd attract time-wasters for sure,' he said. 'Twenty, gaffer? I mean, sergeant?'

And so it was agreed. As we started walking again, Elias asked, 'How are you going to manage with this new lord turning up?'

Burrows coughed. 'Always assuming he is the new lord. I assume someone is checking his credentials, Mr Rowsley?'

'That's the job of the Family's lawyer – and don't forget, his lordship might be unwell but he is still with us. As, thank God, is Samuel. This idea of putting it about that he's no longer in the House—'

'That was Elias' notion, and a good one too, to my way of thinking. Has the new lord asked about him, by the way?' He looked at me shrewdly. 'What do you make of him, Mr Rowsley? Ah, you're too loyal to let on, aren't you! How do you like the idea of him rattling round that great place all on his own? Ah, I can tell you're not happy. And neither would I be, I can tell you.'

'But it must be strange for him,' Elias reflected. 'Lonely. No one to talk to, barring a few portraits – and they wouldn't answer back. The odd ghost, maybe? How long does he propose to stay?'

'Until his lordship croaks, no doubt,' Burrows murmured dryly.

I found myself saying, 'I'd like to offer him my friendship – but he seems a stickler for social class and, of course, I'm the estate's employee.'

'Ah, treating you like a servant, is he?' Burrows sounded half-gleeful, half-sympathetic. 'But it must be hard for you to know what to do with him and it doesn't seem right to have him rattling in the House.'

'With all those valuables lying around,' Elias put in. 'I suppose you can't invite him into your own home.'

'I doubt if he'd accept. The best thing we can do is resume our quarters in the House so he has our company if he wants it. I should like to invite the village gentry to dine, but . . . I am a servant, after all,' I added, with an ironic shrug.

'But you have that professor staying with you. Can't he move into the House and keep an eye on him?'

I grinned at Elias. 'It had occurred to me. At least he's entertaining him later today, showing him the ruins.'

'Let's just hope no one pops up with another stick,' Burrows said grimly.

Perhaps a bad marriage and too many children had reduced Mrs Fairbrother to the slatternly old woman who stood before us. She might have come from a different world from our precise and immaculate friend. She kept us on the doorstep of her cottage – one could blame her landlord for the dilapidated state of the building, but no one had made any attempt to maintain the garden, let alone grow a few vegetables in it. Perhaps either she or her husband was unwell. But even as I made mental excuses, I was aware that our rector's view that there were undeserving poor might be creeping into my judgement. 'Judge not that ye be not judged,' I told myself.

Harriet took the lead in the conversation, greeting Mrs Fairbrother with polite warmth. The woman, after all, would know from her clothing that Harriet was not a poor woman – perhaps she might even have taken her for her ladyship if she knew nothing of the situation at the House. Her curtsy suggested she knew quality when she saw it.

'Mrs Fairbrother, I'm Mrs Rowsley from Thorncroft House. I wrote to you the other day – do you happen to have kept the letter?'

'Letters ain't no use to me. Carn hardly see, can I, and I dae learn my letters. I was waiting till someone learned came this way.' There was a mite of insolence in her delivery, some of which was hard to penetrate. Samuel's vowels and consonants were copy-book pure; hers were so distorted they were more dialect than accent.

'Shall I read it to you?' Harriet asked calmly. 'It's important for you to know what I said.'

Mrs Fairbrother bellowed over her shoulder. A man, ancient but not immediately venerable in appearance, shuffled up behind her, wagging a battered envelope. It had been opened, the crumpled sheet of paper it contained half in, half out.

Harriet held out her hand for it, taking it with a slight nod. Apparently she read it aloud as it stood, but I could see she was paraphrasing her original words.

'"Dear Madam. I am writing to give you sad news about your brother Samuel—"'

'The old bugger's snuffed it, has he?' Mr Fairbrother asked, without any indication of sorrow.

'Shut your mouth and listen! Her ladyship's talking!'

'". . . who was injured during a bad fall and is now resting in bed, unable to perform his duties at Thorncroft House."'

'Well, he core come here,' his sister said quickly. 'We got no room. Where'd us put him?'

'And what about the half-guinea he sends us each week? What'll happen to us without that?'

'It'll be the work'us for us, you mark my words,' she wailed, daubing her eyes with the corner of an apron that had seen better days, but not much acquaintance with soap. 'Thrown on the parish!'

She was probably right.

A half-guinea – about what a labourer might hope to earn in a reasonable week – was the difference to them between survival and disaster. But now Samuel was no longer receiving generous tips from open-handed guests, it constituted almost half his own weekly income. Although he had no immediate need to spend on food, lodging or even his self-appointed uniform, he was being very generous for a man who wanted little contact with his family and who might well have been saving for a safety net for his imminent retirement. On the other hand, his brother-in-law might be indulging in a little optimistic exaggeration.

'Ten shillings and sixpence a week?' Harriet asked, with an inflexion that clearly indicated disbelief.

'When he could. Sent it under the seal of his letters.'

Harriet nodded. 'But now he's on his sick bed . . .'

'He's got this sock under his bed, your ladyship. Keeps a bit by for rainy days. E woe lerrus down.'

Harriet nodded in a way I could only describe as magisterial. Clearly – clearly even to the Fairbrothers – she was evaluating this assertion. 'I shall take it upon myself to ask Samuel if he wants this custom to continue. Half a guinea a week . . .' She shook her head doubtingly. She folded the letter and stowed it in her reticule, raising an eyebrow to me as she did so. Was she to give them some cash to tide this unlovely pair over? She clearly was. She produced three half-crowns.

Mr Fairbrother fell on them avidly; his wife looked genuinely shocked and disappointed. I was beginning to believe the story about the half-guinea.

Perhaps Harriet was too. Raising the authoritative finger she used to remind a housemaid she had not finished what she had to say, she turned back to the trap, returning with a basket packed with food: solid, warming, nourishing fare. So few teeth did either Fairbrother possess that I wondered how they would deal with the bread, but I was sure that they would find a way to soften it; no doubt unbeknownst to his late lordship, many of our labourers had once softened toast in cold tea to mimic meat. I thanked God and my fellow trustees that Harriet and Beatrice now had the authority to provide better rations when times were hard.

'What I would really like to do,' Harriet said, setting the pony into a brisk trot, 'is speak to someone who knows them – for though I pity them, I am not sure I believe the story about the regular half-guineas. As far as I know, there is no sock under the bed. I have had the room stripped and I am sure that little Sarey would have told me if she'd found anything unusual. What do you make of it?'

'It's hard to tell. I'd have thought if he had enough money to worry about he'd have popped it in the silver safe. I'll check when I get back, shall I? It truly is ridiculous that only he and I were permitted to have keys – which reminds me: where is his set?'

'Locked in the cupboard in my bedchamber. But I find I cannot bring myself to use it.' Her laugh was self-deprecating. 'Our roles are very much prescribed, you know. Samuel would not have dreamed of asking me to oversee the removal of the epergne or of any other items of silver, no matter how busy he might have been. As for the best silver-gilt cutlery, he literally counted each piece into the canteen. Even if a high ledge needed dusting, I wouldn't have asked the footman standing directly beneath it, I'd have asked Samuel to ask him. Ah! That wonderful Georgian house next to the church: do you think that's the rectory? If it is, would it be worth consulting the rector about the Fairbrothers and their half-guinea? It needn't be a long visit; we shall be losing the light soon.'

I glanced upwards. 'Ten minutes at the most, then.'

The omens were good. The maid who admitted us was cheerful as well as efficient, installing us in a clean and pleasantly chaotic study while she fetched her master. In fact it was a woman in her thirties who entered, introducing herself as Mrs Richards. 'My husband has just been summoned to a deathbed, but if I can help I will. May I offer you tea?'

We shook hands, declining the offer as politely as we could, making the return journey our excuse. Harriet glanced at me: might she speak woman to woman? I nodded. I would keep quiet.

She outlined the situation succinctly.

Mrs Richards nodded. 'If it is the case that your friend is regularly sending money, then I see no evidence of it. It would be good if he could spare some, because they are right, they will end up in the workhouse. They are feckless; they can't manage money. Mr Fairbrother has always been work-shy, according to his employer, and his wife has no skills worth mentioning.'

'But—' Harriet began, with a heavy sigh.

'But indeed, Mrs Rowsley. But they are human beings, and they do not deserve to suffer in the hellhole that is our local workhouse. I don't know what we ought to do, any more than you do. All I can suggest is this: if money does become available, send it to me here, and I will buy food for them. Fuel, too. The winter has been mild, so far, but the local shepherds say we are in for a cold snap. I will do my best.'

Harriet took her hand, pressing it. 'Indeed, Mrs Richards, that is all anyone can do. Here is an instalment on account.' She produced a guinea. 'When – if! – our friend recovers, then it is for him to decide what to do. Meanwhile – yes, we will all do our best.'

Our route home took us past what Francis assured us we should call the Roman site. We expected to see some village men still guarding it, warming themselves at the braziers Matthew had got Thomas to organize. But though there were plenty of men around, they were all in a bunch. Then a couple of them started jostling each other. We could hear jeers and catcalls. Harriet brought the horse to a fairly anxious standstill, and I was about to leap down to deal with the situation.

But I stopped. 'I have an idea that your presence will calm things down more quickly than anything I can say or do,' I said. 'Will you come too?'

'Of course. I'll tell anyone who is particularly trouble-some that I will inform his mother.' She waited till I had secured the horse, and then took my outstretched hand. 'That man there, for instance: his mother was one of the best housemaids I'd ever come across until she married a forester with all the charm in the world but a temper to fear. They have drifted down in the world. Now they live in one of the worst cottages in Stammerton.'

Our presence had not gone undetected, of course, but there were still a couple of men squaring up to each other as the others straggled back to the braziers.

'John Shepherd, what are you doing?' Harriet asked the smaller, wirier young man, reducing him to a shamefaced skinny ten-year-old.

I was disconcerted when he stood his ground. He jabbed his finger at the trenches. 'All these were supposed to make our lives better. And it turns out a load of people from the time of the Ark are more important than us tenants.'

'Do you really think that, John? New plots are already being laid out in the next field – you can see the posts from here.'

'Won't be done by winter. No, nor the next one neither.'

'Of course it won't be completed by winter: it's well-nigh winter now! But I'm sure Mr Rowsley will move heaven and earth to have everything right and tight by next Christmas. He's already told the professor that all the men working here will have to stop and start new foundations. It's the professor's job to recruit and pay a new team of men.'

Another man stepped forward. 'But Mrs Faulkner, ma'am – beg pardon, Mrs Rowsley – people are getting ill now. Some'll be long dead by the time there are any new places!'

I nodded. This was true, and Harriet and I both knew it.

She continued, 'You recall, don't you, Harry, that his late lordship always sent food and fuel to you so no one would ever have to go on the parish. We know his son is too unwell to make decisions, but knowing me as you do can you imagine that the tradition won't be maintained? And knowing the work Mr Rowsley has already had done on some of the cottages here, can you doubt that he won't make them weatherproof at the very least until you can finally move out?'

'We're not after charity!' he yelled, to a mutinous cheer from his fellow-villagers. Then, slightly shamefaced he said, 'Not wishing to appear ungrateful, ma'am, but we want a say in things. All sorts of things. The vicar tells us one thing, Mr Rowsley tells us another and it's much better than the vicar says . . .' He tipped his cap to me. 'Now, don't get me wrong, it's good we're being looked after – but we have voices, but no one asks us, let alone listens to us.'

'Vote! We wants to vote!' The yells came from several directions.

My heart pounding, I stepped forward. 'And why not? You are right: you should be able to express yourselves. A tiny start will be in the village hall that Stammerton will have. Meanwhile, why do we not all gather in the tent there tomorrow afternoon, and I will tell you all about the plans and you can comment on them?'

Harriet put forward a less nebulous idea. 'There will be hot tea and cake, so bring your wives and children too.'

Had we averted a crisis? Or merely postponed it?

ELEVEN

When we set out for the House for dinner, the fierce wind was gusting extraordinarily hard, driving occasional flurries of rain into our faces. We were all agreed that it would have been much more pleasant to stay in our cosy house; politeness and a sense of duty, however, drove us to ensure that Mr Trescothick was not left entirely on his own. At some point in the evening I would raise the idea of a dinner with the local gentry and some of his lordship's most respectable tenants. At the back of my mind lay Sergeant Burrows' reservations about him being left on his own, but I do believe that hospitality and kindness drove us most.

We accompanied Harriet to the servants' entrance, which she was still resolute in using. Insisting she needed to confer with Bea, she sent us off for sherry with Trescothick. Thatcher was on duty in the great entrance hall, greeting us with his usual deference and summoning a footman to relieve us of our coats. Then, biting his lip, he bowed, presenting me with a letter on a silver salver: he would never have deigned simply to pass it to me. But I sensed that he was rigid with embarrassment.

For once his tactful discretion was outweighed by the outrage he obviously felt. 'With due respect, Mr Rowsley, I believe you should read this in the privacy of your office, and before you speak to Mrs Rowsley. Sir Francis, do you care to take sherry in the drawing room, sir?' He was clearly about to lead the way.

Francis froze at the subtle distinction between the ways in which Thatcher addressed us. 'Thank you, Thatcher,' he said, 'but I believe I would rather accompany my friend.'

Thatcher's face spoke volumes, but his only words, delivered in a tone of deep foreboding, were, 'Very well, Sir Francis.'

My office door safely shut behind us, I opened the note, holding it so that he might read it.

Rowsley

I do not care to dine with servants, so I expect you and your fellows to eat in the usual quarters. Similarly I find it unacceptable that you have granted yourself the privilege of using a guest chamber as your own. If you wish to stay overnight, you might consider the butler's room as appropriate.

There was no signature. 'Might I indeed!' I snarled, with a couple of unrepeatable expletives. 'And I daresay he is too high in the instep – or too cowardly! – to tell dear Harriet to her face.'

'What will you do, Matthew?' He laid a hand on my arm.

I took a very deep breath, fearing I might turn violent in my anger. And another. 'Nothing. Nothing till I have discussed this with her. And with Beatrice, of course.'

'Indeed. I cannot believe Wilson wanted this outcome when we sat down to supper together! Heavens, this is a bad business!'

I nodded. 'If there is one good thing about Samuel's illness, it is that he has been spared all knowledge of it.'

Harriet was in the kitchen, apparently sharing a joke with Bea. Bea was about to bob a curtsy when Francis took her hand and kissed it, a greeting he then bestowed on Harriet.

'If that is tea, I believe Matthew and I might care to join you in a cup.' As he sat at the table, he glanced at me. Was he as apprehensive as he looked? Bea probably was, as she poured.

I took a sip, willing my hand not to shake, willing myself not to dash the cup and its contents against the freshly painted wall. I replaced the cup in the saucer and touched the bruises still tender on my hands. I could do it. I could. I could read the note aloud word for word. When I spoke, my voice was quiet. Perhaps it was too quiet. I knew Harriet would be watching me, trying to conceal her anxiety.

To my amazement, Bea broke the stunned silence with a cackling laugh. 'Thinks he'll insult us and get away with it, does he? I'm sorry, Sir Francis, but we cooks have long had ways of dealing with rude guests. As do the footmen waiting on them.'

Harriet added, 'Actually, Bea, you've put your finger on Mr

Trescothick's problem. For all he is adopting these airs and graces – a very caricature of an aristocrat! – he is no more than a guest here. He can issue all the instructions he wishes. But we are only answerable to his lordship and her ladyship and, in their absence, to Mr Wilson and a quorum of trustees.' She gestured. Yes, us.

'So we simply ignore . . . this?' I asked, poking the offending note with the fury that still lingered.

'What do we all think?' Bea asked. 'I for one would rather eat in the Room amongst friends – but that might be a cowardly way out.'

'And it would leave you, Francis, to eat tête-à-tête with him,' Harriet observed with a dry smile.

'So it would. But I might, with your approval, send him a polite note indicating that since I have a previous engagement I cannot dine with him this evening.'

Bea pulled a face. 'Your eating informally in Harriet and Matthew's dining room is one thing; supper with us in the Room is another.'

'Forgive me, Bea, but I beg to differ. I would be honoured to be your guest.' He bowed to us in turn.

'Thatcher, as butler, would join us for part of the meal,' Bea said. 'And Tim would wait on us.' The warning was clear: any conversation would have to be circumspect. 'No one would think the less of you if you all turned tail and left him to it.'

Perhaps Francis' smile was a little less relaxed. 'But if we agreed to dine at the Rowsleys' home, you might not be able to join us.'

'I can do many things, but I can't be in two places at once. Stupid man, putting us all in an awkward position like this. It . . . it is not *gentlemanly*,' she declared. 'Now, if you will excuse me, I have to prepare dinner, or His Nibs'll try and turn me off without a reference.'

I was conscious of Harriet's embarrassment at receiving Francis in the Room. Friend he might be, but he was now used to seeing her as a woman of status; for all her efforts, there was a meanness about the dimensions and décor of this room that one could not ignore. It was emphasized by the bare shelves. She had transferred all her books to our library when we married. Even the speed with which she summoned sherry and biscuits spoke of her sense of being demeaned by her surroundings. We sat on dining chairs at one end of the table. As far as I know they had never matched. For the first time since Francis' arrival, an uneasy silence fell.

It was time to make conversation. 'Francis, I believe you were escorting Trescothick to the ruins this afternoon. Did you manage to persuade him of their importance?'

'It would have been hard to find anyone less interested. What he did want to do was find out all he could about all the art and artefacts in the House. I admitted I knew about Lely – those portraits we spoke of, Harriet – but when he started talking about value I claimed I only knew about them because there was something like them at my grandmother's house. I cannot persuade myself that he believed me: he was constantly pointing at objets d'art and wanting my opinion.'

'Was he perhaps simply attempting small talk?' Harriet asked.

'Do you think he is the sort of man to do that? My dear friends, I wonder how soon the estimable Mr Wilson will be able to establish he is the true heir. And, assuming he is, how he might guide the man in what is and is not appropriate behaviour.'

'And what power he might exercise,' Harriet said. 'Not just over us, but over the treatment of his lordship. Might he try to have him declared non compos mentis?'

'As a way to seizing control here? Mind you,' Sir Francis continued with a rueful smile, 'if all mentally incompetent nobles were removed from power, I suspect we might not have a viable House of Lords!'

Laughing, Harriet rose to her feet. 'Will you excuse me for a few minutes? I really feel I should check up on the measles patients.' She was not a woman to wink, but she gave her amazing smile as she left.

In an instant there was a tap at the door. Thatcher entered with paper and pen and ink from my office. 'I understand that Sir Francis had need of writing materials, sir. Am I to wait for a reply?'

I got up. 'Let us wait outside, Thatcher. There.' I shut the door behind us. The kitchen was quietly purposeful as ever, everyone going about their business with no need for Bea to raise her voice. But the hum of activity was enough to cover our conversation.

'You did well earlier,' I said. 'Thank you. This whim of Mr Trescothick puts us all in a very difficult position, does it not?'

He nodded. 'He acts like my employer, Mr Rowsley, but I know he is not. If anyone is, it is you, isn't it?'

'Only insofar as the trustees keep me in this position.'

He frowned. 'When Mr Wilson played that trick on him, implying you were all . . . well, you are all ladies and gentlemen, but you know what I mean – did he want you all to get the sack? Surely he should have known better?'

'I hope he genuinely believes that we are his equals as trustees. I believe he is a good man. He certainly wants the best for all of us in the House, and is very keen on the new village. But I do suspect he made a serious error of judgement. Some gentlemen would have laughed at the pleasant deceit—'

'Some would. But tell me – no, I can't ask what your opinion is, because it wouldn't be right. But me and the footmen – sorry, the footmen and I! – aren't sure he is a gentleman. Do you know he expected me to take a letter down to the village?' He sounded genuinely outraged.

'And did you?' I asked, straight-faced.

'I might have taken it from his hand, all folded up and sealed, but I gave it to Alfie.'

I nodded. 'That's absolutely right – that's his job, not yours. I hate to ask, but to whom was it addressed?'

He shifted from foot to foot, a child again. 'Mr Rowsley, he made me swear on the Bible not to tell!'

'And did you make Alfie swear the same promise?'

I was relieved for his sake that before he could reply, his bell rang. 'That's him again. In his bedchamber. Doesn't he know he should summon his valet? Should I go or should I send young Davies? Officially he's his man. No, I don't want him to get it in the neck, do I?' He frowned.

Before he could respond to the summons, however, I remembered the note Francis was writing. 'Just one moment. It may be that Sir Francis has something he'd wish you to convey to Mr Trescothick.'

Francis had. Obligingly he let me glance at his note before he sealed it.

> My dear Trescothick
> I fear I am unavoidably detained and thus unable to accept
> your kind invitation to dine this evening.
> Yours etc
> Francis Palmer

'Let him put that in his tureen and sup it,' he said, reaching for his sherry glass.

TWELVE

Before I went to see Samuel, I spoke to Sarey, curled up in a window seat reading the pages I had set for my little class to study. She sprang up and curtsied as if in one movement. 'Please, ma'am, no ma'am. I've never seen no sock.'

'Are you sure? It might be important?'

She bit her lip – was it guilt? No, it was her usual expression when she was trying to concentrate. 'Please, ma'am, there was a box. This big.' She gestured – about nine inches by nine. 'It rattled. I gave it to Mr Thatcher to look after.' Another gnaw of the lip. 'He said he'd lock it away for Mr Bowman until he was better.'

'Excellent. You did absolutely the right thing. Now I needn't worry.' I pointed to the book. 'Have you written down all the words you don't know so we can look them up in the dictionary?'

Samuel was still unconscious, but Nurse Pegg, who was sitting quietly by the fire knitting what looked like a scarf, assured me he was certainly no worse. 'I was just about to read to him, Mrs Rowsley. But he'll know your voice, would you care to do it? I love a good psalm, myself.'

'I'll read his favourite. And then his favourite passage from the New Testament.'

Under the well-thumbed Bible was a small, unexpectedly heavy box. I shook it. It rattled.

'Ah, that's what Mr Thatcher brought up. He said it'd be the first thing Mr Bowman would ask for.'

I believe I was weeping as I started to read. But Samuel would have hated to hear the great words and phrases punctuated by sniffles, so I dried my eyes, took his hand, and read. As before, I am sure that as I concluded the Sermon on the Mount with a firm 'Amen' his lips moved and he squeezed my hand.

'May I question him? And ask him to respond by tightening his grip?'

'Please do.'

But there was no response to any of my questions.

Nurse Pegg stood to accompany me from the room and joined me in the corridor, leaving the door ajar so that she might watch her charge. 'I hoped to see you, Mrs Rowsley. My colleagues tell me someone has been asking to see his lordship.'

I caught my breath.

'Oh, they denied him access. Dr Page's orders. This story that Mr Bowman is no longer being treated here: is that connected with this person's questions?'

'It is simply what the police recommended. I gather it is not unusual when the attacker is still at large. How is his lordship, by the way – and her ladyship, of course?'

'I see signs of improvement in him: there are days when he is reasonably lucid, but he is very hard to manage if he is crossed. She . . . she rarely has good days, but Dr Page does not think her death is imminent. As for all our measles cases, I'm sure you know how they are progressing!' She left me with a chuckle.

I summoned Thatcher to thank him, meeting him just outside the Room.

'There's a lot of money in it, Mrs Rowsley – not just guineas but notes, too. I really don't like leaving it where it is, just in case anyone might be . . . tempted. I thought about the safe, ma'am – but didn't want to bother you for the key. And now I need to. Mr Trescothick is demanding the silver plates.'

'Mr Trescothick can demand all he wants. You don't have the keys, so it is not in your power to obey his order. However, next time I am upstairs, I will take Mr Bowman's box away and lock it up. Just in case.'

He did not take my gentle nod as dismissal. 'There's another thing, ma'am. Mr Trescothick's telling me not to attend you or even Sir Francis. I had to take him a letter from Sir Francis he didn't like. And, Mrs Rowsley, ma'am, he says he'll dismiss me if I don't do what he says.'

'Come into the Room a moment, Dick.' I opened the door, to reveal Francis and Matthew playing chess, glasses of sherry beside their vanquished pieces. I poured another and put it in Dick's rigid hand. 'Sit down here, Dick, and repeat what you've just told me . . . No, you're not in any trouble, quite the reverse.'

Matthew's face changed so many times during the course of the young man's narrative I might have laughed.

'I believe it is time to summon Mr Wilson,' I said quietly. It was he who had provoked this mess: let him get us out of it. 'If you write to him now, Matthew, Alfie might just catch the last post.' I caught Thatcher's eye and smiled. 'Meanwhile, Dick, please taste that sherry and tell me what you think. No, sip it slowly. No?' He had screwed up his face as if forced to drink medicine. 'People call that "dry". Now try a sip of this one. Better? Now, remember those two drinks. The first is called fino, the second amontillado. You need to know these terms because in years to come people will ask your advice about their beverages. You remember practising your reading and writing? Well, now you have to practise your drinking. Just sips, remember. And concentrate on what you're doing – you're not slaking your thirst!'

Poor Dick Thatcher was terribly ill-at-ease during supper, not least because Mr Trescothick had expected his attendance for the entire meal. The young man's explanation that the House custom was for the butler to be present for formal gatherings only was not well-received, I gathered, but to do Dick justice he stuck to his guns. A solitary footman – Arnold – waited on him.

It must be admitted that the rest of us felt constrained too, not wishing to embarrass him by remaining silent, but unable to relax into chatter. However, I had supervised enough Room suppers to know that hierarchies often caused awkwardness, and such a baptism would not harm the would-be butler, any more than the sip or two of sherry would.

He excused himself as soon as was polite, but was back in the instant, tapping the door and asking to speak to Matthew. The two slipped out together. In a moment, Matthew returned, a schoolboy grin on his face. 'Thatcher will make an excellent butler, even if he does not like fino. Trescothick handed him a note to take to the village, first extracting a promise he would not tell anyone the intended recipient. However, when Thatcher despatched Alfie with it – as any butler would – he asked for no such promise. So Alfie was able to tell me whom he delivered it to.' He paused dramatically – irritatingly. 'Would anyone hazard a guess? No? To the Reverend Theophilus Pounceman.'

The news caused a mixture of disbelief and consternation, enriched by speculation: how were they acquainted? How long had they known each other? They certainly did not seem likely friends or even likely allies.

At last, I looked at Bea. 'It may seem an act of cowardice, but tonight I prefer to sleep at home. Will you feel safe here without us?'

'Bless you, have you ever known me sleep without a rolling pin beside me? And if you were all under this roof, what good would you be? I could holler all I liked and never be heard, the guest corridor's so far away. In fact, why don't you tell little Sarey to prepare another room for you, on the Chinese corridor, the furthest you can be from His Nibs and closest to the backstairs?'

'She'll be in bed now.'

'I'll tell her in the morning, shall I? Before church.'

THIRTEEN

Armed with that curious information about Mr Trescothick and Mr Pounceman, the following morning, all best-bibbed-and-tuckered, we attended morning service. We sat in the House servant pews towards the back of the church. Sir Francis, as we naturally addressed him in front of the junior members of staff, modestly joined us. Meanwhile, Mr Trescothick took his place in the Family pew, his presence acknowledged with a gracious bow from the Reverend Theophilus Pounceman as he surged from the vestry.

As he took his place in the middle section of the pulpit, just like an actor assessing the size of his audience, he cast his eyes over our group until they rested on Francis. He might have attempted to conceal his feelings, but I was alarmed to see subtle shifts in the contours of his face. My colleagues and I had once been on the receiving end of one of his diatribes, delivered in the body of his sermon. We had endured it, scuttling back to work to nurse our hurt and anger. Matthew's passionate response on our behalf had been one of the things that cemented him so deeply in my heart. But for the life of me I could not see why Mr Pounceman's handsome face had iced over at the sight of our friend; nor, from his puzzled frown, could Francis.

Hard as I tried to attend to the service, my apprehension could not be quelled, and when Mr Pounceman climbed to the top of the pulpit my hand sought Matthew's for comfort and reassurance, just as it had in Italy when I was faced with a precipitous bridge to cross. We exchanged a quick glance; he knew my behaviour was puzzlingly out of character. But once the sermon started, Matthew understood.

Mr Pounceman pointed directly at Francis. 'We have among us a man you may think of as a gentleman. He dresses like a gentleman, walks like a gentleman, talks like a gentleman. But I tell you he is an idolater—'

'If I stage a faint,' I breathed, 'can you catch me? We have to stop this!' And down I went.

The commotion was gratifying. The servants shrieked in horror, standing up in their pews to see more of the unexpected sideshow. I knew Bea would be fumbling for her smelling salts, which would quite betray me. But Matthew was ready to play his part. I could feel him gathering me up in his arms, demanding air and a passage to the church door. Francis was offering to help. Still the maids squealed hysterically, surrounding us on our passage to the cold air.

For us and for our friend, the service was over. It might well be for the rest of the congregation. I dared not imagine the general speculation.

And it was over for Dr Page, too, pushing Matthew aside to take my pulse. Not for one minute would he be deceived, so I mouthed to him, 'I will explain later.'

He turned to the little crowd surrounding me. 'There's nothing wrong with Mrs Rowsley that a bit of fresh air won't cure. Now, will someone bring round my trap? I'll take her back to her home.'

'I thought for a moment that we were all going to hear some interesting news,' Dr Page said, sipping his coffee.

I shook my head. 'I'm sure that's what everyone still thinks. I am sorry to mislead you, but I had to stop Francis hearing Mr Pounceman in full spate. And, more important, to stop everyone else hearing his attack.'

'You believe those references to his being an idolater allude to his interest in the remains?'

'I do.'

'Has Sir Francis mentioned a dispute between them?'

'No. As far as I know they have never met. But I do know that Mr Trescothick has written to Mr Pounceman. Secretly.'

He smiled. 'So you're not revealing the source of your information.' He set down his cup. 'Now, why on earth should he do that? Because Pounceman's a trustee, perhaps? Perhaps he's trying to get him on his side in a way he singularly failed to do with you and your colleagues the other night. But how is he settling in? He's in a terribly difficult position, poor chap. I was thinking I ought to invite him to join me in a glass of sherry – do you think he'd come?'

'It depends on which door you use when you come into the House.'

'I beg your pardon?'

'If you use the front door, you must be a gentleman and you are welcome. If you use the servants' entrance, then I'm afraid you'll be persona non grata. This is what he did yesterday.' As I gave a brief outline, his eyebrows rose higher and higher.

'What a foolish man. Doubly foolish to alienate those upon whom he depends the most. How do you propose to improve the situation? More important, how are you going to explain your "illness" this morning?'

'Will not the assumption that it was "women's troubles" be enough? Meanwhile, I wonder if I have the tiniest piece of good news about Samuel. Last night I read to him familiar passages from the Bible. Could it – I hope it wasn't my imagination – but could his lips have been moving at one point? Just as I finished the Sermon on the Mount and ended it with an "Amen". And could he have squeezed my hand?'

He stood, smiling. 'Harriet, you know how I respect your powers of observation. And I hope with all my heart that you are right. But my counsel is to say nothing.'

'Of course! Particularly, of course, as Samuel is known to be in Shrewsbury Infirmary! How is the measles outbreak, by the way?'

'I am confident that there will be more cases.' Abruptly he stopped laughing. 'Tell me, my dear, is there any reason to hope you might one day have another cause to faint?'

I shook my head gently. 'Before our marriage, I went to consult Sir Charles Locock. I felt it only fair to establish before we married whether Matthew could hope for children.' I took a breath. It was hard to speak of such things even to so kind a man as Ellis Page. 'It was his professional opinion that an . . . an assault on me when I was a child left me unable to bear a child safely.'

'An assault – my dear, you were raped? Dear God, what monster would hurt a child? Forgive me!' He rose to his feet and took a turn about the room. Then he sat again. 'I interrupted.'

'There would be danger not just for me, but for the unborn baby. In any case, it was his opinion, based on the evidence I described, that I was no longer at an age when . . .' I had to swallow.

'I am so very sorry, my dear.'

'Please don't be!' I managed a smile, refusing to let it be watery and self-pitying. 'Matthew and I had one short discussion, during which he insisted it was better to enjoy the huge gift that we had received than pine for something we could not have. And we are very happy indeed,' I added.

'So I see every time I see you together. He is a lucky man, my dear. Now, shall we go and assure him that all is well, and see if we can find what Sir Francis might have done to offend our rector?'

Francis and Matthew rose to their feet as we entered the drawing room, Matthew's face as concerned as if he did not know that my illness was feigned. Francis stepped forward to take my hands. 'You are a remarkable woman,' he said, kissing each in turn.

It gave me great pleasure to say to a member of the aristocracy what I should have said many times. 'Fiddlesticks! But you, on the other hand, owe us an explanation.'

'I wish I had one,' he said with an open-handed shrug. 'I've never seen the man before, as you know. So when he pointed his finger of doom at me at the start of his sermon, I simply had no idea why he should be so vehement. And inaccurate, of course. I might not be as well-connected to the Church as you, Matthew, but I am a Christian soul generous enough to the clergy whose livings I hold. Some of them have asked for huge donations to rebuild their churches – they seem to have been convinced by this new craze for knocking chunks off decent country buildings and turning them into mini-cathedrals. I'm sorry, Matthew, I know you want quite an impressive building for this Stammerton of yours, but at least you're starting from scratch and can build whatever shape you like. Round, if it please you – you and the trustees, of course,' he added, with a somewhat ironic bow.

'I'm sure Mr Pounceman will be delighted to hear it,' I said dryly. 'However, although I have no high opinion of him, and am all too aware of his penchant for drama, I have never seen him attack anyone of your status before. He was always inclined to kowtow to his social superiors. When his lordship came into his inheritance and was spending money hand over fist, a clerical word in his ear might have been beneficial. But Mr Pounceman almost applauded the extravagances. It was Matthew who had to rein him in, or there would have been no estate for Mr Trescothick to inherit – just a title without land.'

Matthew nodded, and smiled at me with such love my heart turned over.

Dr Page raised a finger. 'It seems to me that he must have been misled about the Stammerton site, Sir Francis. A careless word from one of the workers, perhaps. Or a note from someone else?'

'Quite,' Francis replied. 'But he is an educated man and should have corrected any misapprehensions under which some colonial idiot might have been labouring.'

Matthew said pointedly, 'He may yet be my master, Francis. In any case, I do not know if we should blame the Antipodes for his churlishness.'

'He is in a very awkward situation, with no one to support him or to teach him our ways,' I observed.

'If I were you, Sir Francis,' said Dr Page, preparing to depart, 'I would arrange to show our irate friend round the site and explain things to him. It would be better to have him as an ally, especially as he is a trustee, remember.'

'In fact, this afternoon,' Matthew said, 'we have arranged to meet the Stammerton families there to discuss our plans with them. It might be useful if you were there too, to reassure them that the site will bring them nothing but financial gain, even if it delays the building by a very few weeks.' He added, 'It cannot be a long meeting – it is too cold – but it might be helpful if you came too, Page.'

The doctor's eyebrows went even further up his forehead. 'To deal with injuries after an outbreak of violence?'

'Neither, I hope. I have been too high-handed. I assumed I knew best. Possibly I do. But I should have asked those whose lives will be most affected.'

'I will come. Shall I bring Mr Baines too? He never opens the inn on the Sabbath, does he, and he knows some of the Stammerton men very well.'

Bea, alerted by my note, worked a miracle: she and a couple of kitchen maids had produced cakes, pies and sandwiches – enough to feed forty hungry people. She had also loaded the trap with blankets, almost burying the maids, who seemed to regard the incursion on their free time as something of a treat. Dr Page brought two baskets of apples, and Marty some balls for the children. Although only a few of the most argumentative men were waiting for us, one despatched his lad back to the village, so within minutes several families were struggling up the slope. Matthew set up an easel to display his proposals. Francis looked as if he would rather be swimming in the lake than standing next to a table on which lay some of the newly returned finds.

Bea declined any thanks. 'It's like the old days, when I had to cater for shooting parties,' she said. 'Only here I'm getting more gratitude.'

Marty laughed, but touched Matthew's arm. 'Look, lad, make sure they've all got food in their mouths or their hands before you speak. All of them. Because I know a few of them from the Royal Oak: barrack-room lawyers, they are. Shout you down as soon as breathe.'

Matthew laughed, but did as he was told. Only when everyone's mouth was full did he pin up his drawings. He explained quickly. The houses built in pairs. The sanitation. The space to grow vegetables. The school – free for all villagers. The village green and pond and a cricket pitch. The church. The village hall.

The only thing he didn't give them was a choice. I'd always wanted choices. So must these people, who'd never had any all their lives, except the bitter one between eating and heating, rags to wear or cardboard to line boots. Why hadn't I spoken earlier? I didn't want to now for fear of betraying him.

But then he nodded to me, and smiled. 'You may have other ideas. All of these things will be built, at the estate's expense, but since you will be living in the village, I would welcome your suggestions.'

The silence was only broken by the chatter of a magpie.

Then a voice: 'Tell us about the privies!' It might have been that of any of the women, but in fact it was Bea's. She'd drifted into the group and called from the back.

Dr Page stepped forward to explain. They listened in respectful silence; they knew he was generous to them, rarely demanding payment.

'How about a pub?'

Laughter. Marty stepped forward. 'I've got a question for you women. How many times have your menfolk come back to you roaring drunk, without a penny of their wages left? No? Because they've had a quiet drink in the Royal Oak and I've kept an eye on them. If you have a pub here, is that going to be the case? I hope so. But I can't run two pubs. Up to you.'

As if on cue, Bea and the maids passed round more food.

One young woman, still to be fed, raised her hand. 'Gaffer, why don't we wait and see? With all the will in the world, this lot isn't going to spring up overnight. When we've got our homes all right and tight, and the school, then it's time to think about other things. And maybe we can think of them on a summer's day!' She shrank into her inadequate shawl. Bea handed her a blanket.

'I think that's an excellent idea,' Matthew said. 'But there is one thing I'd like to ask. I've suggested we put these cottages in pairs, sharing a wall. This should give you more privacy. But they won't be as warm as those in a row.'

The young woman again. 'Pairs'd be quieter. So long as you build the middle wall nice and thick. Breaks my heart people can hear every word I say, every grizzle my bab makes.'

'And kitchens! We need a proper kitchen!' another woman yelled.

'Shut your mouths! Wenches talking in public! Should be ashamed!'

Before I could remonstrate another woman chimed in. 'What's the point of a kitchen anyway, if we've got no food to cook? And no money to buy it?'

Marty stepped forward. 'This is Sir Francis Palmer, who will be responsible for digging up these old Roman stones and other bits and pieces. Am I right in thinking, Sir Francis, that you

won't have enough men to do everything because the estate –
Mr Rowsley here – says he can't spare men from work on the
new village? Won't that bring more work and more money?'

'It will. It should bring work in for your wives, too: everything
we find has to be carefully washed.'

When this announcement wasn't greeted with any particular
enthusiasm, rather a sullen silence, Matthew stepped in. 'And
there should be plenty of other work for you women too,' he
said. 'Because new homes mean new windows and new windows
need new curtains. And new floors need new rugs.' He flailed
comically. 'And all the things as a mere man I have no idea
about.' He stopped: even the blankets were inadequate in this
wind. 'May I suggest you talk amongst yourselves and put forward
perhaps four people to represent your views – men and women?
I'd like us to meet at the Royal Oak on . . . shall we say Tuesday
evening? Mr Baines, would you agree to that?'

Good man though he was, Marty was perhaps disconcerted
by the idea of women entering his snug. A couple of the older
men started chuntering about where a woman's place might be.
In response, two young women catcalled. It was hard not to
join in. But Marty wasn't a good landlord for nothing. 'You'll
be welcome. Nice and early. An hour after nightfall.' Which
meant that later on the men could still nurse their half pints in
masculine comfort.

'Very well: an hour on Tuesday evening it is. Thank you,
Marty,' Matthew said. 'Over to you,' he whispered.

I stepped forward. 'Just one word before you go: there's a lot
of food left over. Could you oblige us by taking it all? Martha
and Izzy will hand out supplies to each family so everyone gets
a fair share. And if you need a blanket, please take one.'

Most needed one.

Matthew joined in with a will as Bea, Martha, Izzy and I
gathered together the remains of the picnic and thrust them
into waiting hands. Marty helped too, as did Dr Page. The
notion was all too plainly foreign to Francis, whose awkwardness
did little to endear him to the villagers whose hearts he had
clearly failed to win earlier. Dr Page, having done his share,
offered Marty a lift back to the village.

Matthew hesitated. 'Harriet?'

Bea said, 'Harriet has a sure pair of hands. I'm sure she'll take us womenfolk back to the House safe and sound. Just help us load the trap, gentlemen. Come on: the heavens will open within the hour – you mark my words! Supper will be served at the usual hour, and if I were you, gentlemen, whatever His Nibs said, I'd bring your night-gear! It's going to be a rough night, and I'll get a fire lit in the Willow Bedchamber. Sir Francis, I've put you in the Dragon Room, which should satisfy His Nibs if he ever gets to hear of it.'

FOURTEEN

Although much goes on behind the green baize door that those living the other side are never aware of, such as our stay last night in the guest wing, for instance, it is hard for those apparently in control to do anything without the whole household knowing. While so far as I knew, the heir was completely undisturbed by even the notion of our presence, we knew exactly what time he sent for his hot water and how long he liked his eggs boiled. We also knew that he was irritated by the late arrival of the London papers, and apparently bored by his new life. And why not? He was not part of it. Suddenly I was a child again, whisked into a strange house amid strange people, all talking about things I didn't understand in words I hardly knew. At least I was born and bred in the country, used to living my life according to the seasons. At least I had people telling me what to do and when to do it, and if I made mistakes and was shouted at, then there was often someone to slide a sympathetic glance – and sometimes a piece of cake or other treat – in my direction. And I was quick to learn. But Mr Trescothick had no one to teach him, even by example, and no one to offer him kindness. And things might get worse when he inherited the title – and its responsibilities. The aristocrats for whom I had worked would regard him as a parvenu, no matter how old his title, if he couldn't pronounce his vowels as they did, or understand their ex-public school slang.

Dear me, I found I was feeling sorry for him. Reason told me he had brought the general dislike upon himself – but one part of my heart longed to go and speak to him in private, and encourage him to mend his ways for his own sake. Would Matthew agree with me? I would raise the matter at a quiet time.

Instead it was time to consider my day. Matthew was going to Shrewsbury to talk to Mr Wilson; Frances, on a whim, set out with him – he needed more clothes, he said. Matthew would be responsible for discussing Mr Trescothick's requirements and relaying them to Bea. So I could return to my regular routine without worrying about any of them. Accordingly, I set out on my Monday tour of the House. From my chatelaine hung all the keys to the House. Today they were joined by two pencils and a notepad, ready ruled and with the names of each room already inserted. There was also a column for the regular maid's name. I used to do all this myself: now it was the task of Ada, the girl I hoped would become senior housemaid, now Effie was training to become a nurse. Of the two I thought Ada more likely to leave domestic work, since she had the looks, the talent and the readiness to undertake hard work to do well in the world. Perhaps she might become a pupil teacher in the new village school, but I could not envisage such a move suiting her for long. I would have taken her round with me today but it was too early in her ad hoc apprenticeship, and would cause dissension among the other girls, whose sense of hierarchy was as strong as Mr Trescothick's. So Ada was currently charged with preparing for what we hoped was the prompt return of Mr Wilson: she was ensuring he could use the dressing room adjoining the Blue Bedchamber as a study, should he need one. Thatcher had deployed a strong but especially spotty footman to move any furniture for her. I did not want youthful love to spoil either career.

In happier times, with a houseful of guests, I would inspect all of the rooms. Now Nurse Pegg took responsibility for her wing, and since so few bedchambers were occupied, even unofficially, and so few state rooms were used, I chose to do what I often did when the House was empty: I opened a few doors at random on every corridor. If there was any sign of neglect, I locked it until I had spoken to the designated maid. I was fairly sure she would not give me cause for complaint in future.

I had reached the floor below the run of attics, where rooms were cleaned but once a month, before I found anything untoward. Anyone trained by a less pernickety housekeeper than I would probably not have expected it to be perfect, but my dear mentor Mrs Cox breathed down my neck if ever I thought of slacking, in cleaning or any other task. There was dust, and dust aplenty, in most rooms – but it would be the work of minutes to restore the room to a pristine state. But in the next room there was a lot of dust, far more than a month's worth. It did not need the thought of Mrs Cox for me to surge inside. I checked the hearth: no, there was no soot, or I might have blamed a bird. I ran a finger along a windowsill; ah, this wasn't just the dust of neglect – it was almost gritty, like plaster dust. Now I felt not irritation but alarm. I did not like the inexplicable on my watch. Taking one last look, I locked the room behind me and moved on to the room to its left. That was no more dusty than you'd expect after a month. But the one to the right? The same gritty dust. But all the others in the corridor were up to standard. Clearly I must talk to Mary who Ada's clear hand told me was responsible up here.

What would the other top corridor rooms be like? Irritatingly, I had to go back to the servants' hall, to supervise their dinner, but I would be back as soon as I could. In the meantime, I would tell no one what I had found – after all, in a sense, I had found nothing.

But I did find something on the place laid for me on the servants' hall table: a tiny posy of wild cyclamen and winter-flowering jasmine, all that was available without raiding a hot house. There was a note: *We all wish you and your baby well, Mrs Rowsley.*

My face burned: I had not thought of this, had I, when I staged my faint? I needed to nip this bud of rumour at once. Lunch would be the silent meal it always was. It was only when the senior staff withdrew to the room for tea or coffee that tongues could wag again. And I was resolved that they should not – resolved at least that I should find something else for everyone to talk about. I thought fast. In the absence of Matthew, and perhaps I would have chosen her anyway, I turned to Bea.

In the hot kitchen, pushing hair back from her face, she laughed when I consulted her. 'And are you surprised? You should have said something to the girls at yesterday's picnic, shouldn't you? Very well, do you want to make a public announcement, or let one or two reliable gossips overhear our conversation?'

'I don't know. It's not the sort of thing one talks about, is it?'

'Harriet, you know that in the country no one talks about anything else. And this place needs cheerful news – that's why they gave you the flowers. If you say nothing, people will be knitting bootees by the end of the week. Come on, if anyone can think on their feet it's you.'

I nodded. 'You're right – as usual. Do you think we could . . .?' I whispered in her ear. Her face told me all I needed to know. 'I'm so glad you agree! Now, can you call them to order?' This was her domain, after all, not mine. 'Thank you.' I raised my voice into the puzzled silence. 'I would like to thank you for your good wishes, girls, for the new baby. Or actually, for the new corset. Very smart it may be, and the latest fashion,' I said smoothing my bodice into the new flatter lines dictated by the magazine advertisements we all pored over, 'but yesterday it meant I just couldn't breathe. That's why I fainted – and for no other reason at all.'

There was a mixture of tittering and sighs.

What had Bea said about cheerful news? I raised my hand for silence again. 'After dinner I shall make another announcement – about something else altogether. Something to look forward to. But it involves all of us in the House so I will tell everyone at the same time. Before you get on with your work, let me thank you for the flowers. They were a lovely idea. What I would like to do with them is place them – without the note – on Maggie's grave.'

There was a gratifying murmur: Maggie, one of our housemaids, had been scarcely more than a child when she had died, and I often found a little posy when I went to check that her grave was tidy, which it always was. She had borne his lordship's child, in quite terrible circumstances – and worse still, there was no one in her family able to look after the newborn girl, who now lived as a much-loved member of the narrow-boat family who had found her.

Bea – one eye on the clock – said swiftly, 'That's a lovely idea, Mrs Rowsley. And we can't wait to hear the rest of the news.'

I still had the House servants to disabuse, and had in fact violated unofficial protocol by telling the kitchen girls first. I just hoped what I was going to tell them after dinner would help them forgive me.

And, even if it delayed dinner even more, I would talk to Thatcher.

'What a wonderful idea!' he said, forgetting he should be on his dignity. 'A proper dance? With music and our best clothes? A Christmas tree?'

'All of those. Some musicians. A proper Christmas, Dick.'

'Is this to celebrate . . .?' His blushes made my early ones look like a mere amateur effort.

'I think people drew the wrong conclusions when I was unwell yesterday,' I said gently. 'This party is to celebrate the birth of Our Saviour, Dick – and to give what we hope will be a joyous end to a very difficult year.'

'What will Mr Trescothick say?'

'That he'll grace us with his presence, I hope. The House has always had some sort of Christmas celebration, has it not? Quiet by many people's standards, I accept. But he is not to know this.' That was both a statement and a warning.

He nodded his understanding. 'A great Family tradition it is, Mrs Rowsley.' He might not actually have winked, but there was very little about him that was sober and subdued. 'What about the former servants – the ones in the Family wing? Can they come? They might be called nurses but they're still staff.'

'That'll be a matter for Nurse Pegg,' I said with a smile, 'but I really can't see any objection, can you?' I raised a gentle finger. 'But you're not to drop a hint, not even so much as a secret smile. Not till I've made the announcement. And then you will be responsible for restoring order, just as Mr Bowman would.'

There was almost as much gaiety in the Room as there was in the servants' hall. I had worried about Bea's response, because it was traditional for the butler and cook to open the dancing, and I did not want to uncover emotions best left buried. But she in particular was enthusiastic. 'It'll be wonderful to do some exciting cooking again,' she declared. 'And so good for the kitchen maids to learn new dishes. Most of all, we'll have fun.'

Her voice dropped. 'Unless her ladyship takes it into her head to pop off and plunge us all into mourning.'

Or Samuel or even his lordship.

'We must ask Mr Pounceman to say special prayers,' I said lightly.

Dick said, 'Begging your pardon, Mrs Rowsley, he's more likely to pray for a quick end for him. So Mr Trescothick can inherit, see.' He took in our blank faces. 'They're as thick as thieves, those two, all of a sudden. When you were taken badly yesterday, Mrs Rowsley, and all the maids left the church to . . . well, they said they were going to look after you, but you know what girls that age are like – anyway, I stayed behind, to instil a bit of decorum into the men. Mr Pounceman . . . he wasn't very happy to have the solemnity of the service disturbed, and he cut short his sermon to denounce frivolity and lack of concentration. Then he and Mr Trescothick shook hands in the porch, as important people do, and kept us all waiting while they had a little chat. And then, without bothering with anyone else, they went off to the rectory together.'

As a decent woman I should be rejoicing that the lonely heir had found company. Instead I wished he'd found it with someone else.

Summoned to the Room before I resumed my inspection, Mary, not a brave child, was adamant that she had cleaned all the rooms in question to the same standard as the others. She was very near to tears even at being singled out from the others. But I needed some explanation. Perhaps we might work it out together.

Accordingly I told her to accompany me up the stairs, trying to balance being stern with being kind. I knew she had no family to ask about: she had been a workhouse orphan when I took her on. So we spoke about the other maids, and about whether she got out in the fresh air as Dr Page has insisted we all must do. Then there was the question of Christmas: was she looking forward to it?

'Oh, yes, ma'am. So very much! And a party with dancing! And the girls say we get real presents here!'

I thought of my first place, where we got work clothes, no more, and even the wrapping paper had to be returned. Worst was having to return the ribbon that tied the package. 'Yes,' I said firmly, 'proper presents. Not useful ones, Mary. I promise.'

Together we peered at the dust in the offending rooms. Screwing her apron into a tight ball, she sobbed. I managed to distinguish a few words. No, she certainly hadn't left it like this.

'I believe you, Mary. Listen to me: I believe you. As for turning you off without a reference, can you believe I'd be talking to you about the Christmas dance if I'd been planning to do that? Now, dry your eyes and smooth your pinny. We don't want the laundry maid worrying about her job, do we?' Not that I could imagine much worse a life than one spent boiling other people's laundry and then ironing it to impossible standards. Thank goodness goffering was no longer in fashion.

By now Mary was looking about her properly. I let her wander over to the window, where she dabbed a finger on some dust, just as I would, and looked at it closely. Then she looked upwards. 'Please, ma'am, sorry, ma'am, you don't suppose someone's been trying to open this window, do you?' She bobbed a curtsy. 'Only it looks as if someone's taken a knife to it. Sorry, ma'am. I'm being silly. Why should anyone want to open a window right up here?'

'Mary, there's no need to apologize. You've had a really good idea. How do you think the dust got everywhere? And what do you think it looks like?'

She examined a few more flakes. 'Please, ma'am, it looks as if someone's been scraping something.'

I smiled encouragingly. 'Go on.'

She turned to show me what she had on the tip of her finger. 'There's paint there – whitewash or suchlike – and then some plaster here. But look, ma'am, this almost looks like gold.' It did.

'You're right! I think we should save it, don't you? Look, I can make a tiny envelope from a page from my notepad.' She watched intently. 'Now, can you tip what you've found inside? Thank you.' I folded it closed, idly passing her another sheet as I popped it into my pocket. 'Could you make me another one while I see what else I can find?'

FIFTEEN

Cold and wet, I arrived back in my office to find a roaring fire. On my desk stood a tray of biscuits and a decanter of sherry, with two glasses beside it. Before I had even shaken my hat dry, there was a tap at the door.

'Allow me, sir.' Thatcher entered in time to divest me of my coat. 'I cannot imagine what Luke Footman was thinking of.' I imagined he was thinking of his job: he knew I was supposed these days to use the servants' door but following my usual practice I had marched through the great entrance hall. 'I will see these are dried, sir. And I will notify Mrs Rowsley of your arrival.'

'Thank you.'

He bowed himself out before I could ask him why he was prepared to disobey Trescothick's orders. I just hoped he hadn't nailed the wrong colours to his mast.

Another tap. Harriet. She looked round the room as if expecting Francis to pop up from under the desk. When it was clear he wasn't, we indulged in the sort of embrace we'd missed during his visit. At last we pulled apart.

'You first,' she said with the sort of smile that showed she was big with news.

'In short, Wilson is coming to stay here in a few days' time, as, no doubt, you predicted.'

'And have prepared for. The room adjoining his bedchamber has all he needs to use it as a study or sitting room if he so prefers.'

'I never doubted it. He has several urgent meetings that he cannot postpone, so he won't be here till Thursday or even Friday – when he hopes to convene a meeting of the trustees. And Francis is staying in Shrewsbury for a day or so – when he returns he suggests he stays here, to allow our life a degree of normality. He asks to remain in the Dragon Room: he likes its distance from Trescothick. But, by coincidence, he too craves the use of a study.'

'I'll show you how I have dealt with Mr Wilson's dressing room; if you approve I can make the same arrangements for Francis.' She poured us some sherry. 'I think you should sit down. I have been busy.'

'There is only one comfortable chair.' I sat, patting my lap invitingly.

'I have no alternative, then. But you may make me stand when I tell you what I have done.'

Was I apprehensive? Surely not.

'I have arranged a Christmas treat for the staff. A proper party with dancing and good food and a tree and presents.' Was she less confident as she continued? 'We have always had one. And I think some jollity will do us all good.'

'Excellent. So long as you save the first and last dances for me. I take it you do dance, Mrs Rowsley?'

'I am sure you will make an excellent teacher. But perhaps in the privacy of our bedchamber . . .' She pulled me to my feet.

At last, as I was lacing her corset – not too tightly, of course – she said, 'I think in Mary we have a remarkably intelligent little maid. You may not know her by name, just by sight. The smallest by two or three inches. Timid. But more observant than you can imagine. I had to ask her why she had left an upper room undusted – I took her up to it to show her why I was dissatisfied. She was terrified of losing her place, but still noticed details I had not. She was very . . . rational. And when I made that little envelope to stow what she had found, I asked her, casually, to make another. Which she did. Just like that.' She showed me. 'Can you tell them apart? Actually, I can't either, because the contents are the same. Some plaster dust, some scrapings of paint, some gold leaf. Not things you usually find in something not much better than a storeroom. Two storerooms.' She was no longer a joyous wife not long back from her honeymoon; she was a serious woman with what she clearly saw as a major problem on her hands.

'Why is it worrying you so much?'

'Because I've never seen anything remotely like it. And I fear – I fear it means someone is . . . someone has access to a room that they should not. I checked all the other empty rooms this afternoon and they are all as immaculate as one would wish. Mary found marks that suggest someone was trying to open a window. For what reason? Who knows?' She bit her lip. 'I know your estimation of their mental powers is not high, but next time we see Sergeant Burrows and Elias, I would like to report it to them.'

'As one whose mental powers are very high in my estimation, have you worked out any explanations yourself?'

'I can only manage one. That someone was trapped in the House and sought a means of escape. Or – I know, this is a second – that someone found a bird somewhere and tried to release it. But there are no bird droppings, no soot. So perhaps there is a third: someone wished to lower something from the window. Yes, I actually fear the last is the most likely.'

I kissed her. 'I think you are right: we should tell the officers. In fact, I will summon them. Meanwhile, this child Mary: what do you want to do for her? What can you do without upsetting the other servants?'

'I'll teach her to read and write, just as I have the others. And then we'll see. She must do well,' she added fiercely.

I kissed her again. 'My love, I am sure she will. I think in her you see yourself at the same age. And you do not think she should wait till she is a grown woman before she sees the world. Now, where would you like to travel to next? I was thinking . . .'

The servants' hall, in which meals were always conducted in silence, was ready to bubble over when Bea, Thatcher, Harriet and I adjourned to the Room. And the atmosphere there was as relaxed as I had ever known it, even the young man shedding his embarrassment at being with his elders and seniors. Soon he would add gravitas to his all-round ability – and then he would be ready to spread his wings and find a better post, unless, of course, his loyalty kept him back. I wondered if Wilson might consider it possible for him to become a temporary trustee in Samuel's place. Perhaps the young man wasn't quite ready for that. Almost certainly Wilson wouldn't think he was.

Unless he admired Thatcher's ability to observe people without their knowledge.

He had not only noted where Trescothick was going yesterday; he was now able to report that he and Pounceman had renewed their acquaintance this morning, walking together in the direction of the Roman site. 'What a shame Sir Francis was not there to enlighten them,' he concluded.

'I do not care to ask how you know about this expedition, Dick,' Harriet said. 'And I will not ask if you are able to give any further information about the heir's whereabouts – unless they concern his exploring parts of the House you consider . . . shall we say, an unusual destination.'

At his most formal, perhaps even expressing a touch of outrage, Thatcher bowed. And then he grinned. 'I am sure the footmen are able to assist, Mrs Rowsley. I daresay the maids will be similarly alert – though perhaps you yourself are unable to compromise your sense of propriety by telling them to be.'

Harriet managed a mirror-image of his bow and his grin. She might have been indulging a favourite nephew. What she had lost when she was raped as a child – the chance to be a wise and loving mother! – Mary and Thatcher were as substitute children, were they not? As long as she was in charge here, all the indoor staff, male and female, would be educated as far as they could be, their ambitions understood and encouraged. I was humble and proud that such a woman had loved me. It was all I could do not to reach across the table and take her hand. At least I could smile at her.

Soon after eleven the next morning Mr Trescothick had sent Thatcher to summon me to the library, where he was ensconced at his lordship's desk. It appeared that he expected me to remain standing in front of him: where had he learned such antiquated notions?

'Firstly, Rowsley—'

At least he pronounced my name correctly. 'Sir?'

'Firstly, I am not having a pregnant woman on the premises. It sets a bad example to the other servants.'

'Indeed, sir? But I am not responsible for hiring and dismissing members of the household. It is a matter for Mrs Rowsley and, in the absence of Mr Bowman, Mr Thatcher.'

'I can hardly expect Mrs Rowsley to dismiss herself.'

'The only person who can do that, until the trustees deem otherwise, is her ladyship, who relies absolutely and completely on her. Sadly her ladyship is too indisposed to be able to discuss the matter. In any case, the first question she would ask is why her right-hand woman should be dismissed.'

'You are being disingenuous.'

That was a charge I could hardly deny. But I did. 'Indeed, sir, there is no reason for my wife not to keep her job and every reason for her to do so. It is she and her team who are totally responsible for the internal well-being of the House.'

'How can she do that if she is about to be a mother? Her place is in her own home.'

'I have yet to learn that our own dear Queen is any less a monarch for being a mother. In any case, though it is frankly no one's business except hers and mine, my wife is not expecting a baby, so let us end this conversation before I forget my manners. Was there anything else, sir? We like to ensure that our guests are happy.' Suddenly I recalled what Harriet had said at breakfast, thinking sympathetically of the man we all found hard to like. I sat down opposite him. 'Mr Trescothick, I am well aware that you are in a most unfortunate situation. You must have expected to be greeted by your family and introduced to the best families in the neighbourhood – in short, treated as his lordship was treated when he returned to the House when his father died. But these are far from usual circumstances, are they not? You are alone, rattling round a vast house. Sir Francis and Mr Pounceman apart, the only people to have greeted you are people with whom you would not normally have mixed. I suspect the little trick that Mr Wilson played on you was to demonstrate that though we are not your equals in society we are not quite like Mr Darwin's monkeys. We are well-educated or at least experts in our areas. If you can accept us on those terms, your life will be much more comfortable. We can offer you company and conversation even if we cannot introduce you to the county set because we are not aristocrats.'

'You're lying again, Rowsley. Your father might be a mere vicar, but your grandfather was a lord.'

The latter term grated for some reason. Perhaps I had expected that when he did his obvious research, Trescothick would have noted the precise rank of my illustrious ancestors. Not a vague lord, but an earl – so by no means in the front rank of nobility. As for my father, I knew he would not mind being reduced to the ranks, as it were.

'Nonetheless, I am a paid employee. As such I do not have the entrée into polite society, which you will have on his lordship's demise. What I can introduce you to is the profession of estate management. And I will do so gladly.' Receiving no reply, I got to my feet, bowed, and prepared to leave him.

'Wait! I called you here to open those bookcases. They seem to be locked and none of the maids will admit to having keys for them.'

'That's because they have none. The only person with absolute control over those cases is his lordship. In his absence, the two most senior members of staff have to open them together, and remain in the room as long as they are unlocked.'

'Except for your friend Sir Francis, no doubt. He was working in here.'

'There are no exceptions,' I said firmly, acutely aware that I had been prepared to make one until Harriet had intervened.

'What on earth is in there, then?' For once he spoke to me as an equal.

'I've no idea,' I said, also man to man, as it were. I got up and peered through the wire grilles. 'I'd have thought one of your first acts when you come into the title might be to appoint a librarian to catalogue everything in here. Whatever these cases hold, I should imagine there's a lot of tedious stuff too. But I wouldn't know t'other from which, as they say round here.'

Perhaps I expected him to reply in kind with some Australian idiom, but he did no more than nod.

The silence grew, becoming awkward. I suspected he would see it as his right to end the interview. Perhaps he expected me to ask his permission to leave, but I found I could not. 'I understand Sir Francis showed you his Roman site the other day. Huge, is it not?'

'I can't understand why you're all making such a song and dance about a heathen temple. No wonder the workers are up in arms, seeing that being put before their needs.'

The first sentence had hints of Pounceman – but whence came the sentiment in the second? I asked quietly, because I was genuinely interested, 'What would you have done, sir?'

Was he silent because he was angry or because he was simply nonplussed?

At last, I bowed myself out.

It seemed to me a conversation with young Davies was in order. Surely he if anyone might understand what was going on between his new master's ears.

SIXTEEN

While Matthew was closeted with Mr Trescothick, it fell to me to welcome Sergeant Burrows and Elias to the House and, showing them to the upper-floor rooms, explain what I had found.

'That could be evidence,' Elias said, reverently stowing one of the little improvised envelopes in a pocket. 'Thank you, ma'am. You did right to tell us.'

Sergeant Burrows broke off from his investigation of the offending window to rebuke him. 'It may be anything or nothing. You did well to keep it, ma'am,' he conceded, 'and better still to summon us, but until we can link it to something – a theft, or something – then it remains no more than an interesting find. Are you sure nothing has been stolen? Something large that might have to be lowered down to someone waiting down below?'

'But why pick this room, sir? This and the one next door, of course. Is it because the windows are larger, ma'am?'

'All the windows on this floor are a uniform size, in line with the symmetrical appearance of the exterior. But it is – to my mind – a very good question. All the rooms up here are equally unused. Why choose two apparently at random?'

Elias peered out. 'Is it easier to lower something from this one than from the others?'

'If it is, that would really worry me,' I admitted, feeling sick. 'Because it would imply that someone knew the House very well indeed.'

Burrows, however, was still thinking about Elias' question. 'Depends on what they might want to lower.'

I pulled myself together. 'You are thinking of a picture, I collect? That was my first thought too. The gold leaf I showed you might have been chipped from the frame?' Before he could argue, I continued, 'I have asked the staff to check each and every room, sergeant, in the hope that they will find a patch of wallpaper a different colour from the rest.'

For a moment he might have looked puzzled. Then he said slowly, 'You mean the rest of the paper would have faded, and any behind a picture would be protected? Well done, ma'am.'

'Thank you,' I said, without irony. 'Sadly the search has as yet revealed nothing of interest.' I had to stop myself gasping at my folly. I had not had the attics searched. However, perhaps I might turn my omission to my advantage. 'Gentlemen, there is one area I thought you might prefer to search yourselves, in case there are any incriminating footsteps in what I fear is a very dusty area – the attics. Shall I accompany you there now?' Of course I could have summoned a footman, but in truth I really wanted to see for myself what, if anything, they found.

'I'd have thought it was unnecessary to lock doors in a place like this,' the sergeant observed. 'You wouldn't expect burglars, not with all the staff you've got.'

Elias nodded.

So did I. 'Staff I've known and trusted for years,' I agreed, affably. Perhaps someone who knew exactly which windows were the most appropriate. 'But if you suspect you might have rats in the kitchen, you don't leave the meat-safe door wide open, do you?' I lit lamps. 'This way to the backstairs, gentlemen.'

The men gasped as they took in the treasure we stood amongst – perhaps at the quantity, rather than the quality, of what they saw. 'This is not generally known,' I said, locking the door behind us. 'Or it wasn't until we had to have the roof repaired. However, the workmen are good men, loyal to the Family, and even if any of them suspected that this was more than just the Family's version of household junk, I can't imagine their speaking of it.'

'This could furnish a whole village!' Burrows breathed.

'Except even this new model village Matthew's planning won't have rooms grand enough for tables like that, or cupboards like this,' Elias observed. He pointed at a particularly ugly Croft ancestor, painted on the Cromwellian principle of warts and all. 'And can you imagine someone like that old bugger – sorry! – watching over you as you break your bread?' He spread his hands. 'How would anyone know if stuff had gone missing?'

I said quietly, 'Those responsible might have left footprints in the dust on the floor.'

Elias said, 'But there isn't any dust on the floor. Looks newly swept.'

'Exactly. Which is why I am worried. That idea we had about the gold leaf coming from a picture frame – there are plenty of frames up here. The trouble is, who would know if one was missing in all this chaos? We could ask Matthew and George—'

'That's the estate carpenter,' Elias put in. Burrows nodded.

'But I doubt if they could remember every detail of every heap and stack and cupboard.'

'It's worth getting them up here,' Burrows said. 'Might I trouble you to summon them, Mrs Rowsley?'

I looked at my watch. 'We will all be gathering for servants' dinner in a very few minutes. Would you prefer to wait up here and look round, or join us? I assure you there will be plenty.'

'I think we should keep this part of our investigation between ourselves, don't you, Mrs Rowsley?' I suspect my hint that it was they who had suggested the origin of the gold leaf had smoothed our relationship. Was it wrong to flatter a little? Who knew? After all, I had spent a lifetime achieving victories by encouraging my employers to believe it was they who had had the ideas that had in fact emanated from me. 'So perhaps you could send the gentlemen in question here as soon as is convenient.' He bowed.

Send? I would assuredly accompany them. 'Of course. And should there happen to be anything left over, it can be served in the privacy of the Room.'

Having agreed with Thatcher that he would take control of the table and the senior servants' dessert in the Room, I approached Matthew and George, whispering discreetly in their ears. Perhaps this encouraged them to eat more quickly than was seemly, and to ask Thatcher's permission to leave the table. I slipped out after them. Everyone would notice, of course, but I was confident he would deal with any impertinent questions with the professional hauteur he was fast developing.

The policemen had unearthed a couple of ugly Jacobean chairs, but it was clear they were not sitting comfortably.

'People must have been a different size and shape in those days,' Burrows said, getting up and rubbing his back.

'That's why they ended up here, I dare say,' Elias said, doing the same. 'Matthew, Mr Rowsley, sir: has Mrs Rowsley explained why we want you up here?'

'I thought I should leave that to Sergeant Burrows,' I said diplomatically. And more or less truthfully.

'I'd like you to look round and see if you can see if anything has been moved, or taken from where you last left it,' he said.

'Like those chairs,' George, clearly not feeling beholden to either of them, pointed out. 'You wouldn't care to put them back, would you, exactly where you found them?'

'We need to visualize things as they were,' Matthew explained with patient authority.

'I don't see what difference a couple of chairs'll make.' Burrows made a great show of dragging the admittedly heavy items away.

'What we're looking for—' Elias began.

'Hush up, my lad. Just let me think. In fact,' George continued, 'I'd rather have your space than your company. So I'd be obliged if you'd just step downstairs for a bit.'

Even I was surprised, but I led the way without protest.

'I had an uncle who was a water diviner,' Elias said eventually. 'He dowsed for wells. I know he used a twig, but he said it was more than that – like listening to things that aren't there. Do you think it's the same thing?'

'Things like you yacking away,' Burrows observed.

I raised a finger to my lips, as if they were my staff.

At last Matthew came downstairs, a grim smile on his face. 'George has identified something that has disappeared. Just one so far. He just looked at things, closed his eyes, and then knew. I've left him on his own for a few minutes just in case he notices any other – though you can't really notice something that's not there, can you?' He gave a self-deprecating grin, the one that always made me want to kiss him. 'What a gift he has.'

'Told you it was like my uncle, the water diviner,' Elias said.

'That's exactly what it seems to be like,' Matthew said. He looked at his watch. 'Two more minutes, I'd say.'

'King Charles has been moved,' George announced. 'But Queen Bess has disappeared. No sign of her.' He gestured with his hands. 'So high; so wide. And not up here, not as far as I can see, leastways.'

'Where should the king have been?' I asked.

'Over here, ma'am.' He pointed to a stack of pictures propped up against the court cupboard he had laid a tender hand on. 'Lovely piece, that, ma'am – deserves to be seen and used, not just left to get woodworm and die. Even in the servants' quarters,' he added, 'given what rubbish they've got. Begging your pardon, ma'am. But you'd know all too well.'

'I do. And am trying to improve things for them. But I can only go so far, George, can't I?'

'One court cupboard wouldn't cause too much trouble, would it?' He stroked it as if it were a living thing. 'Though to be fair, getting it down would cause a mighty lot. I wonder how it got here.'

'Quite. But if the king isn't here, where is he now?'

He pointed to a stack of travelling chests. 'There. He's looking a bit scruffy now, isn't he? Look at that poor frame.'

We all did. There was quite recent damage, just, as Elias pointed out, as if someone had tried to get it through a window that was too small. He patted the pocket into which he'd put my little envelope, which, almost hesitantly, he produced. He knelt beside the king. 'What do you think?'

'We'd have to test it up against the window,' Burrows said.

'And have it known we suspect that someone is up to something?' Matthew asked. 'Could you just write down the measurements, George, and—'

George spread his fingers, and used those to gauge both height and width.

I passed Matthew my keys. 'Why don't just the two of you check? I'll take these gentlemen downstairs. Mrs Arden has cooked a particularly fine shepherd's pie, and I would back her treacle tart against anyone's . . .'

While they ate, I excused myself for a few moments on the grounds that I had two or three urgent tasks to complete. Since one of these involved going outside to look up at the wing from which we suspected Queen Elizabeth had descended, I did not feel the need to explain further. Drains and flowerbeds and even a garden bench would have made it harder to lower anything in a straight line from most windows. But there were a few gaps. One, I judged, was directly beneath the window we were interested in. As if on cue, George appeared above me, shyly returning my wave when he noticed me.

I returned to our guests, their plates now clean. I suspected that they would need no second invitation to try the treacle tart; however, they would have to wait until their business was done here.

Summoning Thatcher, who was, after all, now in charge of half the staff, we all adjourned to Matthew's office to discuss the implications – which no one really wanted to voice – that someone who knew the House could well have participated. No one wished loyal servants to have been tempted by riches of which they were not supposed even to be aware – George in particular was upset at the notion that one of his reliable workmen had been involved. Thatcher was horrified that it had happened while Samuel was too ill to supervise the House, fearing that he himself had somehow been lax, a feeling I knew all too well. Could the finger point at the people who had had the run of the House, Francis and Mr Trescothick?

Sergeant Burrows was genuinely shocked that we might consider it. 'A gentleman? Doing a thing like that? Surely not, Mr Rowsley!'

I knew of gentlemen who had taken far more than pictures, but stayed silent.

Matthew ran his hands through his hair. 'So we have vague suspects that no one wants to consider as suspects. Are we to suppose that the picture has vanished into thin air?'

'Just how many rooms are there in this place?' Elias asked.

Everyone looked at me. I said, 'Yes, once I did count them – those I was responsible for, at least. Sixty-four. Plus the attics and cellars and outhouses. Samuel would know for certain, of course. Are you thinking that someone might have intended to steal Queen Bess but found she wouldn't go through the window?'

'By my reckoning she'd be a damned tight fit – begging your pardon, ma'am.' George blushed. 'And as for a hiding place, there's all those rooms no one ever goes into—'

'Except to dust. And an extra picture on the wall would probably go unnoticed. However,' I mused, 'why not put her back where you found her?'

'Because there was someone around – on the stairs, perhaps, who knows? – who might have seen and asked questions?' Matthew suggested. 'But I am afraid Mrs Rowsley and I can't lead any search now: we must meet the villagers from Stammerton, as we promised. Thatcher, perhaps you might organize some footmen to start the search.'

'Indeed, sir. In pairs, I suggest. And I will ensure that each door is locked after inspection.'

And with that our meeting had to close.

SEVENTEEN

The snug at the Royal Oak lived up to its name. Marty Baines had arranged chairs round a table made by dint of putting stools together and placing a door on them. He had made up a welcoming fire, and even brewed a hot punch for us all, which, he confided, had only the barest sniff of alcohol. He wanted our guests to be happy, not merry. While I paid him – he showed a generous reluctance to take any money till I insisted it came from the estate, not my own pocket – Bea and Harriet unpacked the baskets of refreshments they had thought necessary. Bea herself had agreed to come, largely, she said, to comment on the women's notions of kitchens and ranges.

I propped up two blackboards on the shelves behind the bar. On one were pinned my original drawings, on the other was blank paper, on which I would record their suggestions – for my benefit, largely, since I doubted if any of them could read. I was truly anxious – what if Sunday's anger had been increased, not dissipated, by the chance to express their needs? Would the meeting turn into a litany of grievances, not a list of hopes for the near future? More to the point, would anyone bother to come?

That fear at least was assuaged. Marty politely ushered our guests into the room, settling them round the ad hoc table and putting a tankard of punch and a plate in front of each guest. Bea and Harriet passed round thick sandwiches and slices of pie. Then silence fell. All eyes were on me, some clearly accusing.

At least I had done them the courtesy of learning their names. 'Sukey, Meg, Bob and Ted – welcome and thank you for coming. First I want to thank Marty for allowing us to meet here and for providing the hot drink and the fire. I'm all too aware that you don't always have such home comforts. From the moment I saw Stammerton I believed that this was wrong, and persuaded his lordship to build a replacement village with better houses and gardens and all manner of things I thought important. But before anyone says it, I don't live in Stammerton. You do. And I should have consulted you before I drew up the plans. The slight delay caused by the discovery of the Roman ruins is a nuisance – more than a nuisance for you, I grant – but it means you can be properly consulted. There are my suggestions.' I pointed to the drawings. 'These are the cottages Prince Albert designed – and with a royal brain behind them they must be worth considering. One large dwelling with apartments for four families. Each has two bedrooms for boys and girls, a larger parental one, a family sitting room and a kitchen. A privy, too.' I smiled but noted they did not look notably impressed. 'Here is space for us to write down what you want.'

Silence again. The vocal young woman of Sunday, Sukey, was too busy eating to speak. I waited till she had finished.

'Gaffer, these are all well and good in towns and places without much space. Or these pairs or rows you asked us about. Do we have to be squashed together? Why not nice tidy houses of our own, ones we can have a pride in? And – whatever else – separate privies. Not shared ones. And in the houses – like the prince's. Didn't Dr Page say shared ones spread disease? And he should know. Our own privies for certain.'

SEPARATE PRIVIES, I wrote. 'What about Sukey's suggestion for individual houses?'

Bob, the surly one, surprised me with his observation: 'They'll cost a lot more and be harder to heat. I can't see his lordship's trustees liking that.'

Neither could I, but I still liked Sukey's idea: after all, our own home was unencumbered by noisy neighbours. *IF POSSIBLE, DETACHED COTTAGES.*

'Kitchens with proper ranges,' Sukey continued. 'But I don't know what sort I should be asking for,' she admitted, her face falling. 'Mrs Arden, ma'am, you'd know, wouldn't you?'

'I do,' Bea said eagerly. 'I can recommend a couple of types to fit in a small family kitchen.' She rattled off a few details that probably only Harriet fully understood, but Sukey and Meg nodded sagely.

I wrote down the one Bea wanted them to choose.

Bob sneered. 'All setting up as Lady Muck, are you?'

Bea retorted, 'If you don't ask, you won't get. So in your place I'd ask for what seems like the moon – more rooms. Like the prince says, it's not seemly to have boys and girls sharing a bedroom, however rich or poor you are. I'm not saying his lordship would want you all to go and have more children than you can feed just to get a bigger place, but there should be some larger cottages for those with bigger families.'

Another sneer from Bob. 'It's not as if they're all at home at once, is it? They're out in service or in the fields as soon as maybe.'

Harriet caught my eye, mouthing the word 'school'. But it seemed I was to continue. 'They are now, Bob, but one day that will change – and sooner rather than later. We promised to build a school, remember – and that means children will be educated, not sent out to clear stones and scare birds almost as soon as they can walk. Once they are educated, they can expect better jobs, better-paid jobs. So I agree with Mrs Arden: there must be some bigger houses, and all houses should be able to accommodate their occupants decently.' I wrote on the board again. Perhaps we were winning.

Then Ted spoke. 'I can't see as how all this lot can be afforded. Wouldn't it be better to have a few rows of basic houses – none of this fancy talk about sculleries and privies? Build 'em cheap and build 'em quick, say I. Our place is so bad I'd rather sleep in his lordship's stables. At least the horses are kept warm and dry. And fed regular,' he said. 'What's the point of schools and reading and writing if we're starving now?'

Harriet said quietly, 'You will not starve, Ted, not while I'm at the House. You know that. Some people see our gifts as charity. They're not given with that intention. They're meant as part of your employer's duty to you. As are the new cottages. If his lordship built cheap, miserable houses you'd be no better off – worse off, in fact, because you'd have no land to grow your own vegetables and keep chickens and pigs.'

'He made a fuss about us keeping animals before,' he objected.

'It was not he, Ted, but his land agent. Now my husband is able to do as his lordship wished.'

I noted, but I doubt if anyone else did, that Harriet blurred

the distinction between his late lordship and our present
employer. I did not argue: it enabled us to do good by stealth.

'Until then,' Bea said, in a brisk tone that suggested she
was possibly thinking about Mr Trescothick's supper, 'we will
continue to make up food baskets for you. Bring them to
the kitchen when they are empty, and we will fill them. We
gave out blankets the other day: if you need more, come to
the House and ask for me or Mrs Rowsley. In the past we've
come to you, I know, but there are fewer of us now. But that's
just for now: we all need to think about the future.' No wonder
she had impressed Wilson by more than simply her cooking.

'Meg,' I said. 'You've lived in Stammerton longer than
anyone: what do you think about the new cottages? Quantity
or quality?'

She blushed as deeply as if she were a girl, not a grandmother,
but at last coughed painfully – I'd have to ask Dr Page to talk
to her – and said slowly, 'Seems to me we need both, gaffer.
Mix them up a bit. No need to make them all look the same,
is there? And I know the rector won't like this, but I'd say
houses first, school next, church last. No, a hall. Then the church.
Anyone as wants to go to church of a Sunday can go to the
one here. Or the Methody one there's whispers of. Houses first.
Even if I don't live to see them. There, I've had my say.' Her
cough echoed round the room.

Perhaps it was that that settled the argument.

Marty topped up their tankards, to keep them warm on their
way home, as he said. Bea stowed the remaining food in the
baskets, and handed them to Ted. 'Great lummocking lad like
you can carry them,' she said.

I would not have argued. Ted glared, but took them anyway.
Bob muttered something about a proper workers' union and
proper wages. I chose not to hear it. But I knew deep down it
was probably the only way to get nationwide change.

Had I hoped for a change of heart from Mr Trescothick, and
an invitation for us to dine with him, I would have been disappointed. As it was, he dined alone, and we would repair as usual
to the Room, to discuss our day – but not until I had made
a few swift notes of our meeting to present to the trustees at a

meeting I had arranged for late on Friday afternoon. The next morning Freddie was to copy out and deliver the notice of meeting and a loose agenda. Strictly speaking running errands was not part of his job, but he was looking pale, even peaky, and I thought some fresh air might do him good. He was so efficient it was hard to remember that he was only a child – in other circumstances he would still have been at school. He insisted he was well, but not convincingly. I must speak to Harriet and Bea to see what they recommended.

Needing to change before dinner, I was surprised to arrive in our bedchamber before Harriet. Once I was ready, rather than wait I went down to the Room to find Tim laying the table. He bowed with aplomb. He told me, rather in the manner of Thatcher, that madam had gone to the Family wing to talk to Nurse Pegg about the party. But the mask of dignity soon slipped. 'The missus – Mrs Rowsley – says she wants to make sure as many people as can will be there, even if some of the nurses can only go for half the time. And she specially wants Mr Hargreaves to go.'

Poor Hargreaves: his loyalty imposed a very lonely life on him. His lordship was often so violent that no one else dared approach him, Hargreaves apparently having a special touch.

At this point Harriet arrived, looking as beautiful as if she'd had all the time in the world to spend on her toilette. 'I've been to the Family wing. I hoped to see Nurse Pegg, but she was busy. So I left a note asking her to draw up a rota so that all the nurses and attendants can come to the party for at least half the evening. And there is more. Hargreaves says his lord-ship is having one of his quieter periods, and you might visit him for five minutes tomorrow morning. But to ask first, in case things have changed overnight.'

'That sounds like good news.'

Tim's eyes bulged with anxiety. 'But we'll still have our party, whatever happens?'

Harriet said kindly, 'I'm sure we will.'

Which satisfied Tim rather more than it satisfied me. When he had bowed himself out of the room, Harriet shut the door quietly.

'More later,' she breathed, 'but I am sure that Samuel squeezed my hand again tonight when I read to him. And I will swear his lips moved to say "Amen".'

Bea soon bustled in, but surprisingly there was no sign of young Thatcher. Perhaps he was waiting on Mr Trescothick. Eventually Harriet rang for Tim, asking him if he had seen our missing butler.

The lad frowned. 'Not since he went out for a bit of a walk. Just as dusk was falling, it was. He said he'd got to do what Dr Page had recommended or he'd kill someone. Between you and me,' he added confidentially, 'Dick looked fair furious when he grabbed his hat. Shall I go up to the footmen's room and see if he's back?'

'That would be very helpful. Thank you,' Harriet said with a smile. She added, as Tim closed the door with immaculate care, 'I wish Dick could move into a more convenient room – as acting butler he deserves a bit of status too. One of the nearest bedchambers, perhaps.'

'I'm worried about this furious stuff,' Bea said. 'He had a temper as a lad, but I thought he'd learned to keep a lid on it. Anyway, Arnold is serving Mr Trescothick's dinner. At least he won't be getting on his high horse with us.'

'True,' Harriet said absently. 'You know, I really am worried. It's dark and miserable and Dick's not one for being outdoors when he can be comfortable within. I'll ask the staff now before they all disperse.'

Even as she got to her feet we could hear a commotion.

Dick Thatcher was back. But he was covered in blood.

EIGHTEEN

'It's not all mine!' the poor lad said, as he collapsed on a chair. 'I managed to get a lusty blow or two on one of the men attacking me.'

'Tell us all about it later, Dick. Just sit quietly for now. We may have to send for Dr Page,' I said, over my shoulder to Bea. Then, more loudly, I addressed Dick again. 'Now, young man, I'll get one of the nurses to come and clean you up.'

Matthew didn't wait for a servant, he ran up the backstairs himself.

'But, Mrs Rowsley, I'm supposed to be . . .' Dick quailed under my glance. 'In any case, I don't need a nurse. Do I?' He tailed off, looking at the mess something had made of his hand. 'They started by throwing stones. I think they were aiming at my head. One must have got me – knocked me out cold. I don't know how long I was lying there. But I don't need a nurse, honestly. I'd much rather not—'

'Now, if the nursing staff are good enough for his lordship, they're good enough for you. You're not telling me you can get that coat off without some help.'

Slightly out of breath, Nurse Pegg herself came striding in, carrying a very official-looking box marked MEDICAL EMERGENCIES. 'I'll thank you all kindly for your help so far,' she said, 'but now all I need is some freshly boiled water, a basin or two, and someone with a strong stomach. You'll do.' She pointed at little Mary, who did not quail. I smiled my approval. 'Just listen to what I tell you. The rest of you, shoo! We don't need an audience.'

Bea had to do no more than point as the kitchen maids scurried to their tasks.

'Nurse Pegg, my sitting room – the Room – would be more private and almost as convenient as the servants' hall,' I pointed out. 'It's supper time, isn't it, and there's really nowhere else as warm and comfortable for all the staff to eat together. Tim, clear the Room table quickly for Nurse Pegg, please.'

'Thank you. Very well, in we go,' Nurse Pegg said, easing Dick from his chair. Despite himself, he cried out.

Tim reappeared. 'Thank you. Now will you lay the table in the breakfast room, please. We'll eat in there.' For all my decisive words, I led the way via the servants' corridor. There was no point in annoying our guest unnecessarily.

The fire already laid in the grate started immediately – I hadn't lost my touch – and the cloth and cutlery were on the table before we knew it. Tim promised to bring me word the moment Nurse Pegg had finished her work – or bring her to us if she needed private conversation.

'What if she thinks he should sleep in the Family wing?' I asked. 'Then the cat would be out of the bag and no mistake.'

'I'm not sure it would,' Matthew said. 'Thatcher is trying to follow Samuel's example. I believe he would be as discreet as you or I.'

'The servants don't give that measles story much credence these days,' Bea pointed out. 'They know how many meals we send up each day, and yet I've not heard a smidgen of gossip. Not that they'd like it if I did,' she conceded. 'Even if they did take it into their heads to go and visit him, I daresay they'd keep mum.'

'I'm sure they're too much in awe of you both to disobey orders,' Matthew said.

'Well, someone seems to have been so little in awe of us that Queen Bess has disappeared,' I reminded him tartly. 'This is what's been going on, Bea . . .'

Her face was a study as she listened. 'Someone from the House! You could knock me down with a feather.'

'So I did something I'm not sure about,' I said. 'You know Samuel's box? Thatcher had taken it to his bedside, in case our old friend might worry about it. It might have come to the notice of all and sundry – outsiders might have been called on to sit with him. Given the goings-on, I've removed it and locked it in the safe.'

'You're quite right, Harriet; just a bit late. I had the same thought. Even Nurse Pegg – well, we don't really know her, do we? And I don't know that I could ever trust a person with a voice like that. So I did something too. I emptied the box. All his cash is safe and sound – you've just locked up a collection of buttons!' She laughed so much she choked, and needed a sip of wine to revive her. Embarrassed she added, 'I just thought that the blow to his head might have made Samuel forget about our falling out, and that he might like me to read to him too. So I've been up two or three times,' she said so casually that in my head I doubled or trebled the number. 'I'm sure the money is secure where it is, but if you'd rather it can go where you thought you'd put it – and Samuel can have his box back again.'

Raising a glass to her, I said, 'To old friends, Bea – and that includes you! Now, will you excuse me if I go and see what's happening to young Dick?'

Before I even got to my feet, there was a knock on the door. Tim, clearly aiming to be a butler in Samuel's mould, announced Nurse Pegg. Matthew gestured. Tim pulled back a chair for her and settled her in it before asking me, 'Shall I fetch another glass, ma'am?' I suspect Samuel would have produced one and filled it for our guest without having been asked, but the boy was doing his best. Nurse Pegg kept her head modestly lowered but sipped with gusto. When the glass was empty, she looked about her, putting her hand in front of her mouth like a scared tweeny – and this was merely the breakfast room. All thoughts of Dick Thatcher had clearly been swept from her mind.

'Your patient?' I prompted her gently.

'Oh, Mrs Rowsley, I'm so sorry. I've never seen anything as grand as this before. Yes. Mr Thatcher. I found he's broken his collarbone and I've taken the liberty of asking Dr Page to come and set it. After that, he'll need sleep, but being a strong young man I should imagine he'll be able to sit up in a chair tomorrow or the next day. But he won't be doing any butlering for a bit,' she added.

'Thank you. Now, would you care to sup with us?'

Clearly overwhelmed, the poor woman ducked her head right down. 'Thank you, ma'am, very kindly, but my place is with my patient, and Dr Page may need my assistance.' In her slightly

ungainly way, she got to her feet; Matthew sprang to open the
door for her. I think she was almost as overwhelmed by that
polite attention as she was by her surroundings. Certainly she
turned her face from us as she scuttled out.

It seemed Bea agreed with me. 'It still seems very strange to
me to be moving round upstairs. Until I became Cook, and
had to discuss menus with her ladyship, I'd never left the servants' area. My kitchen maids still haven't, you know. All these
rooms, great and small, and they've never so much as guessed
at what they're like.'

Still on his feet, Matthew nodded. 'No wonder this
Christmas party is so important to them. We must make it
especially memorable for them. Not just the presents, about
which Harriet has particularly strong feelings, but perhaps
prizes for the games.'

'So long as everyone wins some prize or other,' I said. 'As
you say, Bea, some don't have the best of lives; we don't want
them to feel less valued. What about the outdoor workers,
Matthew? In the past they've not been included. Her ladyship
in particular used to object. But now she no longer holds the
reins . . .'

At this point Tim arrived with soup and news: Dr Page had
arrived, and asked Tim to fetch brandy to help Dick bear the
pain. But poor Tim had no idea where it might be.

Bea said robustly, 'Ask one of the kitchen maids for the
cooking brandy; Dick won't know it from his lordship's finest!'

Dick was sleepy when I visited him in one of the rooms in the
Family wing – the closest to the stairs and furthest away from
the other patients. Somewhat slurring his words – he must have
taken a lot of that brandy, cooking or not – he still insisted
he must return to work the next morning – who else would be
responsible for . . .

'Dealing with Mr Trescothick's whims?' I concluded for him.
'At the moment, Dick, your only job is to obey Dr Page's
orders. One of which is probably to go to sleep and get better
all the sooner. Yes? So good night and God bless you.'

'But Mrs Rowsley – I need to talk to Mr Rowsley! About
our search of the building!'

'Suppose you tell me.'

It seemed the footmen had so far searched about a quarter of the House, finding nothing unusual to report, even though they had looked under the covers protecting the furniture in the currently unused state rooms. 'It'd be lovely to use them again, wouldn't it?' he sighed. 'Though not without Mr Bowman here. How will we manage without him, ma'am?'

'As soon as you're better, you will manage admirably,' I said. 'To be sure, you're still learning, but you are learning quickly, and no one would imagine the House having forty visitors for a while.'

'Of course not,' he said, digesting the implications – a death or two, a year's mourning for each. He straightened. 'And I hope and pray that one day Mr Bowman will be back here to supervise me and everyone else, God bless him.'

'Amen.' Perhaps this was not the best time to raise a tricky question, but ask it I must. 'Tell me, how is young Davies dealing with his promotion? Is he enjoying it?'

The battle between the discretion of being a butler and being a young man with a tale to tell was all too visible in his face.

'We will speak of this when you have rested. Good night, and God bless you too, Dick.'

'I wish our dratted heir—'

'Putative heir,' Matthew corrected me with a smile, which I returned.

'Dratted putative heir, then. Anyway, I wish he would take himself off to a Shrewsbury hotel, where he might find life a good deal more comfortable than here. But of course there's the trustees' meeting later this week and he has a legitimate, interest in that. So we will just have to cox and box,' I sighed. 'Davies, the senior footman who would normally take over, is already acting as Mr Trescothick's valet, of course. By the way, I've asked poor Dick how Davies is faring. There's obviously some problem there, but I told him we'd speak tomorrow, provided he's well enough.' I could no longer hold back a sigh. 'My love, I don't know what to do. The only time we've ever been without both butler and under-butler was when we've had the influenza in the House – and by then the Family had already moved to their summer residence to escape the infection. Of course, there are staff there.'

'But all the properties are rented out at the moment,' Matthew said, 'to pay for the lake and the other changes – yes, including the model village. And it would be truly unreasonable to terminate an agreement with a good tenant just so that the heir – the putative heir – has a butler. Even if we tried, there would be legal complications enough to make your hair curl. No, let the next most senior footman try his hand: it'll only be for a couple of days, surely.'

'Very well: Arnold has been waiting on him at mealtimes, but I'd have thought . . . no, he hardly has the presence of a butler, not even a butler-in-training.'

'You know Bea and I will support you whatever choice you make. And it won't be for long, surely. Even if he can't carry anything, I'm sure Thatcher would be outraged to find himself replaced when he can function with his arm in a sling. Meanwhile, and more importantly, has Dick recalled any details of the attack? And do you think he is ready to tell us about them? You, perhaps?'

I shook my head. 'He might have been engaged in something he would be embarrassed to talk to me about, might he not – a young and well set-up young man? Might there be rivalry involved? A job for you, my love – or for Elias?'

NINETEEN

After a particularly difficult meeting with a tenant farmer who had got into debt through no fault of his own and now found himself unable to pay his rent, the last person I expected to see being shown into my office was our rector. Seeing the bandages about Mr Pounceman's head and hand I hurried to push forward a chair, calling upon Luke to bring us refreshments. He was a senior footman, after all, and might as well add to his accomplishments.

'It is not refreshment I seek,' he declared, 'but reparation. Last night I was set upon by a bunch of rapscallions whom I presume are some of your colleagues. I would say, "employees", but of course, you are not their master, are you?'

Perhaps I felt my father's hand upon my shoulder. 'I believe we have only one Master,' I said with probably irritating humility. 'And I fear I do not have too many people I call colleagues who would be in a position to attack anyone. As you know, Mr Bowman is still indisposed; his fate is in the hands of the Almighty. And now poor Thatcher has had a fate similar to yours, and lies sick in the Family wing with broken bones. Where did this gang attack you, anyway?'

'In the village. I was taking an evening constitutional.'

'And were you robbed?'

'No. But they took my hat and played throw and catch and then football with it.'

'Are you sure that these were not idle village louts who should know better? Well, I have already summoned the village constable to speak to Thatcher. He should be here at any moment. Have you complained to him yet? No? Then this could be your opportunity. Ah, Luke, thank you. And will you show Constable Pritchard in the moment he arrives? Yes, and bring another cup, please.'

Bea had stopped buying the very expensive coffee her ladyship preferred, but this morning's brew was very good, as Mr

Pounceman had the grace to acknowledge. Nonetheless, his tone was grudging as he asked, 'Perhaps it was Thatcher who assaulted me.'

'If it was, you more than avenged yourself. His injuries are severe; indeed, he might press charges himself against his assailant, assuming he can be found.'

'I am sorry to hear it. Perhaps he would like me to pray at his bedside.'

For him that was magnanimity indeed. 'That is a more than generous offer. If he is well enough, I will escort you there myself,' I promised, happy to let the ice thaw. 'Now, Pounceman, I am glad to be able to speak to you on a matter that touches us both. You know we shared a dear wish to build a new church for Stammerton. Perhaps we disagreed about the detail, but the intention was the same.'

His bow, if tepid, was nonetheless polite. There was no doubt he was wary, as I would have been in his place.

'Sadly I am going to have to suggest to the trustees on Friday that we defer the realization of this dream. A deputation of people from the hamlet has begged us to put new houses first. Then a school.'

'You know my feelings about schools for people of the lower orders!'

'I do indeed. But I believe it will soon be the law of the land that we educate all our children free of charge. So I hope their wishes have your blessing. In return, I hope they will continue to regard St Anselm's as their home church – though I fear some of them might be attracted by the notion of a new Methodist chapel here.' I confess to being disingenuous. It was what my military acquaintances might call a diversionary tactic. It worked rather too well.

'Methodists! Gracious goodness! By no means!' It seemed that if there was one thing more dangerous than education it was non-conformism, as he proceeded to tell me, uninterrupted. He might even consider he had persuaded me.

Mercifully at this point, Luke knocked to announce the arrival of Elias.

Since I was not a witness to either assault, having invited the men to use my office as long as they needed to, I took a file of correspondence to the Room. Harriet was nowhere to be seen. She would never have left her work on my desk without telling me first, so I carried it with me as I went up the backstairs. As usual I was intercepted by a burly attendant, one whose face I couldn't recollect. 'What is your business here?'

Nurse Pegg called out, 'For goodness' sake, let him through!'

She gave an exasperated sigh as I walked into her office. 'The stupid man doesn't know the difference between efficient and officious, does he? Forgive me, Mr Rowsley – I have the most dreadful toothache.' She covered one side of her face with her hand. 'I fear I may have to resort to laudanum.'

She gave me permission to talk to Dick Thatcher for a few minutes; meanwhile, she would go and see if his lordship was indeed well enough to speak to me. While she was away, I racked my brain for what Shakespeare had said what a woman's voice should be. Was it King Lear talking about Cordelia? Poor Nurse Pegg's would certainly not qualify. And that dreadful bonnet she was wearing this morning . . . It was clear that at least she had no personal vanity.

Dick was propped up in bed, already clearly bored by his enforced inactivity. When I offered to bring him books, he admitted he was not a great reader. 'Though please don't tell Mrs Rowsley, sir – she went to such pains to ensure I learned my letters.'

'I won't. But reading is like other activities, Dick – you need to practise your skill or you will lose it. And it would make her very happy to see a book open on your lap, though I concede it will be hard to turn the pages. How is the injured hand, by the way?'

'Dr Page says he doesn't think any bones are broken.'

'There was a lot of blood, though, Dick.'

'Well, it wasn't just the stone that hit me. I hit someone too. Quite hard, sir. That's why there's no skin on my knuckles. Whoever I hit might have a bit of a bruise,' he added modestly. 'And the shoulder – well, Dr Page says I can run errands in just a few days, whatever that means, but not carry anything for a month. I'm sorry, sir.'

'My dear Dick, a butler is there to supervise others doing the work, not to do it himself! Now, Constable Pritchard will be along shortly – you're not the only one who was hurt last night, and he wants to see if there's any connection between the two attacks. Meanwhile, suppose I find you a book I think you'll enjoy – with any luck my wife may see it and offer to read it to you.' My mind was running on novels by Dickens, but I would have to take Harriet's advice. 'Someone else wishes to visit you too, Dick – Mr Pounceman. He was the one who was also attacked last night. God knows why, but at first he was inclined to blame one of us. When I told him about you, he offered to come and pray for you.'

Dick stared. 'Pray for me, sir? Why?'

'Because it's his job, Dick. That's what rectors do. Don't look so horrified! And actually, between you, you may work out who committed the assault. Now, you are a senior member of the household, remember, and are entitled to his respect, just as he will expect yours. And you are equally entitled to tell me you feel too ill to receive him.'

He was tempted, no doubt about that. 'No, Mr Rowsley, I must see this as part of my job, must I not? Will he be praying with Mr Bowman? Sorry. I forgot.'

'His being here is universal knowledge, is it?' I asked sternly.

'One or two of us – we know there wasn't any closed cab taking him away, sir. And we couldn't work out who's suffering with the measles. But we've said nothing to the junior staff, since we assume the story was put about for a reason. That question just slipped out. I'm sorry. And I promise not to let it slip out in front of Mr Pounceman.'

'Of course. I know you'll be careful, though it must be hard with all that laudanum inside you.'

'Laudanum? Not me, sir. Oh, Dr Page insisted I took some last night when he was putting the collarbone together, but I wouldn't have any this morning. Mrs Rowsley doesn't hold with it, not unless it's essential.'

'She'll be very proud of you. But she wouldn't want you to endure unnecessary pain, Dick. Remember that.'

'I will, sir. And I'll forget all about any other butlers – except in my own private prayers, sir.'

'My wife mentioned you'd spoken about young Davies: do you feel well enough to tell me how he's getting on?'

* * *

There was no sign of Nurse Pegg when I made my way to the
upper floor, so I made my way straight to Samuel's door.
The nurse, whom I recognized as one of our former parlour
maids, greeted me with a bob and a welcoming smile. 'I'm sure
he'd like you to read to him if you can spare five minutes, Mr
Rowsley, sir. Dr Page has promised to look in when he's finished
with his lordship and her ladyship. He wants to see if Mr
Bowman really is reacting when people say he is.'

'What do you think?'

'It isn't my place to say this, Mr Rowsley, sir, but – no, I
don't like to speak out of turn . . .' She bit her lip. In response
to my smile, however, she plucked up courage to continue.
'When Mrs Rowsley trained us, sir, she made us look and
listen and smell all the time – damp, mould, raised voices that
warned us not to go into a room just yet. This sounds silly,
now I say it out loud: could it be that Mr Bowman finds it
hard to hear some voices but not others? We all knew he was
going really deaf when we worked for him. You could stand
behind him and say something and he'd take no notice. And
it was girls he found the hardest. Mrs Rowsley, now, she's got
quite a deep voice, hasn't she, for a lady? So he might hear
her. He doesn't seem to hear me at all, though, and don't think
I haven't tried. Nurse Pegg, now, she sounds like a gate that
needs oiling . . .' She shook her head.

I managed not to laugh out loud. Quickly straightening my
features, I asked, 'Shall I try? Is that his Bible? I ought to read
one of the miracles, oughtn't I? It's a pity a blind man features,
but no deaf ones! Perhaps the miracle of Cana.'

She laughed. 'Turning water into wine? He'd love that! Would
you mind if I slipped out for a few minutes?'

And it seemed Samuel did love the story. At least when
I added 'Amen' at the end, I felt what I was sure was some
pressure on my hand. I put my mouth to his ear. 'Samuel, my
dear friend, it is I, Matthew. You have been very ill. Can you
squeeze my hand if you can hear me?'

TWENTY

'It's a strange business, isn't it, Mrs Rowsley, Mr Pounceman and young Dick Thatcher both being attacked the same night?' Elias said, sipping his tea at the big table in the servants' hall. 'And then Mr Pounceman going to pray over Dick!'

'I beg your pardon?' Could I believe my ears?

'True as I'm sitting here. And no, before you ask, I didn't want to leave them on their own together. For a start, I don't want them to compare notes, not until I've spoken to Dick, and got his statement. But Mr Pounceman insisted he couldn't wait till I had. So now they're both on their honour to say nothing about it. And Nurse Pegg is on hand to stop it – I can't imagine arguing with her, can you? Don't get me wrong, voice apart, and those ugly great strangler's hands, she's a nice enough lady, seemingly, but I wouldn't want to cross her.'

'Do you want to see what's going on? Luke will show you up and Mr Pounceman down.' I rang. We waited longer than I approved of, but the reason was unsurprising: Mr Trescothick wanted his undivided attention. The two set off together, Luke dropping his imitation of Thatcher copying Samuel so they could talk about cricket.

The arrival of Mr Pounceman intrigued me, as did his sudden assumption of Christian charity, an aspect of faith that was too rarely seen in his actions. Perhaps I should by chance encounter him on his way out, which would certainly be via the grand entrance hall. Exchanging my workaday apron for what Matthew referred to as my state one, I drifted through the front corridor towards the main staircase. I listened for voices, but was not surprised to hear none: Luke would be practising self-effacement and Mr Pounceman the opposite. But then I caught the sound of footsteps, and moved forward, immaculately timing my arrival and my surprise.

My curtsy was perhaps deeper than his rank required, and his bow somewhat shallower than a fellow trustee might have expected. However, he paused long enough to ask how I did. Was I feeling more the thing?

'Thank you, I am. And I must apologize for the disruption when I was indisposed.' I curtsied again. 'Do you find Mr Trescothick well, sir?' I asked disingenuously. Did he find himself quite well? All those bandages!

'As it happens, I did not see him. I came to discuss quite another matter with your husband. And then, hearing that one of my flock had been injured, I went to pray for him.'

'That was very kind of you, sir.'

He bowed his acknowledgement, though I might perhaps have preferred him to demur that that was part of his job. Then he frowned. 'Tell me, Mrs Rowsley, is it necessary to have what I can only describe as a guard on the door to . . . you prefer to call it the Family wing, do you not?'

'There is one on the backstairs door too, sir. We are pretty well used to it: the men are former estate workers no longer capable of the physical work their jobs entailed.'

'So this is just charity to paupers.'

'On the contrary. It is responsible work given to people for whom we are ultimately responsible.' I tried hard not to sound tetchy. 'The fear is that should his lordship have an attack of his illness again, he could . . . Dr Page insists he must be confined, for his own sake as much as anyone else's. And it is essential that her ladyship is not disturbed. We used to have bells on both doors to summon attendants, but they caused her . . . anxiety. They seemed to remind her of something that had once distressed her, so now Dr Page insists on nothing more than a gentle knock.'

'I see. And does Mr Trescothick approve of the arrangements?'

'Like us, sir, Mr Trescothick could not override the trustees even if he expressed a wish to do so – which to the best of my knowledge he has not. I cannot imagine any of us wishing to dispute Dr Page's orders, can you?' I smiled, human being to human being. And in the process noticed how pale he had become. 'Sir – forgive me, but are you quite well?'

For the first time in our long acquaintance his smile seemed quite genuine. He sank on to one of the elegant but excruciating sofas that grace the hall. 'In fact, Mrs Rowsley, I do find myself

. . . I am quite dizzy. As you can see: your footman's assailant had another victim – myself. Your husband was kind enough to arrange an interview with Constable Pritchard, who I believe is speaking to the youth – Nick? – now.'

'Dick, sir. Might I show you to the saloon, sir, and offer you coffee? And then I can summon John Coachman to take you back to the rectory.' I even found myself offering my arm as he staggered slightly.

'You didn't! Tell me you're joking!' Bea stood arms akimbo as, in the servants' hall, I regaled her with the tale of my morning's doings. 'And he didn't go and suck up to Mr Trescothick? You amaze me. He'll have to have more bangs on the head if that's what one does to him. Do we know any more about who might have done it? Ah! Elias Pritchard! Come in and have a cup of coffee and tell us what's what, my lad.'

'I wish I could, ma'am. All I can say is that both Dick and the rector have some nasty injuries, presumably inflicted on them at roughly the same time. Mr Pounceman was out for an evening constitutional, it seems, and Luke went out – well, there might have been a young lady involved, though he won't tell me who.'

'So someone attacks our butler, someone attacks the acting butler – I might see a connection there. But where on earth would a clergyman fit in? Or have we got some maniac on the loose? I must warn the girls not to go out alone. I don't approve of them having followers, but if one does, then the young man must come here to meet her.'

'And be subject to your approval? Seriously, Bea, that's a good idea: it should apply to the House servants too – men and women, in fact. We can announce it at servants' dinner.'

Elias bowed. 'That does seem very sensible, ma'am, if I may say so. I don't know if it's a maniac, but it would be good to apprehend him before he does further harm. I understand Mr Rowsley was hoping to see his lordship this morning: how did he find him, ma'am?'

'You can ask him yourself, Elias. Here he is now.' I nodded over his shoulder.

The two men were always slightly awkward when they first

met, largely, I suspect, because Elias was more self-conscious about the social gap between them than Matthew was. Should he stand in a policeman-like way and salute his friend, using his title and surname, or simply address him as a friend whose bowling he'd been able to improve?

Matthew solved the problem by putting a hand on his shoulder. 'Well, my friend, that was an interesting morning.' He looked at Bea and me too. 'I did manage to see his lordship for a few minutes. He is much like his old self—'

'Whatever that means,' Bea put in.

'He can see the lake from his room, and is desperate to be able to take a boat out on it. I sympathize, as it happens. It must be a form of purgatory for him to be pent up indoors, however pleasant the accommodation – they have made the adjoining room a sitting room, and he plays at cards with Hargreaves and his other attendants. But he was always a doer, not a thinker. Hargreaves – the young man is a veritable saint! – sees that he is always smartly dressed, but he now has a full beard, so there is no risk with a razor. Hargreaves himself sports a beard too. I managed to take him to one side and suggest that he joins us for some meals down in the Room, but he declined: no one but he will serve his lordship. Poor lad, his eyes lit up at the thought of a party. I do hope that he and Nurse Pegg can contrive that he comes down even for a short time. But I have other news, news that must go no further, except to Dr Page and perhaps Sergeant Burrows. When I read to Samuel this morning, the miracle at Cana, as it happens, he added "Amen" after the reading, I am almost certain. Then I asked him to press my hand; he quite definitely did so. But he could not move anything else, not so much as an eyelid, even though I begged him to try. And he said nothing else.'

'What a miracle indeed!' I cried.

'It's a shame modern day ones take a bit longer,' Bea said grumpily, turning away – probably so that we could not see any tears. My own flowed freely. The men exchanged an emotional handshake.

At last Bea coughed. 'These here attacks, Elias. I've only got ten minutes before the servants' dinner and I want to know what's been going on? I'd love to hear they just ran into each other and both of them thought they were being attacked and hit back.'

'So would I, Mrs Arden. It's not going to be easy, finding their assailant, and neither of them needing more than a postage stamp to be able to describe him. Or them. Both heard something behind them, then got socked. The rector says he went down like a sack of potatoes—'

'I bet it was something posher than that!'

'And Dick says he fought back, which I can believe, given his injuries. But any attacker'd have to be tough to get the better of a strong young man like Dick. Two men, quite different, just minding their own business – no, it doesn't make sense and if you don't know why someone does something you're less likely to find out who does it, that's what Sergeant Burrows always says. Now, if either gentleman says any more, I'd be glad to hear it. Good day to you all. Oh, thank you, Mrs Arden,' he added, as she pressed a bag of her biscuits into his hand.

Arnold prepared to serve Mr Trescothick luncheon in the solitary splendour of the dining room; a kitchen maid gave a last-minute tweak to the cutlery. It was time for servants' dinner.

'The menservants seem to change by the day,' Mr Trescothick said, later that afternoon, almost before I had entered the library. Somewhat to my dismay, he seemed to have adopted this treasure trove as his sitting room. The most important books might be firmly under lock and key, but his lordship – his late lordship – had prided himself on many volumes in his collection, many of which he had allowed scholars to study. Naturally his son had discontinued the practise, regarding books, as he once said, as things with which to prop doors open. In my leisure hours under the previous regime I had almost had the run of the room, my idea of an earthly heaven. I thought with a pang of the library in our home: Matthew and I had begun to build the collection with such joy, and we had not spent a moment in it for many days.

'Perhaps you have not heard, sir, that our deputy butler was attacked and injured last night. His collarbone was broken, so even when he returns to work he will be on light duties. Currently Arnold and Luke will be taking his place as far as is possible – that is what I came to tell you.'

'Hmph. Surely that husband of yours would do a better job.'

I believe my jaw literally dropped. I breathed deeply – but not I hope too noticeably. 'Mr Trescothick, my husband is running estates upon the health of which depend probably hundreds of lives. Even if he had time, I assure you he would be far from adept in the duties of a butler.' I looked around me. 'There are many tomes on these shelves about estate management, sir, but if I wanted to prepare myself for an inheritance like this I would attach myself to Matthew like a shadow. Forgive me if I speak out of turn, but I would give the same advice if you had already taken your seat in the House of Lords.'

'How do you know so much about the books?'

The question surprised me: it was not the reaction I expected. I tried the sort of smile I had given Mr Pounceman. 'I have dusted them often enough, sir. His late lordship was a bibliophile – he was afraid a clumsy housemaid might damage them.'

'So you have a key to the locked cabinets.'

Had he punched me in the stomach? I felt as sick as if he had. I had set a trap for myself, opened it, and jumped straight into it.

'They may only be opened with his lordship's permission,' I said calmly. 'Will that be all, sir? Thank you.' I curtsied and backed towards the door.

'Give me the keys.'

'I do not disobey orders, sir.' He was not likely to recognize the softer term, breaking a promise. My hand was turning the doorknob.

'This is an order.' He came towards me, hand outstretched. 'The keys. Now.'

The slightest of taps. The door opened inwards. For a moment, I was ready to panic. Then Luke appeared.

'Beg pardon, sir, but Mrs Rowsley is needed urgently in the Family wing. Thank you, sir.'

I managed to turn and curtsy before escaping into the corridor.

As one, Luke and I turned towards the great entrance hall, as if towards the stairs leading to the Family wing. But when I tried to thank him, Luke shook his head. 'You always said we must always look out for each other, didn't you, ma'am? And told us footmen to be on the alert when a maid was alone in a room with a man. And I know you're not just a maid, ma'am, but even so . . .'

'You did well. Very well. Thank you, Luke. Do you think the maids should clean there in pairs?' It was a question I would have put to Samuel, and possibly to Dick.

Luke took it as the compliment it was meant to be. 'I've not heard any murmurs, ma'am, have you? But I'll make sure there's always one of us there hovering, as it were. The trouble is, he doesn't seem to know how to speak to any of us, how to treat us. Not at all. Sometimes he's too friendly with us, sometimes downright rude. You'd think there was someone to teach him how to be a lord, wouldn't you?' He stroked his chin. 'Maybe that's why they go to schools for gentlemen's sons.' He pondered. 'Do they have schools for becoming a lady? That must be just as hard, if you want to do it well. They say that when her ladyship was younger, she was nearly as good about the village as you are. Then . . . poor lady,' he concluded, generously not mentioning the dreadful temper and violent outbursts of her later years.

'Poor lady indeed,' I agreed. 'Now, Luke, am I indeed required in the Family wing, or was that just a very clever ruse?'

'I believe afternoon tea is about to be served, ma'am. So perhaps I may escort you to the servants' hall?'

'You may. Provided you promise to gossip with me very quietly about how Davies is getting on.'

'Surprisingly well, I think. He says he's got hardly anything to do. Mr Trescothick hates disorder, Davies says, and won't wait to have him tidy up. He likes to do it himself. Mostly he's dead quiet, but sometimes he swings round like a weathervane, and suddenly he's very haughty, ma'am, far more than any of the Family ever were. Like he was with you a minute ago. Davies can't make it out. But he says maybe it's because he's so new to the job of being a valet and he irritates him – Mr

Trescothick, that is, ma'am. Or maybe,' he continued slowly, 'it's because Mr Trescothick is new to being a lord.'

'You may well be right. Thank you for the information. I appreciate it. But not as much as I appreciate your kindness and alertness a moment ago. Thank you, Luke.'

TWENTY-ONE

'He threatened you?' My hands bunched into fists.

'It was not a threat. It was just a very forceful demand. In any case, sweetheart, do you not imagine that all female servants learn ways of dealing with assailants? I was taught them too late. Not till after . . . after the . . . assault, and I take care to instruct each new maid. But I was glad that Luke saved me from having to use my skills, and with such aplomb, too.' She bit her lip. 'What worries me is that Mr Trescothick is not the only guest who wishes to inspect the contents of the locked shelves. Sir Francis was quite . . . resentful when we did not immediately hand over the keys, was he not?'

Why had she used our friend's title?

'Here, let me help with those studs. If you fidget, it's very hard to fix them.'

I fancied she took longer than strictly necessary to deal with them.

'Now, would you oblige me by fastening my necklace? I find the clasp very unreliable, you know: perhaps next time we go into Shrewsbury we should take it to a jewellers for repair.' She turned round and bent her neck. The clasp fastened, I touched the little tendrils of hair escaping from her chignon, and wished I could set it all free, burying my face in it. But that would make us very late for supper.

I spun her very gently round to face me, gripping her shoulders lightly. 'I know when you are trying to evade an issue, Mrs Rowsley. And I love you for it. But such behaviour is not acceptable.'

'If you acceded to his wishes and became his butler,' she said limpidly, 'you would be at hand to protect me.'

Despite myself, I tightened my grip, only releasing it as she tried to suppress a wince. 'Became. His. Butler. Did I hear that aright?'

'Don't worry – I told him you were too clumsy. Are you sure that clasp is secure?' She looked at me from under those wonderful eyelashes. And then she could no longer contain her emotion. 'Oh, Matthew, I wish we could just leave him to it and go home!' It came out as almost a sob.

I held her tightly. 'Why don't we?'

'Because of Bea; my promise to his late lordship; our shared sense of duty. Oh, and the trustees' meeting on Friday.'

I nodded as soberly as she could have wished. 'Of course. All of those things.' As I slipped my smoking jacket on, I added, 'And something else is troubling me too: young Freddie is palpably unhappy. He is pale. He is wonderfully suited to his work, which he does amazingly well. I was wrong, I think, to ask him to do it: he has no companions, no one even his own age to talk to. But if I ask him to leave, if I even tried to find him another post of equal status, he would be so humiliated. His parents need his wages. What can I do, Harriet?'

She was all instant concern, touching my cheek in sympathy. 'Have you spoken to him?'

'I've not questioned him directly. I've tried to give him less time in the House – I've sent him on errands, and so forth. But he remains pale and withdrawn.'

'I know what you are hoping I will say – that I will talk to him. But I wonder if I am the right person. We have two very good young men in the House who may have had the same feelings when they were young – Dick and Luke. Despite all those lovely books – I know you did your best! – Dick must be bored already. Why not send Freddie up to him with a message? Any message. Another book. Who knows?'

'You may be right. You usually are right. Very well, I'll try it. And yes, Harriet, I long for a few evenings on our own. In our own home. I could play the piano – teach you to play! Or we could simply sit quietly in the library – talk if we want, not because we have to.' Our embrace was close and long. The dinner gong rang out. When had that last happened when we were not already in situ in the Room? Like children we held hands and scampered. But we were our proper dignified selves by the time we arrived in the servants' hall.

TWENTY-TWO

Most of the rest of the week was given over to the daily mundanities that made up our lives. On Thursday Matthew had to go to Lichfield, to inspect a farm that was up for sale. It ran alongside one of his lordship's farms, and it might make commercial sense for the two to be made one. The weather was fine enough for me to shoo all the staff out for exercise – 'Nothing like fresh air to prevent measles,' Bea declared archly – and for me, ignoring my own advice about walking with friends, to stroll on my own as far as the Roman remains. However, while I did not carry a stick, I carried a trusty umbrella.

The site was still guarded, but Sergeant Burrows had removed the skeleton, which Francis was absolutely sure was Roman. Burrows was supposed to be notifying the coroner, but frustratingly we had heard nothing, not even when the inquest would take place. Whatever the result, the bones could hardly cause more chaos than they already had. The recent rain had uncovered no more similar ones, Roman or otherwise, as far as I could see: But now another arm, strong and muscular, was emerging from the mud, as if an injured soldier was asking for help that would come two thousand years too late. There were pillars. Large and small, they lay at crazy angles. I would be relieved when Francis and his team could excavate and make sense of everything, even though having a fully-fledged Roman fort or villa on the estate would almost certainly bring more problems.

I would be even more relieved when the trustees approved Matthew's revised plans and gave permission for the new building work to begin: the villagers needed – deserved – proper accommodation and a chance to grow food. Since the meeting in Marty's public house there had been a steady trickle of Stammerton villagers asking for supplies. The families in greatest need were those of the men left unemployed when work on the remains had to stop. Matthew announced that they would be paid to cover all the vulnerable cottages with tarpaulins. Then they could chop wood for all the villagers. But none of us wanted such measures to be anything other than temporary.

A twig cracked behind me.

And another.

I was not alone.

I turned slowly, not wishing to show any alarm. More importantly, not wanting to feel any.

Silence. But I was not reassured.

Grasping my umbrella more tightly, I strolled away from the trenches: I had no desire to suffer Samuel's fate. To get back to the House, I would have to pass the woods. Then common sense returned. No one would assault me in full view of the guard. So I made my way to – was it Simon? We could have a short conversation about his new baby.

'A son, I hear?'

'Yes, ma'am. A fine healthy boy.' But his face was troubled. How long could any child stay well in an earth-floored hovel?

'And how is Beth?'

'Tired, missus. More tired than I like to see.'

I would ask Dr Page to call on her as well as Meg. 'I will send down some beef tea. And if I add port wine, you know it is for her, of course.'

'Missus, I only ever touch a glass of mild in the Royal Oak. Only one glass. And I'd walk on hot coals to see her well again.' Tears filled his eyes.

I nodded. 'Of course you would. Now, when do you finish your stint here?'

'As soon as Ben arrives. Could be him there now.' He waved at a distant figure trudging against a growing wind.

'If you care to walk back to the House with me I will put together a basket of things Beth might need. And I will give you a note to take to Dr Page: the Family will pay for any medicines he prescribes.' Another twig snapped. 'Do we have company, Simon?' I nodded in the direction of the sound.

He grasped his cudgel. 'Likely so. Shall I go after him, missus?'

'We don't know who it is yet. It could be someone perfectly harmless.'

'What I hear, someone's been hurting enough decent folk without any more being beat up.' He gestured vigorously: Ben picked up grudging speed.

Suddenly I wondered if we were being ridiculous. It might be an animal moving round – more audibly, now. The men looked to me for instructions. I weighed the odds: one woman in too many yards of fabric; two men, neither well-fed enough to be truly robust. Versus? Who knew?

'I will bid you goodbye and walk along the road – alone, Simon, though I haven't forgotten what I said a moment ago. I will pretend I have a problem with my boot. If anyone comes out and attacks me, then you must rush up and catch him. Is that clear? Pretend to be deep in conversation, but be watchful.'

Ben nodded vigorously, Simon as if I was posing a conundrum. I set out, my hand tight on the umbrella, although I swung my arm as if I had not a care in the world. Before I could perform the boot charade a figure appeared.

'Sir Francis, what on earth are you doing?' Perhaps in my surprise I sounded accusing.

'I thought I'd come and find you, of course,' he said, with his usual charming smile. 'I left my baggage – there's quite a lot, by the way – and my man back at the House. Beatrice seemed to think you weren't expecting me till tomorrow, but turned not a hair. She found a room for Johnson, next to – is it Luke? And Luke showed me to the room you had had made ready for me, complete with study. Wonderful, my dear – wonderful. Now, what are those rustics staring at?'

'You, probably. They took you for a footpad and sent me on as bait. Simon!' I called. 'Don't forget what I told you about the jelly and wine for Beth: I will see to it the moment I get home.'

He and Ben tugged their forelocks: I sensed that Ben would remind Simon if he forgot.

'Tell me, though, why you were scrabbling round in the woods like a squirrel after nuts,' I said. 'I heard you well before you called out to me.'

'That would have been difficult,' he said. I fancied that his voice was harder than usual. 'Because I only arrived a moment ago. It must have been another . . . squirrel.'

'I hope it was only hunting for the nuts it stored, not stray artefacts from your excavations,' I responded as lightly as possible. Francis might be a friend, but he was an aristocrat first and foremost and never had liked to be questioned. I gripped his forearm, pointing. 'Look! A big squirrel with no tail! After him, lads!' I yelled.

Ben grasped the urgency at once, and hurtled into the woods, crashing along and calling out. I was ready to shout at Simon, but to my surprise and pleasure he took a different route, apparently trying to cut off his colleague's prey.

There was a great deal of noise and general confusion. I released Francis's arm in some embarrassment; at least he wasn't such a dandy as to smooth the fabric of his sleeve, but I fancied I had gone several steps too far today. However, we maintained a steady flow of social conversation while the men thrashed around, emerging at last before us, dishevelled but with at least one spoil of war – a battered hat. Soaking wet, it was shapeless and had nothing as sophisticated as the maker's name for which Francis immediately searched. Indeed, it was hard to imagine the identity of its owner – man or gentleman? I had known peers of the realm wear disreputable headgear that a respectable working man might scorn.

At least Francis remembered that noblesse ought to oblige, and pressed what were probably generous coins into the men's hands. He seemed about to discard the hat, but I shook my head, taking it from him. But I found I did not want to carry it. 'I believe the village constable would be pleased to see this. Simon, will you bring it to the House when you come, please? Remember what I promised you for Beth. I expect to see you within the half hour.'

He tipped his own hat, not, in fact, much newer than the one he now held; Ben tugged his forelock.

'Within the half hour, mind!' And Francis and I went on our way.

'How very tactful of you, my dear. I suspect that had he accompanied us we might have had to walk to windward of him.'

'Once a week a tin bath in front of the fire, but only if you have enough money for fuel to heat the water,' I said, my voice rather more dour than he was used to hearing. The rest I did not say aloud: of course the men and women stank. Of course lice and nits and fleas had plenty of hosts. What did he expect? That a worker like that had a man called Johnson to attend to his every need? But he spoke from ignorance, not malice, I hoped, so I embarked on the opening comments of another inconsequential gossip that kept us going as far as the House.

Hardly had Francis been shown to his room than Simon presented himself at the back door, the hat in his hand. It took a few moments to locate the port I had promised, and he had to be content with chicken broth until the morrow, but he went away with a fresh loaf, cheese, eggs and soap in one basket, covered by a serviceable towel, and a quantity of baby linen in another; one of her ladyship's more selfless activities had been the maintenance of a baby-basket, which she used to deliver herself.

I stared at the hat, now lying on the back step. Had I seen it before? I couldn't recall it. So I stowed it in another basket. Who should take it down to Elias? As I wrote an accompanying note I thought of Freddie, in need, Matthew had thought, of fresh air at the very least. Summoning Luke who must tell Mr Trescothick of Francis' arrival, I asked quietly, 'Do you have anything to tell me about young Freddie?'

'Not yet, ma'am. He muttered something about not getting into trouble, that's all. Should I try again?'

I nodded slowly. 'What do you suspect?'

'I don't like to say yet, ma'am. I can't believe he's stolen anything, can you? But why else should he be afraid?' A frown appeared. Briefly he met my eyes. Then he looked away.

'Did anything . . . unpleasant . . . ever happen to you when you were young, Luke?'

'Can you imagine Mr Bowman letting anyone bully anyone, ma'am?'

That wasn't quite an answer, was it?

'Of course not. Thank you, Luke. And now you have some news to break to Mr Trescothick: he needs to know that Sir Francis has returned.'

'I'll go to the library now, ma'am.' His smile was decidedly complicitous.

'Has my husband returned yet? No? In that case, on your way to the library could you ask Freddie to run an errand to the village for me? I'll be in the Room, writing a note.'

Freddie arrived as if he had wings on his heels, but was as pale and anxious as Matthew had said. He gnawed his lip while I explained that all I wanted to do was deliver the hat and a covering letter to Constable Pritchard. 'There's no need for you to hurry. There's plenty of time for you to go and see Marty, but I'd rather you were back before it gets dark,' I added. There was no hiding the fact that his face lit up at the thought of seeing his old employer.

'Yes, ma'am, thank you, ma'am.'

'And why don't you munch this apple as you go? I know there'll be cake when you return.'

'Yes, ma'am, thank you, ma'am.'

The next visitor to the Room was Francis, who sat down uninvited at the table and, chin in hands, asked, 'Do we have a plan of campaign for this evening?'

I picked up his tone. 'If I sent for another cup, we could discuss it over tea.'

'Does tea involve Bea's cake? Wonderful.' He was a different person from the nobleman who had been so curt earlier. My friend once more. 'Now, about this evening. Please do not tell me I must dine a deux with Trescothick, because I tell you plainly I would rather have bread and water in my study. I know I must beard Trescothick in his den sooner or later, but I would like to hear your suggestions about my tactics before I do so. Yours and Matthew's, of course.'

I looked at the clock. 'He ought to be back from Lichfield any time now.' I felt the sick mindless panic that only love can bring. Perhaps he had gone home to change. Perhaps he had missed the train. Perhaps he had been set upon by the person lurking in the woods – no, his route was miles from there. All my fears were groundless. The trap was waiting for him at the station. He must be safe. Must be.

TWENTY-THREE

t gave me no pleasure at all to realize that the sheep surrounding the beleaguered train were not ours but our neighbour's, whose fence was clearly down. The guard and engine crew had tried all sensible methods to remove them, from simple shooing to toots on the whistle. The sheep would scatter, but then regroup. A couple of sheep dogs might have cleared them in an instant, but naturally none were aboard and none visible.

Sending a willing labourer to find one would have worked, but there were no labourers either. My fellow passengers were elderly women or young girls. For all Harriet would tell me that there were few things of which women were not incapable, I think even she would have baulked at the idea of despatching any of them to seek help in the fast-falling darkness. The railway men claimed they would not know their way to the farmhouse, a protestation I had to accept. So in my town suit I forced my way through brambles and other apparently prehensile undergrowth and on to a lane I thought might lead to my target. Fortunately I soon stumbled past a cottage, as dilapidated as those in Stammerton. Within moments I had roused a terrified and half-starved woman, sheltering a huddle of children behind her. Her feeble rush-light revealed a thin cotton skirt that other women would have disdained as a petticoat. Assisted by a coin, she despatched the oldest child to fetch the shepherd. It was hard to tell if it was a boy or a girl. The legs were painfully thin in the boots into which they were thrust, but they ran with satisfactory haste. As I headed back to the track, two other children emerged, calling after me.

'Gaffer! Stop, gaffer! Stop!'

They sounded desperate, so I turned. Was someone ill? I bent to hear what they were saying, their accents so thick they might have been speaking in a foreign tongue.

'Not this way?' I repeated slowly. 'But I came this way.'

'Gaffer – the mantraps! Gorra goo this road.'

Sick to the stomach – how close had I come to a horrible end? – I let them lead me.

'Poaching, see. Farmer Goodman, he don't want no one in his pheasants. Down here, gaffer.'

Road there was none, just a barely visible sheep track.

Slowly and carefully we picked our way down towards the broken fencing. The train had apparently not moved a yard, the perverse creatures milling round as if sent on purpose to disrupt our journey. But when the children called, it was as if the sheep recognized them; they looked alert, and allowed them to usher them back whence they had come. They were inclined to be skittish when I ran after the children, pressing money into their hands.

Mantraps. I must visit Farmer Goodman.

The porter did not need to summon Dan, who materialized out of the gloom like a benevolent ghost. 'Heavens, Mr Rowsley, you look as if you've been fighting a bear! Don't want to let the missus see you like that or she'll faint away all over again.' He turned the trap for home.

But I was late already, very late, and I knew she would be as anxious as I would be if the situation was reversed. Anxious? Frantic! 'I have clothes at the House, so we'll go straight there. For heaven's sake, won't this damned animal go any faster?'

I ran through the servants' door, calling as I went and nearly barging over a kitchen maid who dropped a handful of cutlery. Her scream was even louder than the clatter. Letting her get on with it I hurtled into the Room, where Harriet was on her feet, her face washed with what a poet might call a ghastly pallor. But she did not faint. She did not even scream. She merely gripped my hands and looked me up and down. Fear and laughter battled it out in her face.

'An encounter with a vicious hawthorn hedge,' I said flatly. 'I will explain later. But first I must change: might you help me with my studs?'

'If Francis will excuse me?' She glanced over her shoulder. I had not even registered his presence.

He bowed. 'I might adjourn to my study for a few minutes

if you will excuse me. May we resume our council of war in perhaps ten minutes?'

Harriet, now less pale and ready to be genuinely amused, laughed. 'The state he's in it might be nearer twenty. Matthew, the smell!'

Until I stood in front of our dressing room mirror, I had not realized what a sight I was, my cloak muddied and my suit in shreds. I was splattered with an unlovely mix of mud, blood and sheep droppings. A maid brought hot water; Harriet demanded at least two more ewers, giving her the poor suit to dispose of. 'No! The waistcoat, even the jacket, might clean up enough to go in the clothing box. But the trousers must and shall end their life heating the wash-house boiler.' The noisome garments disappeared, and I was able to wash, spluttering the explanation Harriet desired as I scrubbed and dabbed. I did not argue when she produced salve and anointed the tears and scuffs on my legs. It was only when I could prove that they were in one piece that I told her about the children and the mantraps.

'But they have been illegal for years!' She was white again as she understood the implications.

'As I will tell Farmer Goodman. Thank God the children knew about them. Imagine . . . Now, my studs?' I looked around helplessly. 'What a gem you are, my love.' How damnable it was to be constrained at all hours and not able to show her how much I loved her!

It was the knowledge that she felt the same frustration that sustained me through what Francis called his council of war. All it boiled down to was in fact where he should dine: with us, which might prove awkward for Luke, who as deputy deputy butler might have been expecting to dine in the Room; or with Mr Trescothick, which was socially logical but against Francis' own wishes; or if he should carry out his threat and dine solo in his room, which would totally disrupt the servants' routine.

'There is another option,' Harriet said. 'That we put it to Mr Trescothick that the four of us should dine together. After all, we shall all be together after the trustees' meeting tomorrow. Or perhaps the suggestion might come better from you, Francis: we know he respects your rank.'

'You mean he's a toady. Very well, I will try. How long do I have?'

She checked her watch. 'Luke and his colleagues will need to set the dining table within fifteen minutes. I cannot hold up the servants' supper longer than that.'

Francis was back within moments. 'He is not in the library, and one of the footmen tells me that he is sure he is no longer in the building. He made him summon John Coachman, apparently.'

I gave an exaggerated sigh. 'So we don't have to worry after all.'

'On the contrary, I'd worry even more: where can the pesky man have gone?'

Harriet was already ringing the bell; Luke appeared as if he'd been waiting just outside.

Can a bow be conspiratorial? If so, Luke's to Harriet was. 'I understand that Mr Trescothick is dining at the Rectory, ma'am. Though what he is doing about evening wear I know not: to the best of my knowledge he is not equipped himself. Incidentally, he talks of taking the coach into Lichfield tomorrow to acquire more clothes.' His voice could not have been more casual or more laden with significance.

'Thank you, Luke. Now, do you care to dine with us here in the Room?'

'Ma'am, if it's all the same to you I'll eat with Dick. He needs a hand – sorry! And he's losing his mind with boredom. He says he hopes to come down and start work again tomorrow.'

'Tell him he may, if Nurse Pegg agrees. But I would like you to work alongside him, so that he makes no attempt to use that arm. And he is to work for no more than three hours: he must rest after that. Tell him not to argue – he may save his breath to cool his porridge!' How did she manage to sound both sternly authoritative and supremely kind? My heart turned over with pride.

More alarmed than amused by Francis' story of the giant tail-less squirrel, the next morning I told Twiss, the home-farm manager, to gather some men not otherwise employed and institute a search of the area. I warned a rider about the mantraps on the farm the other side of the railway: there was to be nothing like that anywhere on his lordship's land. Anywhere.

'Saw a man die in one of them once,' he said. 'I was scarce more than a babe in arms, but the memory's stayed with me. And I'll tell the men to be extra careful, sir – just in case.'

'That's the best philosophy,' I agreed. It was a favourite of Harriet's; perhaps he was quoting it back to me with that in mind. 'Oh, and if they find any of those Roman bits and pieces, tell them to put a white post beside them so Sir Francis and his friends can deal with them.'

A ride to the village on my old friend Esau was next. I left a message for Elias about the mantraps. Anything he said would carry the weight of the law, whereas mine would only be a neighbour's complaint – and it meant I was spared a potentially unpleasant task. The railway company could deal with the broken fencing. I had a moment to speak to Marty, accepting half a pint of his finest, about the trustees' meeting. 'All the trustees are invited to dine afterwards. I know you are at your busiest on a Friday night, but I really would welcome your company.'

'T'village publican amongst all t'toffs!' He exaggerated his Manchester accent.

'An honoured trustee, Marty! There is talk of Mr Trescothick being there,' I added, 'and I know no shrewder judge of character than you, my friend.'

He looked at me through narrowed eyes, and nodded slowly.

'Meanwhile, I need your help – it's Freddie. He's turned pale and is clearly miserable. I know he's been working hard – we all have – on the documents for tonight's meeting, and I believe that he ought to be at school with children his own age and running round and getting fresh air. Harriet says she sent him down here for a chat yesterday, and he came back looking perkier. But he's unhappy again this morning. If I talk to him he may think I'm criticising him . . .'

'There's something going on, that's for sure. If you can find another excuse to get him down here, I'll see what I can find out. By the way, I had a bit of news the other day.

That babe of Maggie's – his lordship's by-blow. She's thriving, apparently.'

'With an adoptive mother as determined as that I don't think she'd dare do anything else. I'd love to see her again. I can't think that a life on a narrow boat is ideal. I know Harriet and I have both had sleepless nights wondering if we did the right thing.'

'And who'd have looked after her if you'd brought her back here? His lordship? Aye, it's a sad business all round, but you did the best you could at the time. And no one can say fairer than that. Tell you what, if I hear their travels are bringing them up the Shropshire Union I'll let you know.'

I shook his hand heartily and bade him farewell. It was a pity there weren't more Martys in the world.

Knowing that Harriet and Bea would have made all the necessary preparations for the trustees' comfort – including accommodating Mr Wilson in the Blue Room, of course – I was checking and double checking all the paperwork for the meeting when there was a knock on my office door. Twiss – with a quizzical expression on his face.

'No mantraps, gaffer, you'll be glad to know,' he said, declining to sit, but casually leaning up against the door jamb. 'However, we have found one or two other interesting things. And I'll be glad if you come down there with me tomorrow, soon as it's convenient. Nine-ish? No: I won't tell you now – I hear you've got company due. And it's best if you see for yourself.'

TWENTY-FOUR

Bea and I walked together to the red dining room, knowing that our staff were as prepared as humanly possible. They might have been expecting royalty, with their crisply starched pinnies and shining shoes. The furniture and silver gleamed likewise. The irony did not escape me that there were no aristocrats there to see it all: obviously his lordship and her ladyship would not be coming down. Mr Wilson had decreed that while he was invited to join us for dinner afterwards, the trustees must meet without the benefit of the putative lord's company. Every time he used the adjective he smiled at me, yet I was convinced that it was Bea who drew his admiration; his precise, well-schooled features always softened when he was in her company.

I would have loved to see Mr Trescothick's face – more, to hear his words – when his fate was announced. However, I had to leave Luke to be my eyes and ears. He absolutely did not wink as he pulled out the chairs of each of us in turn after Mr Pounceman's prayer for guidance. Tonight the rector seemed curiously muted.

'I take it there is only one apology for absence – Mr Bowman's? Excellent.' Mr Wilson nodded. 'So let us turn immediately to any matters arising from the last meeting. The chief one is naturally the problem of the new model village and its inconvenient foundations. Now, should the site be moved?'

There was unanimous agreement that it should.

Then Matthew reported on our discussions with the village representatives, and the disappointment he and Mr Pounceman shared that they did not consider a new church as important as other more basic amenities. 'The wish,' he continued, 'was for a variety of housing. This has both advantages and disadvantages, of course . . .'

It did not take long for the proposal to be nodded through.

The next item was the arrangements, if any, for the excavation of the remains.

I had known Francis to be supercilious and dismissive when dealing with his social inferiors, and prayed he would not succumb to the temptation this time. He did not. He had brought a summary of costs of everything from the workers he needed to employ to their accommodation and subsistence. After this dry analysis he showed sketches of items he had found on previous investigations. I had no idea that he was such a talented draughtsman. He even passed around small artefacts, some of which quite charmed us in their delicacy. Even Mr Pounceman was entranced by a stone bearing what Francis called a chi-rho, a Christian symbol used by Romans: it looked like an X crossed by a P.

'What I cannot say,' Francis continued apologetically, 'is if I will find such a symbol here. Scholars believe it was used quite late in the Roman Empire as Christianity became more wide-spread, and as yet I've no idea when these buildings, whatever they are, were built and used.'

'When would you want to start work, Sir Francis?' Mr Wilson asked. 'You understand that the model village will cost more than we anticipated originally, and it may be that the past must make a minor sacrifice to the present.'

'That is why I propose to wait till the summer, when I can bring along some volunteers, history and indeed theology students,' he added with a smile at Mr Pounceman, 'who may well sleep under canvas. Furthermore, I cannot see why they can't take a break from their excavations to help with the harvest, can you?'

'None at all. So are we all happy for the excavations to continue? Mr Pounceman, I believe you had reservations?'

The rector gave an ambiguous smile. 'Sir Francis has surely clarified everything.'

Mr Wilson bowed. 'And now to the most difficult item – the putative heir. Yes, Sir Francis?'

'Mr Chairman, I am only here to discuss one item: I think it would be more appropriate for me to withdraw unless I can be of any marked assistance from now on.'

'I understand from Mr Rowsley that you have probably spent

more time with him than most of us, so if you might bear with us for just a few moments? Thank you, Sir Francis. Now, I have one or two points worth mentioning, but first I would like to hear from those of you who have had the privilege of having met him or indeed, like Sir Francis, have been in regular contact with him. Mrs Rowsley?'

'Mr Chairman, might we keep our comments brief? The gentleman in question knows we are all gathered here in judgement on him. It must be extraordinarily unpleasant for him to have to sit and wait for our verdict, especially as he's taken the trouble to go into Shrewsbury and buy new clothes especially for the meeting.'

'A very good point. Dr Page?'

'I have had but the briefest acquaintance with him. It might be said that it is not right to judge him on the basis of an hour or two. But he certainly does not strike me as a man who is happy staying here, possibly because it is so different from the situation he was expecting. Or possibly because it is so different from anything he has experienced before,' he added meaningfully.

'In other words, you are not convinced that he is our heir?'

Dr Page inclined his head.

'Mr Pounceman? I understand you have broken bread together.'

He looked profoundly uncomfortable. 'He talks like a sensible man. He is undoubtedly feeling isolated. He is more than aware that none of the neighbouring gentry have left cards – unless the butler has failed to deliver them, which in the present somewhat chaotic situation below stairs here would not be impossible?'

'Mr Chairman, may I?' Matthew interrupted, more politely than Bea or I would have managed. Surely if anyone could have helped him meet at least the county set, it was Pounceman himself. 'None of us can do anything about injuries to our staff, or about the depletion in their numbers that some trustees recommended, but I can assure you that my colleagues have worked with amazing dedication to overcome any shortcomings. We are also in the middle of a police enquiry, let us not forget. But I have spoken to Mr Trescothick about his awkward situation. I have apologized for the staff's inability to help him improve; we are simply not members of the social milieu he was part of when he was a visitor here as a boy. I am actually very sorry for him, but he has rebuffed all of our attempts to engage with him on a purely human level. It seems that class is of overriding importance.'

'He certainly fawns over me, or at least my title,' Francis muttered.

'Mr Newcombe?'

'Perhaps I should have tried . . . But it is surely for the lady of the house to make social contact, not us men.' His expression suddenly changed. 'Matthew, did you say he'd been here before? Sorry, Mr Chairman.'

Matthew said, 'He says he was once a regular visitor here and didn't need a conducted tour of the House. He asked about hunting – I assumed he used to ride to hounds here.'

Mr Newcombe was frowning. 'I used to hunt then, and shoot round the estate, and play cricket and fish – my father and his late lordship were friends despite the difference in rank. And I must say that on the couple of occasions we have encountered each other, he has shown no sign of recognising me.' He scratched his head. 'Nor I him.'

Matthew looked very serious. 'Might I ask that none of us mentions this to anyone?'

'Why not indeed?' Mr Pounceman did not trouble the chairman.

'Because, Mr Chairman, I am acutely aware of what happened to another person who might have recognized him. Mr Bowman.'

There was absolute silence.

The chairman broke it. 'Mr Baines?'

'Never having met him, I can't comment. But it seems to me to be queer, dead queer, that he turns up the very day poor Mr Bowman is attacked.'

'Mrs Arden?'

'I don't think he's forgiven any of us for deceiving him that first night, to be entirely frank. He's been rude to all and sundry, pulling rank, you might say. And yet he makes odd mistakes of etiquette.'

'Mrs Rowsley?'

'It is true that he is inclined to see everything as a personal slight – and resents the apparent lack of attention to his needs. He actually suggested that in addition to his other duties my husband should act as butler.' I had to wait while the laughter died down. 'What truly worries me is the fact that he has taken over the library as his personal study. There are enormously precious books in there, not all locked away.' I turned to Francis, who nodded. 'Some are, however, so important that no one may even touch them without supervision. I know that this is irksome but applies to everyone: to me, to my husband, to my distinguished friend Sir Francis.'

'It does indeed, Mr Chairman. And I must say I was inclined to resent it. But now I understand the reason. As a guest at this meeting, might I submit a suggestion that an expert is brought in to examine and catalogue every volume as soon as it is feasible? Would the trustees agree to that? Meanwhile I understand that Mr Trescothick is not prepared to accept this and has been trying to persuade the House staff to produce the keys for him.'

'Thank you, Sir Francis. I think we should nod through that suggestion and act on it as soon as practicable. Have you anything else to add, Sir Francis?'

'First of all I must stress how entirely professional and loyal to the Family Mrs Rowsley has been. It must have been terribly hard to withstand pressure from me and Mr Trescothick to break her promise to his lordship. As for my fellow guest, he has shown great interest in the House contents – but I desperately fear that his interest is more financial than aesthetic.'

'Mrs Rowsley, that last comment has made you look troubled?'

'An attempt may have been made to steal a portrait of Queen Elizabeth from one of the attics used as a storeroom. In another room, the window frame is damaged. There is no sign of the picture. We have informed the police.'

'And you believe Mr Trescothick might have removed it?'

'I believe nothing: I am just stating facts. I gather, sir, that you yourself have facts to impart?'

'You make us sound like disciples of Mr Gradgrind! Yes, I have – like you, my dear Mrs Rowsley – facts. But whether any inference can be drawn I know not. My enquiries have merely confirmed what I knew when I invited the man I believe to be the heir to return from the Antipodes and present himself here. That Mr Trescothick might well be the heir. But − like you − I am not convinced. And it seems to me entirely undesirable that he stays here on his own and − may I use the word − unsupervised. For his own sake he needs company; for ours, he needs to be observed. But by whom: that is the question. I do not know of any of the Family's relatives who might care to offer him an invitation, and why he might wish to accept it: if he is practising a deceit, then being in close proximity to those who might catch him in a lie is hardly an attractive prospect for him. We cannot expect another epidemic illness to rage through the House and thus make a tactical withdrawal advisable. All of you good people have busy lives of your own, as have I. What do we do?'

A long silence ensued. At last Marty Baines raised a hand. 'Mr Chairman, might I ask how many people boarded the ship bringing this man home, and how many left it when it docked?'

'Mr Baines, that is something I will indeed find out.' His eyes were very bright. 'But until I do I can only suggest that the status quo is maintained − possibly with the addition of a few more sharp-witted servants, one or two of whom I might be able to provide. I will discuss this with Mrs Rowsley later.'

At last it was Any Other Business and an extraordinary question from Marty. 'Mr Chairman, would Dr Page tell us how Nurse Pegg was selected for the role she now has?'

'Might I ask why?' Mr Wilson asked.

'A question I might echo!' Dr Page was clearly indignant.

'In the Royal Oak I hear many rumours, Mr Chairman. One more persistent than most is that Nurse Pegg has been turning away out of hand the retired estate workers who were appointed as the guards on the Family wing: men who have served his lordship for long years, men who had had to give up hard physical work. And she − she alone − has appointed absolute strangers. Has she been acting off her own bat? Or does she do it on Dr Page's authority?'

'I know nothing of this, Mr Chairman,' Dr Page replied. 'As

for Nurse Pegg, perhaps she has her own reasons – discipline, perhaps. If Mr Baines likes, I will question her.'

Mr Wilson raised a fastidious hand. 'Thank you, Dr Page. But I do not believe that Mr Baines' question has been answered.'

'Are there any questions about her competence? Surely not. She came on the highest recommendations.'

Marty's eyebrows rose to prompt him to continue.

'Whose?' Mr Wilson asked. 'I do not know the reasons for Mr Baines' questions, but I believe they should be answered. For instance, did you approach her or she you?'

'A medical colleague knew I needed a chief nurse and suggested I interview her. I did not need to seek any further. Neither do I think I need to now. I have seen her work and find no fault with it.' He was clearly and uncharacteristically furious.

'Thank you, Dr Page,' Mr Wilson said quickly. 'We see no difficulty there, I'm sure. But I'm sure we would all be grateful if you could find out why loyal employees are being replaced by strangers; this is quite contrary to what we have all agreed. Is there anything else before we agree a date for our next meeting – which, in my opinion, should be very soon indeed.'

TWENTY-FIVE

A s we drifted to the drawing room to indulge in a pre-dinner sherry, Luke took me to one side. 'Beg pardon, Mr Rowsley, but I am not at all sure that Mr Trescothick will be joining you. When he realized he wasn't allowed to attend the meeting, he flew into a right paddy.' He put his gloved hand over his mouth. 'He lost his temper, sir. I have gathered up the broken glass, but I thought you might want to know.'

'Thank you. Where is he now? Not in the library, I hope.'

'I managed to usher him out while I swept and mopped, sir. He missed most of the books, I am relieved to say. And the wine was not red.'

'Thank God for that!'

'I have taken the liberty of locking the room, sir. I trust I did right. Mr Trescothick stormed up to his bedchamber, but I do not know his present location. I will endeavour to discover it and report to you as soon as I have.' He bowed and disappeared with such discretion he might have been Samuel's younger self.

I could not describe the atmosphere in the drawing room as convivial, and was distressed that I would have to take Wilson, who was making valiant attempts to create a general conversation, to one side.

'Wretched man! I had best go and reason with him,' he said. 'He clearly does not like anyone here—'

'I will come too – and Dr Page ought to be consulted.'

Wilson bowed. 'I will ask him to help. Perhaps a decanter might be sent up too?'

'Unless you think he might have drunk too much already? I think we should ask Luke for his advice first. Ah! Here he is.'

Luke had not yet learned how to school his face into complete impassivity, so we could see how worried he was. 'Sir, I regret to say that although I now understand that the gentleman in question is in his room, he has made it clear in no uncertain terms that he does not wish to be disturbed. He and his bottle of Napoleon brandy, that is, sir.' His voice changed: he became a frightened young man. 'Mr Rowsley, I think he's smashing everything in sight. We could get in and stop him through the service door behind the tapestry, but not without your permission. And maybe, I'm sorry, but even your presence.'

'What about some of the guards from the Family wing?' Wilson asked. 'They should be skilled in . . . let's call it restraint, shall we?'

Luke writhed. 'But they're not . . . us, are they? They might talk.'

'Mr Bowman would be very proud of you, Luke,' I declared.

The group of trustees opening the hidden door from the unlovely backstairs to Trescothick's chamber included Marty Baines, whom I had commended as a man used to dealing with those in drink. In fact, he was invaluable. While the rest of us took avoiding action when a chamber pot and its contents were hurled at us, he simply stepped forward, grasping with apparent ease the arm wielding a broken bottle smelling of excellent brandy. In a trice the heir was face down on the bed and the weapon on the floor. As soon as I unlocked the main door, Luke and his colleagues surged in to gather up the broken glass, quickly rolling up the Chinese rugs and depositing them outside. Then Luke, who had disappeared, rematerialized with two buckets, one empty, one full of cold water, and a tankard of strong-smelling coffee. 'Mr Bowman always said this was invaluable, Dr Page, sir, him having long experience of young lords who couldn't hold their liquor.'

Page laughed. 'I can't argue with that. Goodness knows how you persuade him to drink it, however.'

'I'm sure Mr Baines and I can think of a way, sir. Gentlemen, if you wouldn't mind holding him over this.' He laid the empty bucket on the now bare floor and nodded to Marty and me. As soon as we had forced Trescothick over the bucket, Luke poured the water over his head. Then he simply swapped buckets and repeated the process.

'Now for the coffee, sir. But with due respect I would rather leave the task of pouring it down his throat to you, Dr Page.'

Page gave a grim smile. 'It might still take two of you to hold him still and another to pinch his nose while I do. And beware of vomit!'

It was a strangely attired group that returned to the drawing room. Most of our shirts and coats had suffered one way or another, so Luke had raided the staff storeroom, producing multi-coloured liveries in many sizes and indeed fashions. If we had set off upstairs as gentlemen with professional self-discipline, we came back with a boyish sense of a job well done. Perhaps our voices raised in laughter shocked those waiting for us, but I do believe that none of us cared. How long the camaraderie would last, I did not know.

Over our meal, we vied like schoolboys to outdo each other in tales of our comic heroism, though the chamber pot incident was not mentioned. Harriet threw her head back and laughed, and Bea rewarded one of Wilson's most outrageous claims with a cackle of delight. Even Pounceman found himself laughing, possibly to his own surprise. To mine, he offered to go and pray for Trescothick, but Page dissuaded him. 'Let him sleep it off first. I have left one of Nurse Pegg's staff with him,' he added with an ironic bow in Marty's direction, 'but I have ensured it was a former estate man. And paid him handsomely to ensure his absolute discretion.'

'What an evening that was,' Harriet declared as we retired to our bedchamber. 'I would never have expected it to turn out more like a gathering of friends than a chilly consumption of food for politeness' sake. Even Mr Pounceman was transformed.' Her voice more serious, she continued, 'Mind you, I can understand Trescothick's frustration: to be excluded from a meeting he must have thought he had every right to attend, on top of all the solitude he's been enduring! And wearing his new clothes, too. Actually his behaviour was no worse than much of what the footmen have always had to put up with from soi-disant gentlemen. At least no young women were . . . forcibly involved.'

'Not one of the men complained,' I said. 'Not one. As if it was part of their job to have to deal with urine and vomit. I will ensure they get a bonus on top of our thanks. And we must make sure their Christmas party is one to remember. But enough of work for now, my love, we can talk of that tomorrow.'

While Harriet and her team worked to clean what had suffered during Trescothick's drunken tantrum, Luke and his were dealing with the heir himself, using restorative brews recommended by Bea. I was to go out with Twiss, to inspect his mysterious discovery.

As I rode out on Esau, I came upon Dr Page, heading towards the House. We pulled our horses to a halt, greeting each other with less ease than I'd expected after last night's high spirits.

'Is Trescothick up and about yet?' he asked, without preamble.

'I would not know. I assume, however, that he is sleeping his hangover off.'

'Hmph. Well, I shall prescribe more strong coffee, or one of Mrs Arden's secret recipes. A handsome woman, is she not?'

'Indeed.' And one who would make an ideal doctor's wife. Or lawyer's wife. If my medical friend felt more than admiration for her, he had better move quickly. 'And a good one, too,' I added. I would not mention her other admirers, Marty especially, after yesterday's awkwardness – though the two had worked together amiably and successfully on our drunken visitor.

'And a wonderful cook. How did she manage to produce a dinner as fine as that and participate in that meeting?'

'Because she has trained her staff so well. And because, I suppose, she and Harriet had planned a menu that didn't demand precise timing – very fortunate since it had to be kept back so long. Now, if you will excuse me, Page, I must be on my way.'

'Of course. Tell me,' he said, just as I was about to set Esau in motion, 'why do you think Baines raised those extraordinary points last night? Why did he not approach me in private? I might have put his mind at rest in an instant?'

'He is a man driven by conscience,' I said, 'sometimes to uncomfortable lengths. But I am sure that you will soon reassure all us trustees and see our former employees reinstated.'

'Even if there is good reason – drunkenness, for instance – for their dismissal?'

'It would be good to know that you have made a thorough investigation,' I said, aware, even if he was not, of the keen wind and the passage of time. 'Now, Ellis, I really must be on my way. Good day to you!'

Esau set off with a brisk trot. But there was no sign of Twiss or his horse. He was normally the most conscientious man. Dismounting, I attached Esau firmly to a sound-looking tree. Perhaps I needn't have taken such precautions, because Esau objected in the strongest possible way to being ridden, uninvited, by anyone but me. He was learning to tolerate Harriet, but she attempted to mount him only when I was at hand.

I retained my whip, and then, on impulse I took my pistol from its holster and shoved it into my pocket. If the cracking of twigs here had scared Harriet, it would not scare me.

Would it?

Apprehensive despite myself I advanced slowly into the woods, wishing I were an owl able to look through 180 degrees in one direction and then the same the other way. When I was a boy, some schoolfriends had sworn that in fact owls' heads could swivel all the way round without stopping, and I had almost believed them. Sadly my studies had disabused me.

There was still no sign of Twiss. I called, called again – and there was nothing. Unless that was a groan. No, it was a muttered stream of invective. I headed for the source. It was Twiss, dressed for riding but with no mount.

'I feel so damned stupid,' he grumbled as I knelt beside him. 'Oldest story going. Horse rears. Rider falls. And the bloody horse takes off – he'll be at home by now. No, I'm all right, gaffer – nothing but my pride hurt. Damn!' He winced as I helped him to his feet. 'Right. Let me show you my find.'

I could hear Esau stamping and snorting. 'I'll go and get my old friend first. Better safe than sorry. Just wait here.'

Soon we were picking our way along no more than rabbit tracks.

'Left here, gaffer – along this track, if you please. A couple of hundred yards, that's all. There – that's where we're heading: that old woodman's shed.' He pointed.

The assemblage of planks and sacking barely merited such an exalted term, but I did not demur. Again I submitted Esau to the humiliation of being tied up, largely to prevent Twiss getting anxious. He pushed his way against the apology for a door, which creaked on its leather hinges. It took me a while to get used to the dim light, but eventually I saw what Twiss was pointing at – a straw suitcase.

He undid the strap. 'A gentleman's clothes, see. Nice ones too. A pair of shoes in good order. Now, what I want to know is, who has risked leaving clothes some of our men would kill for in a little place like this?'

'Someone who gambled on the hut never being found or opened. Someone with enough money to risk losing them. Let's leave them there, shall we? But we should check on them from time to time – and definitely follow anyone we see heading in this direction.' I snorted with ironic laughter. 'Neither of us has an important job to do, of course; both of us have hours to spare! But I don't think we should ask anyone else to do it – it might give rise to speculation. I think the best we can do is check when we happen to be passing.'

Twiss nodded with something like relief. 'World's so topsy-turvy, isn't it, what with the new village and the old one. Not to mention the new lord.' He closed the door, checking there was no sign it had been opened.

'What do people say about him?' I asked casually, as I unhitched Esau.

'Most don't bother overmuch. They'd rather you and your good lady stayed in charge, to be honest – you get things done and know when to leave well alone. Tell me, though – will we be needing a barn cleared for a Christmas party for the farm workers and their families? They've heard the House servants are having one and it doesn't seem fair not to have one for them.'

'Is it a tradition?'

'Not really. His late lordship liked them, same as he liked a harvest home, but we didn't have them every year – we reckoned her ladyship put her foot down because they turned into drunken romps, you might say.'

'I think we should, if we can have a romp without it being

drunken. I don't fancy any of the barns being burned down! Could Mrs Twiss organize it? Some presents for the youngsters? The estate will pay for everything, it goes without saying.' I unhitched Esau. Then, leading him, I asked, very casually, 'Has Mr Trescothick been seen around much since he arrived?'

'Not much, gaffer. And he keeps himself to himself, no doubt about that. No stopping for chats and asking about old acquaintances. To be honest, I worry about him – he's got such a bad seat on a horse, and the heaviest of hands. And that way he strides along as if he's too busy to talk: one day he'll stride his way into a rut and then where will his dignity be? I offered to show him round the farm and explain the improvements we're making, but he wasn't interested. The only person I've seen him talking to is the rector, but you know him – toadies up to them with titles and ignores ordinary folk, unless he happens to be telling them what's what. Lonely old life for him too, of course – like his new lordship, he's neither flesh nor fowl, nor even good red herring, though of course he does dine with the gentry. He needs a good wife: rumour has it he's got his eye on Mrs Arden. Do you think he should try his luck?'

'I never understand what women seem to pick up on instantly,' I said, which was the most diplomatic thing I could think of. 'You'd have to ask Mrs Twiss about that too.'

And I would have to ask Harriet.

TWENTY-SIX

'Three guests to cook for! It's almost like old times!' Bea was saying as I walked back in through the servants' entrance. 'Though I've never had to think about serving them in separate rooms. Mind you, Mr Wilson says he'll insist on us all eating together, Harriet – oh, and you, of course, Matthew. He says he's talked to Mr Trescothick like a Dutch uncle, and that he's probably got even more of a headache now than he started out with.'

'We even have to take luncheon with him!' Harriet told me. 'I think we're supposed to polish him up a bit.'

'Will we all be eating in the Room?' I asked, helping myself to one of Bea's biscuits. 'It might be less artificial, you know.'

'In the breakfast room, I thought,' Harriet said. 'I know Nurse Pegg found it a bit grand, but since I moved my belongings out the Room does look a bit . . . tired.'

'Tired?' Bea repeated. 'Exhausted, more like. A coat of paint would help, and some new curtains.'

Harriet frowned – I knew she was reluctant to spend the Family's money on things they would probably never have considered of any importance whatsoever. But then her whole face lit up. 'Bea, your rooms are worse than mine. Let us ask Mr Wilson if we can accompany him when he goes back to Shrewsbury. We can both choose fabric there. And wallpaper. And we can start thinking about Christmas gifts for the staff! Matthew, next time there is a wet day, could you get one of the outdoor men to whitewash the ceilings – yes, and the whole of the servants' hall. And one by one the servants' rooms must be improved.'

'Whitewash will just make everything else in the rooms look shabby – and I include ours in that,' said Bea.

'Might I make a suggestion?' I asked. 'Might you explore the attics and other storerooms? There are some beautiful rugs there just attracting moths, and furniture that would be far better used than simply waiting for woodworm. As each room is painted, the occupants could choose – I have to say within reason – what they would like.'

'That sounds an excellent idea,' said Mr Wilson, surprising us all. 'I do apologize: I did not wish to interrupt the flow of your conversation. And yes, Mrs Rowsley and Mrs Arden, I would be delighted to escort you into Shrewsbury. There I will put my carriage at your disposal so you may truly enjoy your visit to the shops.' He spoke to Harriet but I fancied his words were for Bea. Certainly his smile was, as like me he reached for a biscuit. Then he frowned. 'I wonder if we might have a reprise of this conversation over luncheon – excluding our travel arrangements, of course. I would like to see how Mr Trescothick reacts to our talk of the attics.'

'What if he wants a tour?' Bea asked.

I said, 'I think we should indulge him – provided that we contrive to have George, the carpenter, working up there. You know how some people have perfect pitch? George has the visual equivalent: let him see something once and he'll remember every detail. He's already been able to help the police investigating our missing Queen Bess.'

'In that case George must certainly be there. But there must be a watertight reason for his presence, especially on what I assume is his one half-day of the week.' For some reason he flashed a smile at Bea, who raised a mocking eyebrow. 'Or we could tell our guest to wait till Monday.'

Harriet shook her head reluctantly. 'Mr Trescothick's behaviour does not match his years. You would not offer a child a treat – but tell them they would only get it days later. If George, for a considerable financial consideration, was prepared to come in, then let it be today. And if George's time is wasted—'

'Then it must still be paid for,' Wilson agreed, again catching Bea's eye.

In the event, George almost got paid for doing no more than checking the attics for signs of leaks. Lunch had not been a success, with our guest silent and the four of us making increasingly stilted conversation. All attempts to find a way to encourage him to talk, including enquiries about his adventures the other side of the world, ended in failure.

Over coffee, however, out of the blue Trescothick asked, 'Is this place haunted?'

Wilson looked at Harriet and Bea. The latter replied, 'If it is, I've never heard of it. I've never heard anything either.'

'But you wouldn't, not down in the kitchen, would you?'

'Like Mrs Arden, I've never been aware of any rumours,' Harriet said. 'Why do you ask, Mr Trescothick? Have you heard anything?'

'One always thinks one might, as the house settles down . . . creaks, odd noises,' he mused. Then he continued, more brightly, 'An old place like this, it's bound to have the odd ghost, surely. Shaking chains, moaning. Things going bump in the night. What about you, Rowsley?'

'You almost make me wish I had. But my nights here are unbroken by clanking suits of armour or fiendish wails.' I smiled at a sudden recollection. 'When I came to talk to his lordship and Mr Wilson about my becoming the agent, I did sleep here for the night, in the corridor under the eaves. And one night an unholy scream woke me. Then there was the scrabbling of feet. And a tremendous thud, which silenced the footfall. There was little more sleep for me that night, I promise you.'

There was a most satisfactory silence.

'And yet you accepted the position – you're a braver man than I, Rowsley.'

'I am also a very nosy man,' I added. 'So when dawn finally broke, I had to find more. What I found was a flat roof just below my window – you will appreciate that the accommodation was where the oldest and the newest parts of the house join. So there were all sorts of nooks and crannies accessible to animals. Under one brick there was some sort of nest – the right size for a rat. Elsewhere, there was the sort of pellet you associate with owls. So my daylight deduction would be that during the night, I heard rats scurrying round, and that one of them became the owl's supper.' I dropped a claw-like hand over one of the salts to illustrate.

Even Trescothick laughed.

'At one point, Mr Wilson asked – I doubt if you remember! – what I saw was the immediate priority if I was offered the post.'

'So I did! And you said—'

'Killing the rats in the eaves!' we concluded as one.

'Well, you never got round to killing the beetles in my kitchen,' Bea said, arms akimbo. 'So what do you have to say for yourself now, Mr Rowsley?'

'Do you really want to know? One of the labourers' children found an injured hedgehog: John Coachman managed to stop it becoming a football. Currently it's in the stables, hopping round on three legs. But I am sure it would consider coming into the warm and dry, and overnight it would come out on beetle patrol. You might be left with . . . some evidence of its being there, of course.'

'At least the maid can sweep up the evidence, which she can't with all the wretched beetles.'

'I will introduce you as soon as it is well.' I offered her my most courtly bow. 'Trescothick, you must have known the attics from your youth? His lordship recalls games of hide and seek.'

'They are not one of my clearest recollections. But on a wet afternoon – is it never fine and dry in Shropshire? – a visit might refresh my memory. Let me see, the best way up is . . .?'

'I can do better than tell you. I will take you. We have been discussing with Mr Wilson the best use of some of the items in store. The servants' quarters were neglected when her ladyship held sway. Perhaps we might find discarded furniture, any rugs or even curtains that might be used to refurbish them.'

'Good stuff wasted on servants, Wilson?'

'Old items, no longer deemed of use, Trescothick,' Wilson said. 'That has always been the way of it. Many employers are reluctant to buy new things for their staff, and not all employers know the value of what they are discarding.'

Francis, who had been unwontedly silent, smiled suddenly. 'One acquaintance of mine gave an Aubusson carpet to his butler to have cut up for the footmen's dormitories. The housekeeper recognized it and had it rescued. I believe that once cleaned it graced his wife's dressing room. But I am not sure it should have done.'

'You mean she did not deserve it and the footmen did?' Bea asked, with an answering smile.

'Actually, yes. I do. But I wouldn't have wanted a carpet of that quality hacked into pieces. I'd have liked – something more in keeping, by which I do not mean plain painted boards. The labourer is worthy of his hire, is he not, Harriet?' He smiled at her. 'Most people of our class, Trescothick, simply do not know that the people who wait on them are human. I have known Harriet for some twenty years, and been honoured to call her friend for most of them. My family has always been abolitionist, of course, and I'm glad to say that my father voted the Factory Acts and the Public Health Act. But knowing the theory is one thing, knowing the people is another. I loathe the very idea of transporting felons to the colonies – but do not know anyone to tell me what it is like for the criminal transported.'

There was a tiny, possibly shocked, silence.

Wilson straightened. 'You do not wish criminals to be punished, Sir Francis?'

'I do not wish crimes to be committed in the first place. And I am not sure that all the punishments are appropriate. That is in part owing to my Whig family background, but thanks to my good friends here my own prejudices are being challenged. I confess, I was shocked, nauseated even, by the prospect of walking with two exceedingly smelly labourers the other day – was I not, Harriet? Then came a quiet observation from her . . . I confess I want to keep some of my undoubted privileges, ladies and gentlemen, but I want everyone else to have . . . better lives, not dependent on the whims of others for food and shelter. I apologize: this is hardly appropriate for a luncheon table.'

To describe the silence as stunned would be an understatement. Bea's face glowed. Wilson was trying to look impassive. Harriet – how did she feel about being praised for what was a veritable Road to Damascus moment? She seemed proud but almost embarrassed, apparently. Trescothick? His features were unreadable: as the heir to huge wealth, did he not have views? Apparently none he wished to share. Yet I thought, as he drained his glass, that his hand shook.

I nodded to Luke: it was definitely time for coffee.

*   *   *

The excursion to the bitterly cold attics came as something of an anti-climax. I introduced Trescothick to George, wondering if either might expect to shake hands; neither did. And poor George was disconcerted, juggling his tool bag before setting it down altogether, when the newly egalitarian Francis seized his hand, pumping it enthusiastically, before asking him a number of discerning questions.

Trescothick looked blank as he stepped inside: he did not have the air of a man reliving a childhood adventure, not even when I pointed to a set of wickets optimistically chalked on a chimney piece in one of the less cluttered areas. The women prowled round with Wilson, but found nothing they thought could be used to improve the staff accommodation. I had forgotten that the furniture was made to display in big rooms. More appropriate items no doubt lurked in other storerooms. Here there were also the battered remains of long-dead children's playthings, paintings galore – good and bad – and chests the keys of which had probably been lost generations ago.

What I wanted to do was separate George from Francis, who might be relied on to amuse Trescothick, but it would not be easy. Francis was an entertaining talker but knew how to listen, and it was clear he and George, after the awkward start, were getting on very well. So it was left to me to entertain our guest. I hoped it wasn't that prospect that left him looking thoroughly dismayed.

'Where would one start?' he asked, spreading his hands. 'Chaos. When you plan your pet village and clear the land, at least you must have some idea of what you want and where to start. But this!'

'You're right. Absolute chaos. That's probably why no one has ever got round to clearing it out. Perhaps one day an historian like Sir Francis will come up here and find it as fascinating as he finds his stones and statues. Meanwhile, the chaos grows, as each generation adds to it, rather than taking away.'

'If you can have an archivist to sort out the books in the library,' he said, surprising me further, 'why not get a historian to go through this lot? If books can be priceless, what about that old chest? And what's inside it?' He was transformed into an impish schoolboy. 'Shall we take a peep?'

By a stroke of fortune the one he touched was unlocked. It opened to reveal piles of documents, some written in a hand and language I could not read.

'Sir Francis! Sir Francis!' Trescothick called, more animated than I'd ever seen him. 'Look at this! Here is history for you!'

As he peered inside, I waited for the response I had always had from historians at university.

'Sadly this is not my period,' he said, as superciliously as I'd have predicted. Then he thawed. 'There's a decent enough man at Balliol. Send it to him.'

'Let us invite him here,' Harriet said firmly. 'We have plenty of room for guests, after all, and Bea and I flourish best when we have work to do.' Her words were unremarkable in themselves but I suspect we all understood the implication. 'Now, my hands are so cold I'm afraid they will drop off. Shall we take tea to warm us?'

George dawdled behind the others, though he would know that he was welcome in the servants' hall. I slipped the coins I'd promised into his hands as I prepared to lock up behind us.

'Everything in order?' I prompted him.

He pulled a face. 'That Sir Francis is a nosy old bugger, isn't he? Begging your pardon, sir. But he knows his stuff, no doubt about that. Taught me a couple of things – but then, he said I taught him some.'

It wasn't the educational aspect of the visit that particularly interested me. 'Did you notice if anything had been moved – if anything was missing, indeed?'

'Funny thing was, he kept picking things up and putting them down somewhere else. Wouldn't want to be one of his servants having to tidy up after him. I like things just so, gaffer, as you know.'

'I do, and I value you for it. Do you think anyone else might have moved anything before he did?'

'Like poor Queen Bess? Don't suppose she's turned up again, has she?'

'Not yet.'

'Everything else is where it should be. The stuff he pithered with, anyhow. But I've got this niggle. There was a pile of pictures stacked together. And I reckon two of them might have changed places. Both still here, mind!' He dug in his tool bag. 'Here, I've got a new lock. Work of minutes to fix it. One key for you. One for Mrs Rowsley. One for your safe.'

'Excellent. I'll go and tell Mrs Arden to get the kettle on, shall I?'

'If you please. She's a fine woman, isn't she? I wonder why she never remarried.'

TWENTY-SEVEN

C hurch on Sunday was more pleasant than usual, with no pointed remarks to make me stage another faint and a sermon – on the Prodigal Son – decidedly short and to the point. Mr Pounceman even managed to shake hands with us all, asking about Dick and whether the police were ever likely to discover his assailant. He demurred when I pointed out he was also a victim of violent crime, saying that his bruises were nothing beside the poor young man's broken bones; he prayed daily for him.

What had happened to transform him? And indeed Mr Trescothick, who was also showing signs of change? Assuming both men were sincere, of course: they could be displaying acting skills I had never suspected.

The weather being fine, a walk after lunch was most certainly in order. For some reason Mr Trescothick was decidedly averse to going in the direction of the remains, and voted strongly against the woodlands which gave the most picturesque vistas. So we all drifted towards the pleasure gardens, which the gardeners had clearly maintained as if her ladyship was still inspecting them every day. But there is something very doleful about a garden heading into winter. I thought longingly of the two of us sitting before a warm fire in our own sitting room, the curtains firmly drawn against the gathering dusk and against all visitors. Instead there was afternoon tea in the drawing room, and a light Sabbath supper ahead of us, both involving hours of polite and pointless chattermagging.

Bea, on the other hand, was in her element, charming us all with dish after delightful dish. Francis would have eaten any dry crumb from her hand, had Mr Wilson, plainly smitten, allowed him to get anywhere near her. However, I doubted that Francis was much more than an agent provocateur, spurring Mr Wilson on. Even so, would he come up to scratch? And would Bea ever be more than flattered by his attentions? She had spoken of a post with a wealthy family, where she could indulge her organizational skills and brilliance in the kitchen. As an employer, Mr Wilson, middle-class professional man, able and successful though he was, would not meet her standards – but what if he genuinely was a suitor? He might well be, because she had blossomed recently in a way I'd never seen before – perhaps because she had always tried to conform to Samuel's ideals, not her own. Could the marriage be as happy as Matthew's and mine? Love, deep passionate love, apart, the fact that he always treated me as an equal had so far given me more happiness than I had imagined possible. Would Mr Wilson be capable of that?

As I often did, I went up to read the day's collect and psalm to Samuel. His bruises were fading now, and his wounds visibly healing. As for the damage inside, who knew? But his hand was warm and dry, and when I stroked his forehead, I found no fever. Did he register my touch? I was tempted to think so. And did he follow the familiar words of the Lord's Prayer, his lips moving almost imperceptibly? I was sure of it! But the familiar bustle of Nurse Pegg brought me up short. Today I did not feel like engaging in any more talk, apart from a brief enquiry about her toothache; her response was equally short – it was showing signs of improvement, though she still cradled her jaw.

And yet, as I ran into Hargreaves in the corridor, I drew to a halt. Somehow we fell into step, entering a yet unoccupied room and leaning on the windowsill together, breathing in the gentle winter's breeze at the open window.

'Jeremy,' I said at last, 'we always ask about his lordship and her ladyship, but never those who are devoting their lives to them. You, in particular. You never expected a life like this, almost monastic. You were expecting tours of all the great houses, making friends and in time carving out a career for yourself. Am I right? I thought so.'

'But how can I leave his lordship, Mrs Rowsley? I'm the only one who can calm him, when he's in one of his moods. And sometimes I look in on Mr Bowman. I know you do too.' He shifted awkwardly. 'How do you think he is?'

'He seemed a lot better today.'

'It worries me. What if, when he gets better, someone wants to finish what they started?'

I turned to look him in the eye. 'Have you any idea – do you care to speculate – who it might be? You're worried about someone, Jeremy, aren't you?'

We heard a door slam, footsteps coming along the corridor. His posture changed, as did his voice. 'I'm really looking forward to it. Musicians and dancing and games and all that!'

'And who are you planning to ask to dance?' I said in an equally carrying and jolly voice. 'I always thought you had your eye on Maisie.'

'Ah, you've caught me out there, ma'am,' he said with a laugh. But his face was ineffably sad.

'Come and talk to me in the Room,' I mouthed. He nodded. Out loud I said, 'Whoever it is, she's a lucky girl. Oh, look at the time! I must get back to Mr Trescothick.' And, though I couldn't see or hear anyone watching, I made a very public exit.

Neither Mr Wilson nor Francis had given us any idea how long they might be staying. Neither, of course, had Mr Trescothick. Monday morning's grey, misty weather reflected the sense of inertia that had settled on the House. Matthew withdrew to his office, Beatrice to her kitchen. I made my regular inspection of the House and found nothing amiss. Francis lurked in his study, and Mr Wilson in his. Mr Trescothick was unable to ensconce himself in the library because the carpet was still recovering from the thorough clean it had needed to remove the wine stains; Francis had suggested a bookbinder who might be able to restore some of the damaged covers. Had one of the Family been using the library, the carpet would probably have been replaced, but Mr Wilson had still not made a conclusive decision about the putative heir's status. So he mooched about the place, popping up in the rooms I was inspecting with irritating regularity, like a lost mongrel. Eventually I explained in great detail what I was doing and why, showing him a curtain that had started to rot in the sun. And there someone had put a wet glass on a mahogany table, leaving a ring: this was how we would repair it . . . For the first time, he was as animated as he had been in the attic, poring over those old papers, and we had a genuine conversation. Suddenly, however, as if someone had turned off a tap, he stopped and, excusing himself with no more than a nod, he turned on his heel and left me. I finished what I was doing, and headed thoughtfully towards the servants' quarters.

I soon ran into Dr Page, who looked quite hang-dog after his routine visit to the Family wing. I urged him along to the Room, not by direct invitation but simply by keeping him engaged in conversation while we walked in that direction. I doubted if he would tell me what was troubling him, nor did he. But he did ask an interesting question: 'Tell me, was that Constable Pritchard I saw earlier?'

'I'm sorry – I was out on my rounds, as you saw. Perhaps he has come to tell Dick his assailant has been found. Though I would rather he discovered Mr Bowman's attacker. How is my old friend, Dr Page?' I continued, when he made no comment. 'Am I imagining an improvement?'

He bit his lip. 'It's hard to tell, isn't it?' Why should a medical man equivocate like that? 'I hope so. I truly hope so.'

'And his lordship?'

'He will never recover his senses fully on a permanent basis. But he is in a good phase at the moment. As is her ladyship. And Dick – yes, I can give you unreservedly good news about him. He should be back on duty tomorrow – but he can only convey messages and gravitas, not carry trays.'

'Excellent. With such good news, Nurse Pegg will be looking for another post!' I joked.

His response was extraordinary. 'Why on earth do you say that? It is not like you, Mrs Rowsley, to make such outlandish suggestions! I fear I must bid you good day before I forget myself.' And, gathering his case, he was stalking towards the door.

'Ellis, pray forgive me. You must know that I was only joking, and would no more advise you on your staff than you would tell Bea how to make a soufflé. As for Nurse Pegg, is it possible that you are more sensitive than usual because of Marty Baines' tactless questions? As for me, I just want what is best for my dear friend. And – pray sit and hear me out – I have only this morning noticed something truly odd. Sometimes when I am alone with him – entirely alone – I sense that he is better. Yesterday he repeated the Lord's Prayer with me. He has given similar reactions to other members of staff. But I have noticed that there are times when he is as unresponsive as a log of wood. Is this usual in a case like this?'

He frowned. 'Do I detect an implied criticism of anyone?'

'You detect nothing but puzzlement. Why should he only respond when we are on our own?'

He shook his head dismissively. 'How could he even know you were alone? Entirely alone?' As he spoke, however, he stared with stark amazement at me. His face changed. 'You must be as aware as I am of the implication. More than one implication,' he reflected, with obvious anxiety. 'The first – let us call it the positive – implication is that Mr Bowman is conscious at least part of the time, is it not? The second – to my mind, and perhaps yours – is that he does not want it to be generally known that his health has so improved.'

I danced on verbal eggs. 'Samuel is a man quite rigid in his ways. Once he has conceived a dislike for someone, he rarely changes his mind. I am sorry to refer to Nurse Pegg again, but she has quite an unusual voice, has she not. Is it possible that that might have irritated him?'

He sank his head in his hands as if faced with an impossible situation. 'It is hard to raise an issue like this with such a highly qualified person, who cannot be other than offended by the criticism. Impossible!' He managed a dry smile. 'Harriet, you must have managed many awkward situations like this – staff not getting on well with each other, or, worse, held in sudden dislike by their employers.'

'In the second instance, the solution was sadly all too easy. They had to be let go. In the former, I could move one to duties in another part of the House.'

'The spurious measles epidemic apart, there is no work for Nurse Pegg to do!'

I clicked my fingers. 'Let me think – and I often think better when sharing a pot of coffee and some of Bea's biscuits.'

Meg was not the only sick woman in Stammerton, as Dr Page soon found out. By the end of the day there were ten invalids for Nurse Pegg and her team to attend to. Since most of their clothes were fit for nothing more than the furnace, there would be plenty of plain sewing for the nurses and the remaining maids to do in quiet moments. There were poplin and serge on the shelves in the sewing room, but I would buy more when Bea and I shopped in Shrewsbury. Quite when that would be I had no idea. Mr Wilson seemed quite settled in his new study. Perhaps I had made it too comfortable, as I observed to Matthew as we eventually retired to our room for the night.

'Wouldn't it be wonderful to escape again?' he asked. 'Just the two of us. No one to have to talk to. No one to be answerable to. No policemen asking questions but in reality not expecting answers.'

'Did Elias mention any new developments?'

'How could he? But I did, in fact. Those clothes Twiss and I found in the woodman's shelter. I sent him off with Twiss to find them, but they had gone, along with the case. But Elias did find something – threads that had caught on a rough patch on the door. I should imagine he'll want to come and check them against the maids' uniforms.'

'Maids?'

'Some sort of cotton poplin, he thought. He's a bright young man, isn't he? How must he feel working for a clod like Burrows! But enough of this, my love. Work dominates all our working days; we must save some moments just for ourselves.'

I did not argue.

TWENTY-EIGHT

Tuesday dawned as bright and sunny as yesterday had been dull and grey. Harriet told me that she resolved to take the trap over to Stammerton to see how the families of the sick men and women were faring and offer emergency food. Her delight to see who led the trap to the back door was quite disproportionate. 'Matthew!'

'Is there room for a passenger?' I asked, looking askance at the bundles and baskets beside her.

'Provided he does not have to talk about work,' she said as I helped her aboard, kissing her hand as I did so.

'I thought we might find time to go to our own home on the way back, just to see that all is well. Not that I imagine anything could be amiss. But I've almost forgotten what it looks like.' I squeezed myself between two overflowing baskets, eventually taking one on to my lap.

'Before or after our errand?' She cracked the whip to set us in motion. 'Shall it be after, so we have something to look forward to?'

Stepping out of her cottage, Sukey eyed me with her usual latent hostility, but greeted Harriet with relief. 'I knew as you'd come, ma'am, or one of the maids at least. But I'm glad it's you and I'm glad Mr Rowsley's here too. I need a strong man, begging your pardon, to shove the prop under the beam in there a bit more upright.'

Stepping inside, I waited till my eyes grew accustomed to the gloom. The prop she referred to actually seemed to be supporting the whole failing roof, weighed down, no doubt, by the tarpaulin that was at least keeping the inside fairly dry.

She gave a snort of laughter. 'Your face, gaffer! Yes, even the rats have run off.'

Outside again, I said, 'I'll get a team of men up here at once, Sukey. It's too dangerous for you to stay here as it is now.

Meanwhile, can we look to you to distribute the food and blankets according to need?'

She looked at the baskets Harriet had unloaded. 'You'll trust me with that lot?'

Harriet pressed her hand. 'If I can't trust you, who can I trust? Sukey, can you sew?'

She pulled a face. 'I can darn.'

'In that case you're halfway there. If you want some work, come to me at the House and I'll add you to the team at work there.'

But Sukey shook her head. 'I smell something shocking, ma'am. I've got nits and fleas. I'm not fit for decent company, am I?' She produced a lop-sided grin. 'But maybe once I've given this lot out I can help the lads you're sending over, gaffer.'

'Maybe you can,' I agreed. 'I'll tell the foreman to look out for you.'

So much for a little time in our own home. The journey back to the House was noticeably brisker, with Harriet decidedly quiet. What was she planning now? Leaving me to despatch a team of workers to Stammerton, she strode – there is no other word – through the servants' door.

There was no sign of her when I followed, hoping for a cup of tea at least in her company, so I retired to my office. She had already been there: there was a note for me.

My own love, how many need to be present for a trustees' meeting to be quorate?

What was she planning? A tap on the door, and Dick himself, wearing his sober butler's suit, announced the presence of Wilson. Normally I would have asked for refreshments, but did not wish to embarrass the young man, whose arm was still in a sling, of course.

Wilson took a seat, his eyes a-twinkle. 'Your good wife directed me here,' he announced. 'There is no doubt about it, she has a plan for something. Ah!' He himself responded to the tap on the door, taking the tray that Harriet carried. It seemed appropriate for me to pour.

'I have to say,' Wilson said, 'that many cities now have public baths and laundries for the poor, but I have not come across many on an estate like this. That does not mean, of course, that I in any way disagree with the suggestion. My only question would be how they could be achieved.'

'When in the past we had a houseful of guests, we employed one part-time and two full-time laundry maids. Even with the bedlinen in the Family wing, including the influx of new patients, we need no more than two – the part-time woman is no longer needed. That means there are certain days when the laundry and its huge coppers aren't used at all. On those days they could be thrown open to the poor of both villages, who would also be able to use the drying room. As for baths, and here I am less sure, there are hardly any horses in stabling built for forty beasts. And there is the grooms' accommodation occupied by four men at most. Is there some way it and the stables themselves could be employed?'

'Are you thinking of lodging these indigent men and women in them?' Wilson asked sharply.

To my relief she shook her head. 'Much as I would like to, particularly that poor woman whose roof is falling down, I cannot feel it is . . . appropriate. Matthew?'

'I agree. It would set precedents. But Sukey must be offered safer accommodation if, as I fear, the whole structure is about to collapse. Why were these repairs never done before?' I groaned.

'Because of your predecessor, Matthew. But his inactivity makes it all the more difficult now. Which is why I asked about the quorum. Do we need the permission of the trustees to extend the laundry room, which after all adjoins the stables, so that the poor may bathe – if in rather spartan surroundings?'

'As chairman, I would say that could be nodded through. As for the woman you allude to, what would you suggest? If she were ill, she would be admitted to the Family wing. But to admit someone who is not even slightly unwell would set another unwelcome precedent. I would say, Matthew, that even if your men have to work by the light of flares, that cottage must be made safe.'

I nodded. 'That's what I ordered. And I have authorized extra wages. Harriet, do we need to call a meeting? They could not read a notice!'

'A risk to your health should be avoided. Tell the foreman to make the announcement once you have decided which days are to be allocated.' He looked round. 'What an admirably short meeting. I rather think we deserve to adjourn to somewhat cosier surroundings and some more coffee to celebrate.'

Which would give him another excuse to flirt with Bea.

For one reason or another, dinner was quite a pleasant affair, with everyone joining in the conversation. Both ladies took sewing baskets into the drawing room; the portraits did not, as one might have predicted, drop from their frames in horror at seeing working-men's shirts being hemmed in such normally leisured surroundings. Neither did I gasp aloud when Trescothick asked if he might join me when I rode out in the morning to see how Sukey's house repair was going. Francis invited himself along too.

Wilson, on the other hand, did not. He said, astoundingly, that he was to visit the rectory. And then, looking around, suggested that we men read aloud to entertain the seam-stresses. Was there a reason for him to choose *Julius Caesar*? If there was, I did not know, but I found enough copies of the play for us to proceed, which we did with far more vigour than I expected after the monotone of schoolboy readings. I believe we were all disappointed when the clock struck ten, but there was a unanimous decision to continue on the morrow.

'Mr Wilson visit Mr Pounceman?' Harriet squeaked, the moment we were shut firmly in our room. 'Surely that can only mean one thing! He is going to ask to have the banns read! Oh, Matthew, how wonderful!' She danced me round the room as if we were children.

Much as I enjoyed the moment, I had to ask, 'Are we sure? I noticed no conscious look between them which there surely would have been if they were betrothed. She did not even redden, as I would have expected. Or look unnaturally calm, on the other hand.'

She stopped abruptly. 'And of course she would have whispered to me . . . Oh, Matthew, I was hoping for some joy!'

'Then we will have to make our own.' I set off whirling her round and round again.

As the three of us set out for Stammerton next morning, each with yet more provisions in our saddlebags, Francis brushed against me. 'Keep your pistol to hand!' he breathed as he patted me apologetically on the shoulder.

I dared not ask why lest the groom overheard. Instead I set us off at a smart trot; I had a day's work to attend to even if they did not. As no one started a conversation I was left to wonder how the others passed their time. Presumably Francis was engaged in some aspect of his historical work, but what about Trescothick? Harriet had told me about their time discussing housework, but try as I might I could not imagine his offering to wield a feather duster. The letters in the attic had certainly engaged his interest, yet Francis had declared that the putative heir generally had more interest in market value than true worth. Now he was interested in repairing down-at-heel dwellings? It seemed less than likely. And what of Francis' reason for joining the party? And his extraordinary warning? What on earth was he expecting? Nonsensical as it might seem, allowing the others to precede me along the bridleway, I did indeed arm myself.

At length I drew level. Conversation was very general, from taking a gun to the pigeons that made farmers' lives so difficult to the prospect of snow for Christmas, a notion that Mr Dickens seemed to have made popular despite such weather making life so hard for country people, especially our poor. 'Cold,' I observed tartly, 'is a luxury only the rich can afford, tucked away in their great houses.'

'And not always then,' Francis pointed out. 'Harriet and I share, if you recall, horrible memories of bitterly cold great houses. The Romans had a much better idea – the hypocaust, whereby hot air was pumped into living rooms. I am in hopes that we will unearth one here. Why on earth did it lapse? And with their notion of flush sanitation, what would they think of us and our chamber pots and privies . . .'

'I understand a Birmingham engineer devised an excellent way of heating his home,' I said. 'The distinguished Matthew

Boulton. Hot air comes into the house through holes in the stair risers. Of course, Soho House is quite a compact dwelling: I fear his system would not work in the House, not without many adaptations. At least you never had that problem in Australia, Trescothick. You'd be having more problems with the heat, by all accounts. And more fearsome beasts than that pheasant, by all accounts.'

'I was never much interested in things like that,' he declared, shifting awkwardly in the saddle. 'I thought this village of yours was next to the ruins. How much further is it?'

Fortunately it was not far. For all their talk, I was the only one to dismount and check on the progress. The men had done an excellent job, beams as solid as pit timbers supporting the roof along its entire length and at all four corners, with extra supports halfway along each wall. I praised the foreman, asking him to check if other cottages needed the same. 'Already looked, gaffer – see, there's another load of timber coming along now.'

So I returned to my companions well-satisfied – but it seemed they were no longer at ease with each other. I sensed I was stepping between two schoolboys squaring up for a scrap. Neither spoke as I mounted, and we turned in silence. Esau chose the route home, taking us past the Roman site and the woodland.

Francis broke the silence. 'This is where Harriet saw her giant squirrels the other day!' he chuckled, pointing.

Apparently despite himself, Trescothick responded sharply, 'I beg your pardon?'

'When I returned the other day I walked to meet her, alarming her greatly as I took a shortcut through the woods. But then we were both alarmed – another figure appeared and then ran quickly away. Two of the labourers gave chase, but they found no one. He left a hat behind, Matthew. Did anything ever come of it?'

'Not that I know of, so it couldn't have been important,' I said lightly. 'It was probably dropped by some tramp or other. At least the man would be safer here than on a neighbour's farm – they've still got mantraps there.'

I had created the diversion I'd hoped for and also got the others speaking to each other again. But before Esau returned to the warmth of his stable, he and I would go on another errand – an invented one, as it happened. In fact, I made my way into the village hoping to speak to Elias. There was a note pinned to his door: he would be back in half an hour, though naturally I did not know when he had pinned it there. I had no desire to wait around, and there was nothing to take me to the village shop, the post office or even the newly-opened haberdasher's. As I turned away, slapping my riding boot in irritation, there came however a breathless shout. Elias came running towards me.

'I got my friend who is a gentleman's outfitter's assistant to look at it,' Elias said, putting the hat on his desk. 'And he spotted what I had missed. Right in here – see? Tucked away there. Yes, the label of the shop where it was bought. An emporium in Cambridge. Goodness knows how it got all the way here. I've spoken to the regular tramps and to people like Jem the Hawker who comes across a lot of folk on his travels; he doesn't just sell ribbons, he garners snippets of news no one else hears. But no one has reported anyone who might have come so far comparatively recently. Even the gypsies.'

I picked up on one word. 'Recently?'

'It was in a sorry state when I first saw it, but it dried nicely and would brush up a treat, my friend said. So not an old battered poacher's hat. A gentleman's hat. And I was thinking of the gentleman's cane we found.'

'So all we need to do is find a gentleman with a depleted wardrobe,' I said dryly.

'That's right. All!' He brightened. 'But does it remind you of anything?'

'It does. The case of clothes in the woodman's hut.'

'Has anyone been seen there since?'

I shook my head. 'Not as far as I know. But it's a big estate, isn't it? And all the workers I can spare are working on the new Stammerton site. Not surprisingly we've got an influx of sick from the old dwellings. I suspect one or two of the domestic servants will offer to become nurses, so I can't organize a search unless you officially order me to. As it happens, though, Mr Wilson thinks it might be wise to introduce a couple of new servants into the House, to act as detectives. They may even be detectives, for all we know. Their aim would obviously be to protect the House and its contents.'

'Ah – to keep an eye on this heir of yours? About time too, I'd say.' He scratched his head. 'I hear your womenfolk are all busy sewing for the poor basket. My missus Rosie is a dab hand with a needle. And as bright as a button. Do you think your missus might find some work for her? She trained her up, after all.'

'I'll speak to her as soon as I see her.'

Elias gave me a strangely compassionate pat on my shoulder. 'Not much of a way to live your first year together, is it?'

TWENTY-NINE

Marty was just opening up the Royal Oak as I left the police house. He gave me a welcoming wave. 'Come along in and try my latest brew!'

'Who could resist? How are you?' We shook hands enthusiastically, and Esau consented to be led to the stables at the rear.

'I hear you and your missus are doing great stuff over in Stammerton,' he said, polishing a tankard for me and filling it.

'We only need to because no one did before, when they should have done. But while the finances are unencumbered by vast weekend parties and balls and hunting, I might as well invest in the workers' future. And it is my job, Marty. I am not being a philanthropist with my own money!'

He laughed. 'How is his lordship?'

'He has much better days, but time will tell if he ever recovers sufficiently to lead a normal life.'

He hesitated. 'Does he know he has a daughter?'

'Not yet. But if he asks I will tell him, and how her poor mother died. The life of a narrow-boat family can't be secure, can it?' I drew on my half. 'Is there any prospect of them coming this way soon? If there is, I would love him to have the chance of seeing the little mite.'

'I'll let you know as soon as I hear. Pray God he's in one of his sane spells then. Did I hear, by the way, that Elias is looking for one of your pictures? An old one?'

'Indeed. Good Queen Bess used to go on royal progresses, didn't she, and now her portrait seems to be following suit.'

'Valuable?'

'I wish I knew. I can tell at a glance how much a flock of sheep is worth, or a field of corn, but I'm no expert on art. I just wish it was where it was supposed to be, and not going missing on my watch.'

'To be realistic, Matthew, there aren't many suspects, are

there? Most of the servants would die rather than steal so much as a Family pin. Perhaps you should consider one of your visitors, perhaps even this Trescothick man.'

'If you had been outside, you would have spat in the dust, wouldn't you?' I laughed grimly. 'At least you will not run away if I ask why? Come, it was clear at the trustees' meeting that you smelt a rat.'

He spread his hands. 'I've not met the man, except to nod to when he graces the village with his presence. But to see you lot giving a complete stranger the run of a place – I can't believe it of a sensible man like you. Trusting to a fault you are, Matthew, and that's the truth.'

'The truth is that I simply had no authority to turn him away, not when Mr Wilson declared the heir had returned. And as you know he seemed hardly to doubt him. But may I guess what you believe? That our Mr Trescothick was a passenger or even a crew member aboard the vessel bringing the true heir home? And that he tipped him over the side and took his place?'

'If you think that too, why are you not taking action? I tell you straight, I think you and that Wilson fellow have been too lax.' Suddenly he smiled. 'Yes, him much more than you, to be fair. He should have checked the man's credentials at once. And it isn't as if you're not a bit busy doing other stuff, is it? Do you ever get a quiet moment now you're living at the House full-time? Come, you've got a beautiful bride, man – you need to spend time on your own. I rue every moment my dear wife and I spent apart.'

'If only we could! But if *noblesse oblige*, so does being responsible for the welfare of so many people, from his lordship down to the smallest, dirtiest urchin on the smallest of his estates. Look at you: you could make far more money if you let the men drink as much as they wanted. Clearly you have a prickly conscience too!'

'I can't argue with that. Anyway, has Mr Wilson heard from the shipping line yet? No? And how long does that Sir Francis mean to hang around? He's not dangling after your wife, is he?'

'After Bea Arden, more like. But somehow he doesn't strike me as the marrying sort – a dilettante scholar.'

'Is "not the marrying sort" a roundabout way of saying he prefers men or pretty boys?'

'Good God! He's a friend of Harriet's . . . I never even suspected it might be possible.'

'I didn't say that. And I can't imagine any friend of your wife . . . no, no. Anyway, now he's not digging up pieces of stone, what's he doing at the House?'

'He's both educating the heir and keeping an eye on him.' And urging me to carry a pistol. Perhaps it was time to turn the subject. 'As Mr Pounceman might be. But they make an unlikely pair, do they not?'

'Chalk and cheese. I can hardly believe that Trescothick has turned to Pounceman of all people for spiritual guidance. But they say that since his illness there are signs that he's showing more humanity: he's even visited the deserving sick – so long as their illness is as genteel as they are. The postmaster and his gout, but not the old postman and his ulcerated leg. The village shop's owner, but not the assistant – you get my drift. But even that is an improvement.' He gestured: another half?

I shook my head. 'I hate to refuse such good ale, Marty, but I must get back to the House. Apart from anything else, I need to prod Wilson, don't I? It's time we had some answers.' I picked up my hat and whip.

'True. Just one thing, before you go. Is there any news about that Nurse Pegg? I know my question got up Page's nose, and I'm sorry. But we can't have a stranger coming in and sacking estate people who were promised the work, can we?'

'That's been stopped, and the original men reinstated. But Harriet tells me he's still very sensitive about his protégée, so I'm loth to press him. Have you got any more out of young Freddie, by the way?'

There was a long pause. 'How well do you know all the people in the House, Matthew? Because I got the impression that someone might have tried to . . . tried to touch him.'

'Which was why you were asking about Francis?' I asked, aghast.

'Not really. But remember, Freddie would die rather than admit if, let alone who. Let's just say I think it would be kind if you kept him beside you as much as you can – it'd do him no harm at all to ride with you on errands so he can learn his future profession first hand.'

I believe I had swayed in horror as he told me. Who could be so unspeakably vile? Oh, I know it was almost common practice in some of our great schools for older boys to seduce or rape younger ones – but here, under his lordship's roof? Our roof, since ultimately I was responsible for everything now! Every feeling was revolted. And if it were Francis!

'Marty, I implore you to persuade him to tell me who the miscreant is. I beg you. Or shall I speak to him myself?'

'I fear he would simply run away if you did. Or, before you ask, even if your wife did. He seems just as frightened of women now. I wonder, Matthew, if the man involved might be – I hate to say this – but someone the boy sees as important. And he's afraid if he snitches even to someone he ought to trust, that person will betray his secret.'

I stared. 'Frightened of women?' Those big hands, that squawk of a voice! 'Marty, I must get back to the House. Summon Elias and Dr Page for me, and send them up! Tell them it's vital. Life and death. And Freddie shall come to you: look after him!'

'What's going on in that head of yours now?' He smacked his forehead. 'Ah! Nurse Pegg! Of course!'

'Yes! Nurse Pegg – who is a man!'

THIRTY

'I can't, sir! I dare not! Look – she's coming after me now!' Freddie screamed. 'I can hear her skirt in the corridor!'

I froze.

'She? No, that's Mrs Rowsley. You've no cause to be worried by her, have you now?' That was Dick Thatcher's voice. 'A kinder woman never lived. You know that.'

There was a murmur that might have been reluctant agreement.

Gently, Dick continued, 'So it's a lady that's hurt you. There aren't too many of those in the House, are there? So why don't you just whisper to me and I'll make sure it never happens again. Come on. Her ladyship used to be unkind, but the poor soul's not left her chamber in months. Mrs Arden, who makes sure you get those lovely cakes? No. So who might it be?'

I did not wait for an answer. Could not. It had to be Nurse Pegg! But a woman hurt a child? Surely not! Not like that! But what if gawky, squeaky Nurse Pegg was not a woman but a man? I flew up the main staircase and was battering at the Family wing door. One of our old gamekeepers, blind in one eye after a poacher's pot-shot, caught me as I tripped. Staggering, I ran on. No, she wasn't in Samuel's room. I sped back to old Sampson. 'Make sure no one leaves, man or woman. Understand? No one. But if Thatcher comes up, tell him to guard Mr Bowman with his life.' I ran on, my skirts bringing chairs and tables down. Dear, reliable Hargreaves would help, even if it meant locking his lordship in his room. But before I got there, I saw my prey.

'Don't move! Stay just where you are! You've done enough harm!' I yelled. 'Hargreaves! Come and help me. Help!'

For the prey had turned attacker. However strong I might be, she – he! – was stronger. Soon I could not breathe, I was falling into darkness. And my dear Matth . . .

THIRTY-ONE

As I almost fell through the back door, Bea was anxiously looking at the big servants' hall clock. Servants' dinner was overdue, and the men and women were gathering. 'Matthew, what on earth's the matter?'

'Harriet—' I gasped.

She blinked. 'Harriet? She's disappeared, Matthew. She set off somewhere about half an hour ago – no, inside the House somewhere. Look, there's her hat and cloak. And no one seems to have seen her.'

'Have you asked everyone here?'

'I didn't like to cause any panic.'

'Panic be blowed. I'll speak to them now! Hang on, where's Thatcher? Have you seen him?'

'He said he was going to have a word with young Freddie – so he might still be in your office.'

I pointed. 'Tim! Go and find Mr Thatcher – tell him he must send Freddie straight down to Marty's. He must go straight down. Through the main hall. Understand? He must go nowhere near Nurse Pegg!' This was not the time to offer my theory; it would cause too much discussion when we needed action. 'As for Mr Thatcher himself, he is to go to the entrance hall with him, whatever he's doing, and lock up after him. Now! And the rest of you: listen to me. Dinner will be late. Two of you will lock up here and make sure no one, no matter how important, gets out. Man, woman. No one. You two.' I pointed at the strongest-looking lads. 'As for the rest, men and women, every last one of you will be looking for Mrs Rowsley. Go in pairs. Check each room in every corridor on every floor. Mrs Arden will be in the entrance hall with Thatcher. Report straight back to her when you have finished a floor. If you have found . . . nothing, you will go to the floor to which she directs you. Before you go, has anyone seen Mr Trescothick or Sir Francis? Or Mr Wilson?'

'Please sir, Luke is serving their lunch in the breakfast room,' some lad piped up.

'Thank you. Now, men to the ground floor, women to the first floor – follow me!'

I burst into the breakfast room, yelling incomprehensibly, I dare say. But all three men responded as quickly as I could wish.

'The Family wing, sir?' Luke repeated.

'Yes. But – no, Luke. Go out of the front door – tell them to lock it behind you – and ride as fast as you can to the village. Elias and Dr Page. Bring them here. Come back to the front door and give your name. No one else but those two and you may be admitted. The door must be locked behind them when they come in. Understand all that? Go!'

I turned to the others. 'I fear for her life. Upstairs with me now, I beg you, all of you.'

I did not wait to see who was following.

I believe I would have battered the door down had the guard not opened it promptly. 'Sampson, Mrs Rowsley?'

'Ah, her came through in a great panic, gaffer. Told me to stay here and let no one out. So I didn't. Might be half blind but I'm not half deaf. So I turned him back, the gentleman that wanted me to let him through. A stranger: not seen him before. Hope I did right.'

Was it Nurse Pegg in male attire? And I'd told no one about her – him! – yet. 'I'm sure you did. Where is he now, this gentleman?'

'Don't rightly know.' He touched his blind eye. 'But the missus was going to Mr Bowman's room. Maybe she's still there.'

I turned to the others, now beside me. 'We're looking for Nurse Pegg. Or this stranger.'

'I believe we'd be safer in pairs. Trescothick, come with me. Wilson, Francis, go to the topmost floor and work your way down. Yes, even his lordship and her ladyship's rooms. Stay together for safety!'

As we ran, we shattered the calm of the wards of Stammerton sick, startling nurses and patients alike with our shouted questions. But the answers came back sickeningly the same. No, no sign of Mrs Rowsley.

'Nurse Pegg?'

'Not for half an hour, when she went off for something urgent, she said,' volunteered one of our former maids. Agnes?

'How did she seem?'

'Angry, I'd say. Mr Rowsley, sir, is the missus all right? There's four of us here: shall we help look?'

'Please. The nurses' quarters. But be very careful. Two of you must stay here, of course.'

She bobbed a curtsy, turning to her colleagues. Hoping she was as capable as her manner, we left her to it.

Trescothick gripped my arm. 'I think we should follow them. If Pegg is holed up anywhere, isn't it likely to be in her quarters? Aren't they likely to be in that area?'

I needed no second bidding, and started to run.

But again Trescothick took the lead, touching his lips. 'She might think the appearance of two women quite normal and they might get to see what – I beg pardon – who they are looking for. But if we go galloping off in pursuit . . .'

I nodded. We progressed like cats and, like cats, waited to pounce. To no avail. The nurses emerged shaking their heads.

'But there is something strange, sir. Nurse Pegg always keeps her door locked—'

'Double-locked,' her colleague corrected her. 'And now the door is wide open and her cupboards and drawers empty. Her valises have gone.'

'Thank you. That's very helpful,' I said. 'Now, if you hear anything—'

Agnes couldn't suppress a snigger. 'That voice of hers wouldn't be hard to miss, sir.'

'Quite. If you hear anything, call some of us men. We don't want you to put yourselves in peril.'

Her smile reminded me fleetingly of Harriet's. 'Don't worry about us, sir. Mrs Rowsley's taught us a couple of ways to deal with importunate men.'

'Except Nurse Pegg's a woman,' her companion said.

'Are you sure?' Agnes asked.

'Well—'

'Pegg's a man,' I said, closing the discussion. 'And we must find my wife now!'

We had all searched room after room, with Trescothick meticulously recording which were locked. Some were his lordship's and his mother's, of course. Others were clearly labelled in what was presumably Nurse Pegg's clear but uneven copperplate: *Linen Store; Medicine Store; Bandages and other Dressings.* And there was one that chilled me to the bone: *Poisons.* ***To be kept locked at all times.*** *Apply to Nurse Pegg for the key.*

I was groaning with despair when I heard Luke's voice. 'Sir! Sir! Where are you?'

I hardly knew. 'Stay with Sampson: I'll come and find you.'

But there was no Sampson. Just an old man in a pool of blood. He was staring towards heaven with his only eye. Dr Page stepped forward to check his pulse. Both eyes were blind now. He closed them both, covering his face.

Heedless of reverence, I stepped over him and ran out to the landing. 'Luke?'

'Down here, sir!'

'Go and find George. We need locks removed or doors broken open. Is Elias here yet?'

'There's a commotion going on outside. Shall I—?'

'Find George first. Life and death, tell him.' I turned back to Page. 'Harriet?'

'We will find her. Calm yourself. Your head is clear, man, and we need it to stay that way.'

I stared as a memory flashed into place. 'If Pegg has Harriet, she – he! – has all Harriet's keys. To every door in the House.'

'What do you mean, he?' Francis asked.

Page blanched and turned half away. Then he faced me. 'Let us assume that Matthew is right. Let us assume Pegg is male. Let me explain—'

'Surely to God!' I feared Francis might strike him.

So might I, but now was not the time. 'Explain later, Page! Pegg has the keys, I tell you! And can get away!'

'Not if us servants have anything to do with it,' Thatcher said. 'I wonder—'

'Trescothick, what is it?' Francis asked tetchily.

'Ghosts. Matthew, do you remember our talk of ghosts one night? Creaking floors, that sort of thing? I did not want you all to laugh at me, so I made a joke of it. But what if I heard real creaking, real footsteps? Above my bedchamber: what rooms are up there?'

'Attics and storerooms. We'll go by the backstairs. Quicker!' I said. 'Thatcher, get some candles – there'll be plenty in the wards – and light them. Trescothick, back to your bedchamber, please, and shout – oh, hit the ceiling, anything, to let us know if we're in the right area.'

We ran upstairs. Thank God the new key shone brightly on the key ring. Thank God it opened the lock sweetly. We were in. Time to listen for Trescothick's call.

But I might not hear anything for the beating of my heart.

Thatcher did. He grabbed my arm. Yes! A shout. 'You're right over my head now!'

And this door too opened sweetly.

Eyes closed, she is lying on her back on the unmade bed. Her hands are crossed on her breast.

She is in my arms. Motionless.

The room resounds to screaming. Sobbing.

Mine.

My face hurts, once, twice, three times. Thatcher's face appears. His mouth moves.

'The missus. She's still breathing. Calm yourself, gaffer, and take her hand and talk to her. I'll get Dr Page. Two minutes, most.'

The longest and the shortest two minutes. The longest because I fear he will never come. The shortest because I need to tell Harriet all she means to me, in the hope that she is still able to hear.

And then I am jostled out of the way, and Page is touching her throat, feeling her wrist. 'Yes, she lives. Open the windows, one of you!' He opens her eyes, peers at them, and shakes his head. 'Enough damned laudanum in that body of hers to make a horse sleep. Can we get her to the Family wing? There's equipment there I need. And I'll want a couple of the women who've trained as nurses. Thatcher, run ahead and

organize a lot of water, a jug and my bag, will you? Good
man. Matthew, you take her head and shoulders; Trescothick,
you take her feet.'

I blinked hard, shaking my head. I hadn't even realized he
was in the room.

We set off with our precious burden, slowly, painfully slowly.
Tears trickled unchecked down my face, falling on hers. And
then I saw his hands were wet too.

We had to stop, and when we reached the stairs we had to
let two of the strongest young footmen take over. We followed
them into a room, bare but for a rubber-sheeted bed and some
cupboards. Two scared-looking young women stood in the
furthest corner. Page was with us in a trice, shooing all us men
out without ceremony.

'And shut the door behind you!' he growled.

Staring at the still wet blood, Wilson was waiting where
Sampson had lain, a hip flask in his hand. 'Brandy, my friend?'

I shook my head. 'I need to think. I want to stay by that door
and howl, but more than anything I want to make sure that
Pegg doesn't escape. And when I think that he wouldn't be
here if Page hadn't been so lax . . . I trusted him! And he let
this happen!'

He reached for my shoulder. 'He might not be the only one
to have been lax. I did what your friend Mr Baines suggested.
All might not be well with our Antipodean friend's story.'

'We'll deal with that later. My God, it's Page I'm trusting
to keep her alive!' I pushed aside the flask and was ready to
barge in and tear him apart.

'Indeed, and he will answer to us all for that later. He may
have made one terrible mistake, but surely you know he is a
good doctor. And,' he added bleakly, 'there is no one else to
turn to. Now, shall we join the teams searching for the
miscreant? I think you should know that one good thing has
come of all this, by the way.'

I shook my head. 'I have to be . . . have to be within earshot.'
Then I realized what he had said. 'What good thing?'

'That young man looking after his lordship – what's his
name?'

'Hargreaves. Used to be his valet,' I added, almost automatically.

'Yes, Hargreaves. He had something to confess, and found it easier, he said, to talk to a stranger. Something about a picture his lordship should not have had.'

'Queen Elizabeth?' I said stupidly.

'Possibly. Apparently his lordship got out one night, and found his way to the attics. Hargreaves found him rummaging through the pictures – he had this idea that someone wanted to steal them and he wanted to save them by dropping them through the window. Hargreaves could only soothe him by letting him bring the picture back to his quarters for safe-keeping. It's safe in the back of his lordship's wardrobe. Hargreaves checks on it each night. But he doesn't want to remove it, in case he brings on one of his lordship's bad spells. He's in a good phase just now, and Hargreaves wants to keep it that way.'

'Of course.' Another day I would worry about his lordship's escape. And Hargreaves' tale – did it make sense? Today . . . Why bother about a portrait of a dead woman when there was a real one to worry about? What a strange man Wilson was, to see such a trivial discovery as some recompense for all this terrible trauma.

He pressed my shoulder. 'Why do you not go and sit with your friend Samuel? You will hear there if anyone is calling you. In fact, I will tell a nurse to fetch you when you are needed.'

So while everyone else in the House was being useful all I could do was kneel beside my sick old friend, holding his hand and reading our favourite psalms aloud.

THIRTY-TWO

float. I float. I float nearer the light. Nearer my God to Thee.
Though I walk in the valley of the shadow of death. Forgive
us our trespasses.

Hands lift me up. Not my will but Thine.

But the hands – I can feel them. Human hands. Human
voices?

Matthew? Matthew! Matthew?

THIRTY-THREE

'She still lives! You may see her!' the little nurse gasps as she runs into Samuel's room.

I am on my feet in an instant.

'But Dr Page asks you to wait five minutes. Just five, sir. To give her . . . dignity, if you please, sir. She needs a night-gown, sir.'

'I will fetch it. Myself. Get back to her – no, stay with Mr Bowman and hold his hand and talk to him. And observe very carefully.'

I fly to our room, and bring a night-gown from our press. And a hairbrush. I know she will want to brush her hair. And one of those loathsome night caps. But surely, surely, she will want to come back to her own bedchamber? If only I could think!

I am dimly aware that as I head for the entrance hall there is a lot of noise. A hubbub. As I enter I hear applause.

The tiniest maid is pushed forward. 'Please, sir, we're so pleased about the missus.'

'Thank you. Everyone. Excuse me if I say no more.' Awkwardly showing them my little bundle, I turn for the stairs.

'Two minutes, Matthew. Not a second longer. She needs sleep – and I fear it will not be restful. Unpleasant problems call for unpleasant solutions.'

'Can you not give her something, Page?'

He shook his head. 'She has a strong constitution. Let it work for her. Sleep is often the best remedy as well as the kindest. Ah! I will give those garments to the nurses and ask them to make her presentable.'

'Let me see her now. She may not forgive me later, but I need to . . . to . . .'

'Very well.'

She was green rather than white, shaking and trembling as

if icy cold. I took her hands and pressed them gently. The beautiful eyes opened. The white lips smiled.

Page was waiting for me as I emerged. 'Matthew, how can I ever apologize?'

'Enough of that for now, man. Just do what you are so good at. And when you are satisfied with my Harriet's progress, look in on Samuel. I would welcome your opinion.' The words sounded collected enough, but had Wilson been there I would have emptied his flask in one draught. Then I would have prayed long and hard.

As it was, I had to collect myself and remember that there was still a criminal at large. Vengeance must be left to the Lord, but the least I wanted to do was deliver this evildoer to justice. I joined the ranks of those on patrol, asking everyone I found, but gaining no news of the criminal. The murderer. But at least I could tell them that one would-be victim lived!

At last I found myself in the entrance hall.

Calm she might appear to the servants milling round, but Bea was white and shaking as she sat at her place in the entrance hall. I went straight over and took her hands.

'Someone else can take over here,' I said.

'I'd rather stay at my post, thank you,' she said. 'While people need me I have to hold myself together. All this business about Nurse Pegg being a man! I still can't believe it! All the time she – he! – was supposed to be nursing Samuel. And now he's . . . When the news about him becomes general,' she said on a sudden sob, 'then I don't know how I'll manage, and that's the truth of it.' She stared at me. 'You've not heard, have you? He's spoken to a nurse. He's back with us, Matthew. And what does that mean for me?' Her voice rose to something like a wail. 'No, I shouldn't even think about that now. But I can think of little else, to be honest. And I know it's wrong and selfish, so there's no need to look at me like that!' She straightened her back and controlled her voice. 'Now, this list. All these rooms have been checked, and all the doors to the outside have been locked. There's a couple of burly labourers outside each. Elias has sent for Mr Burrows, and had a trap despatched to the station to meet him. Luke left Freddie at the pub, and he and Elias have got as many villagers as they can lay hands on patrolling the estate boundary. Oh yes, Farmer Twiss has got the farmhands to patrol the woods by the ruins – he said something about a hut?'

I nodded. I knew that hut.

'Mr Wilson and Sir Francis were having a row to end all rows so I sent them outside to cool off. And ever since he came down, Mr Trescothick has been working his socks off. He says he'll take over from me so I can organize cups of tea for everyone. It'll have to be here, he says, so we can check everyone coming and going. He's off looking for trestle tables even as I speak.' But her efficiency was snuffed out. 'Oh, Matthew, what shall I do?'

I almost shouted at her, 'Pray for my Harriet, you fool!' But she was almost as pale as my dear wife. 'Go and do as Trescothick suggested. I will stay here.'

I may have stared at the lists and columns before me, but all I could see was Harriet's face. I was deep in prayer when I heard footsteps approach.

'Trescothick?' I smiled. 'Thank you. Your help . . . I couldn't have managed without it.' I patted the chair beside me.

But he stood, awkwardly. If he had been a labourer he would have twisted his cap in his hands. 'There are things I need to tell you—'

There was a terrific pounding: even the grand front doors quivered under the onslaught. Like footmen, one on either side, we opened them. 'Twiss!'

'Got him. My men are taking him to the police house now! Your stable lad is bringing that great beast of yours round now!'

'My wife—' I spread my hands.

Trescothick put a hand on my arm. 'They won't let you talk to Pegg, you know. Even if they did, they wouldn't let you throttle the truth out of her – or rather, him! Go and see how Harriet is,' he continued, giving me a gentle push. 'If she's going to sleep for a long time yet, you might be able to leave her? And you will feel much calmer, less violent. It won't do Pegg any harm to have to cool his heels. Let him wait till night. Till noon, if necessary.'

As I ran up the stairs, I tried to work out why his words were

familiar. Harriet would know. I must ask her when I see her.
When? If! No, it must be when. Please God, it must be when.

Now beside the bed were two chairs, as if she might receive
visitors. And the nurses had worked wonders, as if they were
ladies' maids. Her hair was neat, under the cap. Her nightgown
was tidy. She was still pale, but I fancied her breath was more
even. Her hand was no longer icy to the touch. But even as I
held it she tossed and screamed aloud.

'Just a nightmare, sir. She'll have a few of those, Dr Page
says. He's with Mr Bowman, if you please, sir. Shall I fetch
him?' She bobbed a curtsy and glided away.

Page looked worse than Harriet, grey and dishevelled. 'Matthew,
I'm sorry. I don't know where to start,' he stuttered.

'As I said earlier, you start by doing what you do best: tending
the sick. Harriet . . . but I must ask about Samuel, mustn't I?'
I fought to keep my voice low.

He gripped the back of the nearest chair. 'I have never been
so wrong about anyone . . . But yes, there is good news about
Samuel. I suspect there might have been some progress, some
return to consciousness, days before this, but there was no
obvious sign of it. Why was there nothing? Because he was
drugged. Pegg simply continued with the laudanum, and didn't
tail it off, as I requested. Samuel still has a long way to go,
weeks, months, maybe, but now I am sure he will live. And
Harriet: I believe she will too. Let her sleep a little longer if
you can bear to.'

I gazed at the beloved face. Looking at her it was easier to
speak quietly. 'Is it better for her if I do?'

'The longer she sleeps the better she will feel when she wakes
up.' His smile was bleak. 'Come back in two hours.'

I held his gaze. 'Pegg has now been apprehended, which is
why I will accept your advice. But I want you to accept some
of mine. I believe you made a grievous mistake when you
allowed this person into our household – a murderer!'

'Not just a grievous mistake – a criminal one! When I think
what has been done . . . Harriet . . .'

'Had she not lived, I would have killed Pegg with my bare
hands.' I took a deep breath. 'Now, Page, you must promise
me not to make an even more grievous mistake and . . . I want

to see you alive and well when I return. We understand each other, do we not? Do nothing foolish.'

He nodded. 'I promise. I will repay your generosity. Though I cannot imagine staying in the village after this debacle.'

'You know, I think that's exactly where you should stay. But now – dear God, must I go?'

He put a hand on my shoulder. I tried not to wince. 'Matthew, leave Pegg to the police. And I will ask someone to bring a more comfortable chair and your Bible.'

I wanted to pace and scream. How I did not hit him, knock him silly, knock him into the depths of suffering that Samuel endured, I did not know. I took a very deep breath. Then another. 'Thank you. But not until you've told me what I hoped to get out of . . . I will not call him your accomplice, because I think better of you than that. Tell me why you brought Pegg here! Here of all places!' I pointed to the bed.

He nodded. 'Let us sit. It is harder to shout when one is not standing, is it not? And for Harriet's sake, we must be quiet. Pegg is my second cousin. He is a qualified doctor, though clearly of late he has misused his knowledge, shall we say? Like me he had a thriving practice. Mostly middle-class, some wealthy patients, in Oxford, not the countryside. He enjoyed the best of relations with his patients. But one day, not many days . . . he misused his position most grievously. Boys, Matthew, boys. He lost most of his patients, as you can imagine, as word went round. He begged me for help. At that time Freddie was safely working for Mr Baines. The House needed medical staff. He beseeched me to employ him, in no matter how menial a capacity. And so he became Nurse Pegg. And now' – his calm voice became a sob – 'I find he has drugged one of my patients, assaulted a young boy under your protection and tried to kill a woman I am proud to call friend.'

It took me a few moments to collect myself enough to speak. 'Was he also the one that attacked Samuel in the first place?'

'I don't know. Why should he?'

'That's something to ask him when I see him!'

He coughed gently. 'Remember what I said about the police. It is possible that you will not see him again, Matthew, till he is on trial. If you have questions that need answers, Elias and that pompous sergeant from Shrewsbury will have to put them to him on your behalf, will they not? And I hope that they will also ask him if he attacked Thatcher and Mr Pounceman – and if he did, why he did. I thought I knew him, Matthew. We played together as children. Yet now I find I know nothing of him. How is it possible?' He literally tore his hair.

To my amazement I found myself comforting the man I had wanted to blame as he wept on my shoulder.

At last he pulled himself together, turning to his patient. 'Her pulse is stronger already,' he said, 'and her eyes are improved too. Matthew, permit me to prescribe something for us both. A tot of the entirely medicinal brandy that Trescothick ran to earth the other day.'

THIRTY-FOUR

I steadfastly refused to be carried downstairs. True, I needed a strong arm either side of me, not because I was weak but because I did not trust myself not to stagger like a drunkard. The main staircase was the only one with treads wide enough for three people to walk abreast, so I made my descent like a grand lady on the arm of a lord. It was better than any lord, however, it was Matthew on my right side. After some discussion we asked Dr Page to take my other arm. If I knew villagers there would be all too many ready to heap opprobrium on his head, forgetting all the unsung and unpaid kindnesses he had done to so many. If the servants in the entrance hall saw that we still valued him, that might help him if he chose to stay in Thorncroft.

I had expected one or two of our colleagues. I was not prepared for the entire household to be my audience. And I found it hard to be calm in the face of my colleagues and their chorus of good wishes and cries of 'God bless you'.

Two or three steps from the bottom I paused and smiled. 'Thank you. It is good to be back among you: it seems much longer than just two days. We have some difficult times ahead but they will pass. To help us through them, let us keep to our routine as best we can. You probably know more than I do about what's been going on – and you'll certainly have heard more rumours! But as and when we learn facts, I promise you that you will hear them too. And, most important, our Christmas party will go ahead!'

I felt like Moses going through the Red Sea as they parted to let me through. Our little procession came to a halt by the breakfast room. Bea ran forward and hugged me in silence. She looked paler than I did, and had clearly shed tears. Mr Wilson and Francis waited by the window, through which gleamed some welcome winter sun, though the sky threatened something quite other; it was full of heavy clouds driven by what looked like fierce winds. Thatcher was quite unnecessarily supervising the minutiae of the table layout as Luke polished the silver and the glass as if preparing for the Queen herself. I counted the places. Six? 'Where is Mr Trescothick?'

Mr Wilson coughed. 'His words were that he did not think he was entitled to join the gathering. He is packing his bags, Mrs Rowsley.'

I gripped Matthew's hand, praying that he would agree with me. 'Mr Wilson, while he is a guest under his lordship's roof, we must treat him with courtesy. Thatcher, would you invite him down, please? Thank you.'

Luke exchanged a glance with me and relaid the table.

There was an awkward silence.

On the sideboard lurked a silver ice bucket, promising with two protruding necks.

'I felt that just a little champagne, well diluted with water would not hurt you,' Dr Page said.

'Ellis, if I promise to have plenty of water separately, may I have my champagne as it should be? With life-enhancing bubbles?'

'Are you sure, Harriet?' he demurred.

'Positive,' I assured him. 'Thank you. Ah, Mr Trescothick. Please join us. No, stay for a moment, Dick. And you too, Luke. The doctor has news that you should hear.' For all my bravado, after that I had to sit down rather hurriedly. At least that meant that the men felt they might too. Bea sagged, rather than sat.

But the doctor remained on his feet, as did Mr Trescothick. 'Our good friend Samuel Bowman is now fully conscious. The long rest has enabled his body to begin to heal. He can speak again. He can recall some things but not others. Soon I will have him moved back to his old room in the hope that the familiar surroundings will help him. Obviously we will need to find rooms nearby for the nursing staff who will still be on constant watch.'

Thatcher stepped forward. 'Beg pardon, sir, and I'm sorry to interrupt, but might I ask a question?'

Clearly taken aback, Dr Page nonetheless nodded.

'Sir, does Mr Bowman recall who attacked him? And why? Surely he doesn't have an enemy in the world!'

'He made one, Thatcher: Pegg. Mr Bowman is more

protective of what he sees of his family than anyone could imagine. And he suspected – before the rest of us realized it – that young Freddie was afraid of Pegg. He could make nothing of it – after all, why should the youngster have anything to do with the woman? And then, one day, on one of his constitutionals, he came face to face with a smartly dressed middle-aged man. Something about him was familiar, though he knew he had never met him. At the moment he recognized the face, Pegg swung at him with his cane. After that Samuel remembered nothing.'

Now Luke stepped forward. 'And what does the evil two-faced bastard have to say about it? Begging your pardon, ladies.'

Matthew replied, 'Believe me, if I had been allowed to see him I would have found a way of making him confess. But Elias tells me that Pegg insists he did no more than strike him – that all the other damage happened when he accidentally fell.'

Dr Page nodded. 'But as the doctor who treated him, I will be testifying at the assizes that Mr Bowman suffered more than a simple blow and a fall. I will testify that he was the victim of a prolonged and vicious attack. Samuel may not be dead – but it will take him a long time to recover. And I have told Mr and Mrs Rowsley that he may never be well enough to work again.'

'So what'll happen to him? Not the workhouse!' Luke was close to tears.

'Never. Not as long as I live,' Matthew declared. 'I beg your pardon. I should have said that the trustees will be meeting very soon to ensure that he has both compensation and a pension. He will never want for anything in his old age. For that is what he has become, I fear – an old man. Nonetheless he lives! We should celebrate that. Mrs Arden has arranged for a parallel celebration in the servants' hall, I understand.' He smiled. 'Poor Thatcher is still unable to use both hands, of course, so I must ask Luke to do the honours.'

Not a drop did he spill. The two young men joined us in our toast.

As if nothing unusual had occurred, Dick bent towards me. 'Luncheon in twenty minutes, ma'am? Very good.' Luke and he withdrew, though true to form – and probably as a good butler should – he remained within earshot.

There was an awkward silence.

'Matthew tells me you were a tower of strength when I was ill the other day, Mr Trescothick. Thank you.' I offered him my hand. At first I thought he would decline, but at last he bowed, and kissed it.

'It was the very least I could do,' he said. 'And Mr Wilson and Sir Francis would be the first to say so. When you are well, you need to know what I have told them. I would have told everyone before, after the trustees' meeting. But it went on and on, and the tot of brandy I needed became two and then three and more. I am very sorry.' He looked it.

'I am ready now to hear whatever you want to say. Let me prompt you. You are not who you claimed to be. Who are you, then?'

He took a deep breath. 'My name is John Timpson. It's pure coincidence that I shared my initials with the real heir. I was Julius Trescothick's cabin steward aboard the SS *Great Britain*. He was a sick man, that much was clear, and he needed my arm to take the air on deck, for instance, as his medical man had said he must do. During that period we became friends. He might have been travelling in a first class cabin—'

'Which the estate paid for: he was not a rich man,' Mr Wilson interjected.

'Exactly. Though he spent some of his school holidays here, his family left the country. Far from enjoying the trappings of a nobleman's life, he was an ordinary clerk in a Sydney office, so we had something else in common. "No fortune ever made or ever sought," he told me. He was terrified of what lay before him. As a steward, I could teach him about table etiquette, but little else. Dimly, very dimly, he recalled visiting the estate – or it might have been another of the Croft residences – as a boy, when he had been scared beyond measure by the formality. We became friends. Much as I tried to deny it, he was dying, and knew it. On his deathbed, he gave me all his papers, and even scrawled a note absolving me of any blame.' Mr Wilson nodded. 'And then, much though I protested, he made me promise, my hand on his failing heart, that I could benefit where he could not. That is how I came here.' He took a breath. 'And I am sorry. As I told Mr Pounceman, I would not be here but for that promise.'

'That damned wretch Pounceman knows what we do not!' Francis shouted. 'My apologies, ladies.'

'He knows nothing except that I was very troubled about an undertaking I had made. Had he been a kindly priest, I might have made a confession and sought absolution, but . . . He would be a much finer heir than I would ever be, would he not?' He snorted with grim laughter as he added, 'He did his best to educate me in the ways he expected me to follow, but clearly thought I was a poor student. He told me straight out that I was not yet ready for society, and I suspect he thought I never would be. And now I don't have to be. I can go back to what I know best.'

Matthew asked quietly, 'What will you do?'

'Go back to sea. Or seek employment on dry land over here. And as I said, like Julius, I was once a clerk. I worked for the late Mr Brunel – what a sad loss that was. A fine man, a brilliant man, but so driven. And he drove us too – too hard at times. So I tried an easier life. I should have stuck to my place, shouldn't I? But I came here and hated every single moment until . . . until I saw the stuff in the attics. And I wanted to stay.'

'The attics?'

'That case of old documents, Matthew. The moment I saw and touched them I believe I would have died sooner than let anyone harm them. The pictures, the china, the furniture – they don't excite me one scrap. But those old pieces of vellum, yes, and some of the books: if I could do anything to keep them safe, I would.' I had a glimmer of an idea, but would mention it to no one until I had discussed it with Matthew.

The sun had given way to snow – a sudden flurry hid the garden.

'Make no hasty decisions,' I said. The advice might well have applied to Bea, who was wringing her handkerchief. Had she secretly – not even admitting it to herself – hoped that Samuel might die, and spare her making what would now be an unwelcome match? Or had she hoped for another proposal, only to find the gentleman not coming up to scratch? Or if there was an offer, was it of uncongenial work, not marriage?

Fortunately Thatcher appeared to top up our glasses. Concern written all over his face, he gave Bea extra; she managed a pallid smile.

When he approached me, I felt Dr Page's eyes upon me. Dutifully I shook my head. 'Dick,' I began quietly, 'did Elias ever find out who attacked you and Mr Pounceman?'

'He reckons it was a band of gypsy lads who attacked Mr Pounceman, ma'am. There was a large group on the common, and when they ran away they went in that direction.'

'And you?'

'Not gypsies for sure; they'd not have got through the gates, would they? No, Elias and I reckon it was Nurse Pegg as he was then. I think he was out and about in gentleman's clothes and didn't want to risk being identified. And the next day he wasn't much in evidence – nursing a few bruises, I'd say.'

'Ah! The toothache! The toothache and that weird nurse's cap! More like a bonnet!' Matthew exclaimed. 'You must have landed a really good blow or two!'

'Thank you, sir.' Thatcher bowed with consummate calm. 'Now, ma'am, may I tell the kitchen that you are ready for us to serve luncheon?'

Matthew and Dr Page tried to insist that I return to our home after coffee, but I was determined to speak to Bea, following her down to the kitchen. 'Your room or mine? Come, Bea, it's clear you need a shoulder to cry on. Come on, no one will disturb us in the Room because they'll assume I've gone home to rest.'

'Which you should have done, no doubt about it.' But she took off the working apron she'd been donning and let me lead the way.

We both sat down, our glad rags making the décor look even shabbier. 'Tell me,' I said.

'What about?'

'I don't know what about! That's what I want to know.'

She sighed and rolled her eyes. 'Samuel for a start! Oh, Harriet, I can't marry him, not now, not ever, and that's the truth of it. And everyone will think I've led him on and hate me for it.'

'Our small household isn't everyone, Bea. And we all know

that Samuel is an old man, who would have retired in other circumstances and is now an invalid, needing a nurse, not a wife. And you are in your prime, full of life. Where do you see this life taking you? That's what I want to know.'

'And me too! I don't know if I'm on my arse – oh! pardon me – or my elbow. And that's the truth.'

'Does a stand-up row between two of our guests have anything to do with it? The one you mentioned to Matthew?'

'Yes and no. Harriet, they both want my services. One for a wife and one for a cook.'

My eyes rounded. 'Which is which, Bea?'

She got up, pacing as much as the tiny space would permit. 'Mr Wilson wants to marry me! And Sir Francis needs a cook-housekeeper – but he admits he's hardly ever in either of his residences, and rarely entertains at either. The thing is, I'd marry him in the twinkling of an eye if I could. Urbane, handsome. All the travelling he does. What have I said now?'

I got up and took her hands. 'This sounds brutal, but you're my dearest friend—'

'Apart from him!'

'Dearest woman friend, then. Yes, he's become a dear friend. But in all the years I have known him I have never, ever seen him look at a woman the way a man ought . . . if he's interested in women. His interest is in relationships that would be illegal if he engaged in them. You understand? As it is, I think his life is probably celibate, though obviously not at all monkish.'

She made a valiant attempt at her old laugh. But it ended on a sob. 'So I can cross him off my list then.'

'I'm sorry, but yes, I think so. Mr Wilson? Marriage?'

'I'm not sure. I'm just not sure. I don't know the first thing about middle-class life, and that's the truth, except what I've read in books, of course.'

'You aren't so deeply in love with him that you want to take the risk?'

'Not the way you are with Matthew. And the trouble is, oh, Harriet, the man I like best is really not eligible at all. I'd never be able to mix in your circle ever again.' She turned to the window in tears.

'Marty?' I asked quietly.

'Oh, he's so full of life! And kind too – the way he treats young Freddie! But a landlord, and not even of a respectable hostelry. No! It'd better be Mr Wilson, then.'

'You make it sound like having a tooth drawn. So I'd really advise you not to choose him, not on those grounds. Bide your time, Bea. The way this snow is settling, no one will be going very far very fast. And tomorrow we'll all be needed to make soup for the poor villagers. Just bide your time, and if anyone presses you, tell them frankly what you've told me. If they can't deal with honesty, they don't deserve you.'

There was a knock on the door. Matthew popped his head round. 'My love, if we don't go home now we won't be able to.'

'Do we have fires lit and food in our kitchen? No? It looks as if we'd better stay here, then. But I do find myself weak. Might I ask for your arm to our bedchamber?'

THIRTY-FIVE

One might have had a sense of déjà vu as we all took our dinner together that evening. But though all the drama of the previous days might have created even more tensions, many seemed to have been resolved. The seating arrangements were slightly different, with John – how strange it seemed to use his real name – beside Bea, with me to her left. Harriet separated Francis and Wilson, though clearly she was having to force them into a civilized conversation. Page had declined to join us, despite our pressing invitation; he had a baby to deliver, he said, though he would do his best to join us later, bringing, at Harriet's insistence, an overnight bag so that he could stay here. Some of us found it harder to forgive him than others, and I feared that some villagers would see this as another instance of people with power protecting each other. However, immediately after lunch, driving through that shocking blizzard, Ellis had set out to apologize in person to Marty and his protégé, ready, as he'd told us, to make every reparation he could to young Freddie. At the very least he would pay for a proper education – first a tutor and then a good school – so that the lad would fulfil his undoubted promise. He would even send him to university if that was appropriate. He couldn't undo his dreadful mistake, but he would do his best to remedy the appalling treatment the boy had had to endure.

How I would manage without help I had no idea – not until last night when Harriet had tentatively voiced what she said would be an elegant solution. 'We saw how Mr . . . how John made the library his chosen sitting room; we know how he fell in love with the old manuscripts you found in the attic. He doesn't yet have the skills to catalogue books or manuscripts, but he can do routine work for you. If he was good enough for Mr Brunel, he might meet even your high standards!' Seeing me reluctantly weaken, she pressed further. 'In this weather, where can he go? Let him stay here, and help you. If he is prepared to, of course. He may, of course, feel that a hair shirt is his only option, but he does not deserve to be driven out in this, so close to Christmas too. As long as Francis is trapped too, he can really educate him about the paintings and the furniture.'

'Another lame duck for you to help over a stile, Harriet?'

'People I did not know helped me when I most needed it, my love.'

Given the weather and the possible awkwardness I was somewhat surprised when Page returned to the House, just as we left the dining table. He was so cold when Thatcher showed him into the drawing room that Bea bustled him straight down to the kitchen to thaw out properly and drink hot soup. Only when he had returned did I understand why he had made the journey. He had called in at the police house for more news of Pegg. Burrows was apparently still stuck in Shrewsbury, currently under a foot of snow, but Elias had acted on his own initiative and opened Pegg's valises, in which could be found an interesting mixture of men's and women's clothing. Then he had produced the walking stick found near the scene of the attack on Samuel. Essentially he confirmed what Samuel had said, apart from his insistence that he had hit him but once. Would his story stand up in court? Especially since he had killed the poor guard? Surely not. But now he was claiming that he had actually saved Samuel's life! Yes, by keeping his patient drugged he had helped his recovery.

Page was clearly more puzzled than outraged by this assertion. 'I have always believed that sleep assisted suffering bodies to heal more quickly, but never have I risked extending the treatment for so long. As soon as I can, I will write to my colleagues to see what they think of the notion. Meanwhile, I have good news: mother and baby are doing well. I'd never have chosen to be born in Stammerton myself, but the cottage is windproof and as warm as I've even known one of those hovels to be. Blankets. Food. You good ladies have excelled yourselves. But I pity those not living on such a benign estate.'

Harriet sighed. 'Samuel's sister, for instance, and her deplorable husband.'

'She is deplorable too, my love. And the rector's wife has her eye on her.'

Bea nodded, 'And I'll wager those half guineas you sent her didn't come from Samuel's store. Oh, is someone reading the Bible to him tonight?' She half rose.

'I asked his nurse to,' Harriet said with slight emphasis. 'The two Ellis has allocated to Samuel were once two of our very best maids. They already know him well: I think they see him as their grandfather.' The last word was very carefully articulated.

Once again, I produced our copies of Shakespeare, and the evening passed more harmoniously than I could have even dreamed of yesterday.

The snow cleared as quickly as it had come. The invalids from Stammerton were able to return to their home, most at least. Page's best efforts could not save Granny Butler, who died a day after her seventieth birthday. Since Page made no charge for any of his services, his mistake was tucked to the back of the villagers' minds, though perhaps it would never be forgotten completely. Just now topmost in everyone's thought were preparations for the next, but most important event: Christmas. Bea and Harriet did a lot of shopping, both in the village and in Shrewsbury, where Wilson had returned to his office in pursuit of the next heir in line. He was as good as his word and lent them his coach. He showed no signs at all of umbrage at his rejection. Harriet wondered if he was secretly relieved that he could continue his comfortable bachelor existence, answerable to no one but himself. Francis too was gracious in defeat, conceding that our need in the House was greater than his. But he secured Bea's hand for the first dance of the Christmas party, narrowly beating Ellis Page. Yes, it seemed that Harriet's bachelor friend had decided to extend his visit.

Harriet watched everything with amusement now she realized that her friend would survive her disappointment. And perhaps she foresaw another romantic development.

Meanwhile John Timpson was proving an invaluable clerk, quickly grasping the needs of estate management as if they were a mere offshoot of engineering, and in his spare time trying to catalogue the documents we'd found. Occasionally I

could take a day off; on one of them Harriet and I travelled to
Wolverhampton to meet his lordship's love child, a baby who
had inherited more of her pretty mother's looks than her father's.
She was flourishing, but her new parents were worried about
their work if the cuts froze. In vain did I remind them of the
money we had left with a trusted clergyman for the family's
benefit; that was for the future not just of the baby but of all
their children, they insisted. But one thing they did consent to:
that they would accept help if they needed it.

Harriet asked gently, 'And if his lordship was ever well enough
– in the spring perhaps – would you let him at least see her? That
can do no harm, surely.' I could almost hear her adding under her
breath, *And it might bring the whole family untold opportunities.*

'Her's still our Lizzie, ain't her?'

'Of course. Your daughter and the other children's sister. But
a father might want to know his daughter is doing well – and
growing up as pretty as her mother. He really loved Maggie,
you know. But his mother . . .' She shrugged.

'Old bat, is her?' Mrs Stride asked, arms akimbo. 'What'd
her say if she knew this precious lord wanted to see Lizzie? A
lot, I reckon.'

'I don't think she will still be on this earth by then. And to
tell you the truth, his lordship does not enjoy good health.'

'Oh, ah. Locked up in a loony bin, I hear.'

'No. He lives quietly at home. Very quietly.' She was a mistress
of understatement, was she not? 'There's no need to make any
decisions now, Mrs Stride. But I beg you to consider at least
what I have said. And promise me, never go without, any of you.'

'All right. Seeing as you ask. But only for the children's
sake, mind.'

'Of course. Please will you do one more thing for me? As
you can see, we have been shopping for Christmas, but we
don't know what your children would like. Would you be
kind enough to buy a small gift for each of them, a real treat!
Something they might never dream of? Thank you, and God
bless you all.'

Mrs Stride weighed in her hand the little purse. 'Ah, I reckon
He might have done already.' But since she was looking at the
baby, I am not sure she referred to the money.

EPILOGUE

I t was time for the party. The long gallery was decked in the traditional greenery, picked with a will by the outdoor staff who were included in the House party for the first time. At my behest, there was a modern addition: we had never had a tree in the House before. Its branches were hung with ornaments most of us had never even heard of, let alone handled. At its foot were the presents Bea and I had selected for each individual. Yes, it all looked as magical as human effort could make it. Food waited on tables at the far end. Drink too, thought the punch was not as alcoholic as it looked and smelt.

It needed one last touch: the guests.

Would Samuel be able to come down? His lordship? Yes, I hoped so. George had converted two comfortable chairs into invalid chairs, easily pushed by a single attendant. We all needed some joy, especially the uniformed young men and women penned into the Family wing. Tonight they could dress as they wanted, as could everyone else. I knew how much of an effort the women and girls were making with their finery; I hoped the menfolk would match them.

The little band was already tuning up.

In other houses the Family would often act as servants for the night. On this occasion Matthew and I would – though we would dance, we had promised each other that. So in a moment we would throw open the doors.

'Yes?' Matthew asked.

'Yes!'

We flung open the doors, the band struck up, and Matthew took me into his arms. The party had begun.